THROUGH THE DOOR

THROUGH

THE DOOR

Jo Anne Yarus Randall

STEIN AND DAY/*Publishers*/New York

Lines from "Husband and Wife" and the complete poem "The Order of Life," by Allen Grossman, from *A Harlot's Hire*, Walker-deBerry, Inc., Cambridge, Massachusetts, © 1961, used by permission of the author.

Lyrics from "Tea for Two," by Caesar and Youmans, copyright © 1924 (Renewed) Warner Bros., Inc., all rights reserved, used by permission.

Lines from "Que Bonita," from *The Selected Poems* by Federico Garcia Lorca, copyright © 1955 by New Directions Publishing Corporation, reprinted by permission of New Directions.

First published in 1985
Copyright © 1985 by Jo Anne Yarus Randall
All rights reserved, Stein and Day, Incorporated
Designed by Louis A. Ditizio
Printed in the United States of America
STEIN AND DAY/*Publishers*
Scarborough House
Briarcliff Manor, N.Y. 10510

Library of Congress Cataloging in Publication Data

Randall, Jo Anne Yarus.
  Through the door.

  I. Title.
PS3568.A4955T45 1985   813'.54   84-45212
ISBN 0-8128-2991-3

For Robert and
Joshua and
Abigail

So high you can't get over it,
So low you can't get under it,
So wide you can't get around it,
You have to go in through the door.

—Traditional Spiritual

This, then, is the end of speculation—
This certainty about the way you go
Night or day, loved or unloved. The darkened sky
Brings rain, rain yields to starlight,
Stars to the somewhat misty morning,
And clear day, clouding towards the afternoon.
These things like loving have no place in time.
The road runs through them for it can't go round.

from "Husband and Wife,"
by Allen Grossman

THROUGH THE DOOR

My father is a large, shadowy figure with heavy glasses and a reddish mustache. He descends wearily from buses carrying a brown leather briefcase, his face brightening momentarily as he sees me selling lemonade at the corner or daredeviling it down the street on one roller skate. Where, I wonder, are my little sister and brother? Even after eight years of analysis my stomach occasionally tightens when I see a man with his vague outline. But I am better now, for I used to follow such unsuspecting strangers for blocks, not really knowing why.

My father stands in front of mirrors making sucking sounds of concentration with his lips as he arranges his bow tie. He wears a navy blue cashmere overcoat, for in my memory it is almost always winter, the season that somehow best suits his burly frame.

Sometimes, though, it is summer. Once I remember seeing him do a serious breaststroke in a local lake. His head, with its high forehead and receded hairline, looks infinitely intelligent, and his face, with the thick glasses still on it, appears oddly sphinxlike floating, disembodied, through the water.

Too, I remember him in the garden patting the black topsoil lovingly with his hands and in the kitchen cutting the cucumbers and potatoes he had grown. He slathers them with sour cream, slices up an onion, adds salt and pepper. He stands at the open refrigerator, a jar in his hands, swallowing the brine from the green tomatoes he has pickled. My mother looks on disapprovingly or mutters, "Honey, please . . ." For this giant of a man with his positive craving for cholesterol and salt has a bad heart that will very soon give out. And I will stand bewildered in the front hall closet wrapping the soft arms of his cashmere coat around me and sniffing in the faint odor of tobacco with my tears.

When my father died it was November, gray and cold. The landscapes that I walked through for years after retained that climate.

I lie in the twin bed next to my sister, listening to her heavy breathing. In the living room Aunt Goldie is laughing. I am angry with her and her laughter, disturbing me so late at night, so early in the morning. My glasses are across the room on the dresser, and I cannot see the clock to tell what time it is, nor can I hear too clearly through the muffling doors of bedroom and of hall.

By morning the laughter translates itself into sobs. My mother is sitting on the other bed, staring at me and my sister or at the wall. Later, she will tell us about Daddy and that we needn't worry about sleeping late, as we are not going to school.

I stand in the doorway to the kitchen, my face pressed to the wall. Uncle Marvin, his hand on my shoulder, tells me I am a brave girl. My sister sits on a chair much too large for her in the living room. Her blond curls frame her face angelically, and her blue-rimmed eyeglasses give her an oddly wistful expression. Mother mutters over and over again "my poor baby, my poor baby," and it is impossible to tell to whom she is referring. My older brother, adolescent and angry at not having been at the hospital when it happened, is not in the picture I retain. But my baby brother, also angry, is. He defiantly insists that he *will* see his daddy again, as if the strength of his stubborn belief would make it so.

The house is always filled with people and their quiet buzzing.

16

There are never enough chairs. My mother is on the sofa. Is she sick? She looks very small. Do I have to kiss all these relatives good night? It seems odd, somehow, to be having a party at a time like this. Cousin Burt is here, looking strange in his army uniform. Fruit and flowers fill the room. Although I have my glasses now, everything still looks blurry. It takes a long time before it begins to get clear again.

Dr. Edwards is not a very large man, and he wears glasses only when he writes down addresses, appointment hours, or prescriptions, which is not very often. This is one of those times. He hands me a card with his name and address on it and a date, too. He tells me how to get there. I try to concentrate on first his face, then the card, but both remain fuzzy. I find myself looking somewhere past his nose. Although I cannot really see him, I can hear him clearly. His voice is soft and steady. Years later I will wonder whether someone taught him to talk like that or whether he always did. But now it doesn't matter. The gentle words telling me to come to him next day penetrate my haze. I am to be given permission to leave the hospital in order to visit with this quiet, slow-gestured man. For one brief moment I plan to run away, but for some reason I know I will not. Maybe it is that I do not want this kind stranger to be disappointed by my absence. What if he should wait and wait and I do not come?

1

THURSDAY——

THE sound of water running in the bathtub interrupts my reverie. I shake myself and strip, rushing past the ugly reality of my sadly damaged body, then slip gratefully into the deep water that makes no distinctions between my right side and my left. How can I be so distracted, I wonder, as I lie back in the water, letting it cover me, even letting my long hair float out behind me, like so much red seaweed, before it sinks beneath the surface at my back.

For a moment I try to concentrate, to conjure up some image or some clue that will clarify my thoughts, illuminate the haze that seems to have shrouded me too often at the office these past weeks or days. But soon I give it up and lie there, mindless, listening as the water laps up toward the overflow hole with every movement of my body. I am always at peace in the water and have often dreamed of the delight of being reborn as a porpoise, intelligent but buoyant.

At last I raise myself and reach for the soap. Before the surgery I never used a washcloth, always preferring to let my own hand or the soap itself glide gently across my skin. Now I surround myself with mounds of terrycloth, bathmitts, loofahs, sponges, anything that will protect my fingers from knowing the hard ultimate truth of my new contours.

I choose a bath brush and scrub my skin back to life until the combination of scent and sensation alerts me to the fact that my hair, wet as it is, demands washing. I pull the plug to drain the soapy water, then turn on the hand-held shower. Where is the damn shampoo?

When first I notice the ringing of the doorbell, it is so distorted by the noise of water rushing out and spraying in that I think I must have water in my ears. But no amount of head-shaking rids me of the annoying sound. It is the doorbell I hear. I am perplexed. It was after ten o'clock when I stepped into the tub; it must be ten-thirty by now. The persistence of the bell is disturbing. It sounds as if someone is leaning on it the way the twins used to do when they first grew tall enough to reach it.

I wrap my wet hair in a bath towel, grab my slightly steamy glasses, and pull Daniel's blue corduroy bathrobe from the hook on the bathroom door where it has been hanging since May when the evenings were still cool. As I tie it hastily around me, I wonder if Daniel misses it in Spain. But no, surely it is too hot there now for heavy corduroy.

I run quickly down the stairs in a hurry to silence the noisy intruder. I am curious but unafraid. After all, no self-respecting burglar or rapist would announce his presence by ringing the bell for five full minutes. I note with satisfaction that I have remembered to double-lock the front door, then pull aside the batik curtain that covers the full-length glass and switch on the light. There, blinking in the sudden light, with his left forefinger still on the doorbell and his right hand holding a rumpled madras jacket over his right shoulder, there stands Mark Harrington. He grins at me in his usual engaging way, and I wonder for the hundredth time whether his teeth are capped.

"Dr. Buchanan, aren't you going to let me in?"

I hesitate for some reason before I unlatch the door, think about clicking the lever on the screen door as I open the front door, then decide that might make him think I am afraid of him. Am I afraid of him? This is certainly an unorthodox situation. Mentally, I run my mind through myriad journal articles and texts. I can't remember ever having seen one about patients who show up on your doorstep late at night. Surely someone must have written about it.

"Dr. Buchanan, please, I need to talk to you."

"Mr. Harrington, you've chosen a very peculiar time and place for our talk. Is something troubling you?"

I wonder if that is a good opening. Have I put him on the defensive? Have I sounded unsympathetic? What would my old supervisor, Saul Rabinowitz, have said? I look at Harrington, trying to determine if he has been drinking. It is then that I realize how intently he is looking at me. Another grin flashes across his handsome face.

"That's a very fetching outfit you're wearing."

I look down at myself, nonplussed, and then hear the click of the screen as he lets himself in. "You've caught me at an awkward moment, Mr. Harrington. I was just taking a bath."

"I see," he says appraisingly, letting his eyes run up and down my torso, and he is in my living room.

"It would be best if we talked in my office tomorrow."

Does that sound all right? His eyes are too bright, and he keeps walking toward me. I turn sideways to him as if to let him pass. He stops, turns, and he is directly in front of me. My back is to the wall near the doorway. I try to look dignified. It is difficult to look dignified when you are barefoot and you can feel water trickling down your body and see it making little puddles on the waxed floor.

"What is it you want to talk about?"

I can hear his breathing, or is it my own? I know he is going to try to touch me, kiss me, and I don't know how to prevent it. My mind ranges quickly over all the possibilities. I make several alternative diagnoses I haven't thought of before: psychopath? no, borderline? maybe, narcissistic character disorder? hmmmm.

21

Meanwhile his right hand has dropped the madras jacket onto the sofa, and he is standing only inches from me.

"Mr. Harrington," I repeat for the third time as if addressing him formally, as I always do at the office, might remind him of the nature of our relationship, "it's obvious that you are in the grip of some rather strong feelings. But the same rule applies here as in the office. It would be best if you could tell me what those feelings are. Then we could talk about them, learn something from them. Acting out has been a pattern for you in the past, and it has never solved anything for you. It needn't always be that way. There are other, better ways."

I'm not sure he can hear me. There are beads of perspiration on his upper lip, and there is a small blood vessel throbbing near his left temple. My God, is it possible he is psychotic? I reject the notion. It doesn't fit in with what I know about him. But I do know that his rational mind is not with us in the room at the moment and that the treatment, and maybe my own safety, depend on what I say, what I do next. Should I reach out for him, take his hands, which he does not seem to know what to do with now that they are both free, and lead him to the sofa where we can talk? Would that convince him that I am in control of the situation, that I am not afraid?

"You're much smaller than I thought you were," he says breathlessly, from the advantage of his six feet two inches, as his tongue licks the sweat off his upper lip.

"I'm not wearing any shoes," I point out to him irrelevantly, then recovering my analytic cool, "perhaps I appear larger to you in my office for reasons we haven't clearly understood yet. Shall we talk about that a little?" I add lamely.

I've lost him again. He is staring at my throat and collarbone exposed by the V of Daniel's bathrobe. I feel vulnerable. I am a woman. I don't want him to notice the absence of my breast. I don't want him to see my scar. I raise my right hand slowly, crossing it over my chest, clutching the neckline closer together, hoping he hasn't seen.

I move slowly as I have taught Hanna and Jacob to do with little woodland animals. All the while, I look into his eyes to distract him from my hand's motion. He seems hypnotized, yet I'm not sure he really sees me. For a moment I am piqued. I realize I want him to see me, not as I am now with my mutilated body and my husband's too-large bathrobe. Not with strands of wet hair peeking out limply from under a thick towel. Not with my heavy eyeglasses sliding down my still damp nose. But as I was five years ago, or ten, or more—a thoroughbred, as Daniel once said, long of limb and light of bone. My vanity embarrasses me, and I feel guilty as I wonder whether my only partly conscious wishes that he want me have communicated themselves to him and become translated into whatever obsession has brought him (unbidden, I hope) to my door.

"Dr. Buchanan."

"Yes, Mr. Harrington."

"I have to talk to you." His hand reaches out and rests itself lightly on my left shoulder near where my own is clutching at the lapels of the bathrobe.

"Mr. Harrington, if we're going to talk, let's go sit on the sofa. Perhaps you'd like a cup of coffee."

I take one step forward toward the kitchen and run smack into the wall of his body. My hope that a purposeful move on my part would bring him to his senses does not materialize. I feel his hand close over my own and begin the now inevitable effort to unclench the fingers that hold the bathrobe shut. Should I fight him?

"Mr. Harrington," I murmur into his silk necktie, "try to get a hold of yourself," and I push gently but firmly against his chest with my free hand.

"Shhh," he whispers, as he uncurls one of my fingers, then another, and he pulls the towel off my head and begins stroking my wet hair.

His hands are deft and gentle, and when I feel myself begin to tremble, I am not certain fear is the only reason. I give up my battle to hold the bathrobe shut and use both hands to push against his chest. He hushes me again and steps forward, using one knee to pin me quite effectively to the wall. For a moment I think of screaming, then reject the idea in the interest of the therapy. Perhaps I should slap his face the way men used to do in the movies with women having hysterical outbursts. But I cannot free either of my hands from between our two chests.

"Please, Mr. Harrington, for your sake and mine, stop what you're doing and consider what it means."

Whether or not he hears me I cannot tell, but I feel his hands begin to slip the bathrobe down my shoulders, and a breathy kiss plants itself on the back of my neck.

Panic overcomes me, and I shout "Mark, please," then, hearing the words, wonder how many times he has heard them with various other women, and what they have meant.

I know I am defeated and for a moment am tempted to enjoy the patterns he is tracing with his fingers and his mouth along my neck and upper back, when suddenly I remember what will be revealed to him if he manages to slip off my robe. Vanity succeeds where fidelity to husband and psychoanalysis might have failed. I jerk his necktie hard, hoping to startle him. His head comes up, and he steps back to have a look at this new development. I seize the opportunity to move sideways out of his reach, but as I do so the robe falls open, revealing what he would have guessed before if my arms and hands hadn't braced themselves between our upper torsos.

"Oh no," I hear, and "Oh my God," and I bite my lips to keep from saying more, before I realize it is he who has spoken.

I pull the bathrobe closed and start to turn aside, then remember he is my patient. I look at his face, drained of all color by what he has seen, and I feel like the Gorgon head Medusa who turns men to stone. He feels sick, it is clear, and his sickness transcends the waves of nausea and dizziness emanating from somewhere inside my own body. He begins to look frantically around the room.

"It's at the top of the stairs, Mr. Harrington. This is an old house. There are no bathrooms down here."

I point him in the right direction, and, as he plunges toward his destination, I move into the safety of my kitchen.

Automatically, I turn the burner on under the teakettle, then reach for the ceramic pot, hoping it isn't full of stale leaves. Mercifully, it is clean. I turn on the hot water in the sink and let it fill the pot, then pull a cannister of English tea from the shelf. While I wait for the water to boil, I rewrap Daniel's bathrobe,

24

circling my waist twice with the long sash. I double-knot it and straighten the lapels.

My hand moves to my hair. I am surprised to find it still quite wet and realize that only minutes have passed since I answered the door. My trembling fingers refuse to make a braid, but I am able to twist it in a kind of makeshift chignon, which I fasten with a large bobby pin I see lying on the windowsill.

The water boils. I measure four teaspoons of tea into the pot after emptying it of water, then pour the steaming liquid over the waiting leaves. Done. I find a tray, a sugar bowl, and two large glass mugs with trigger handles. I have always enjoyed the beautiful amber color of strong tea and prefer to drink it out of glass.

I go into the living room to wait for Mr. Harrington. The sounds of running water from upstairs tell me that he is through with being sick and is now washing up. Out the living room window I see his green Mercedes sports car shining under a street lamp. Remembering the two others he has totaled in six months, I go to the telephone and call a cab, asking for it to come in thirty minutes. Then I return to the living room, adjust the Buchanan-plaid tea cozy over the pot (Daniel's and my first trip to Scotland, 1965), and wait again.

Mr. Harrington descends the stairs. His hair is damp and rumpled. I picture him as he must have been moments ago with his head under the faucet.

"Feeling better?"

"Well, at least there's no danger of my throwing up on your rug," he answers, shifting from one foot to another like a sheepish schoolboy.

"Sit down, Mr. Harrington." He does. "Do you take sugar in your tea?" I ask, as I begin to pour.

"Yes, two." He adds "please" in a whisper, almost as an after-thought. Still whispering, he says, "I'm sorry. I'm really very sorry."

"Yes," I reply, "I know you are."

I hand him the mug and pour my own tea.

"Don't you take any sugar?" he asks.

"No, I like it this way."

I cannot control the trembling of my hand as I try to bring the

25

mug to my lips. The hot liquid splashes on the coffee table and on the lap of Daniel's robe.

"Are you all right?"

He is on his feet over me, looking confused and concerned. I wish he would sit down.

"Dr. Buchanan? Are you all right?"

"Yes, fine, just a little shaky."

Should I tell him how I feel about what he has done to me? Should I tell him what it means to me to be exposed as I was ten minutes before? I can't let Daniel look at me yet, not in the daylight. I can barely look at myself. I must not tell him. But I must tell him something.

"It has been a very difficult evening, Mr. Harrington, frightening and confusing. For both of us."

He looks at me, sits down, covers his eyes with his hands.

"I'm so ashamed. I don't know what I was thinking of."

He pauses. Should I encourage him to go on? Should I tell him we can talk about it tomorrow at our regular appointment?

"I had been thinking about you all day. All week maybe. I knew I had to see you. I knew it couldn't wait until our regular appointment. Then, after work, I went to a bar and just sat there drinking vodka martinis until, until . . ."

I interrupt him. "We can talk about it tomorrow, Mr. Harrington, at our regular appointment. Drink your tea."

He drops his hands from in front of his face. "No, no, I can't come to my appointment tomorrow, how can I ever face you again?"

"You're facing me right now, Mr. Harrington. Drink your tea. We'll talk about it tomorrow."

He has a dazed expression on his face. I put down my mug, pick up his, and hand it to him. "Go on," I say.

I am on strange ground and do not know if anything I am doing makes sense in terms of the treatment. My actions are instinctive: I am a mother, he is a sick child, he must have something warm in his stomach. It doesn't matter anymore that he has uncovered my nakedness and found the sight so repulsive that he vomited. I am, after all, only his doctor, not a real woman at all. I must heal him.

It is my profession, my calling. He drinks his tea. While he drinks it, I tell him the plan.

"I have taken the liberty of calling a taxi for you. It will be here in a few minutes. I will drive your car to my office tomorrow, if you will give me the keys. You can pick it up there when you come for your appointment."

It sounds rather neat to me, actually. I guarantee his safety and his arrival for his hour with one neat stroke. He nods agreement and hands me the keys obediently.

"Your house keys, Mr. Harrington. You'll be needing those, surely," and I begin to detach the double-ringed mechanism separating car keys from house keys.

"No, no, Monica can let me in," and I am stabbed with envy as I wonder what it must be like to be beautiful and rich and young and to grow up with a name like Monica. "Wait a second, she's not there. I just remembered that Monica left today for Connecticut. She took Kelly Ann up to see the grandparents."

Connecticut. It figures. Something clicks in my brain, and the jealousy is swept away while insight rushes in to take its place. His wife is gone. And Daniel is gone. Something he said last hour if I can only remember. The pieces will fit together; his behavior tonight will be part of a pattern. In his acting out he has shown me what he has not been able to tell me. What has he needed to hide? What made him feel so lost, so frantic that he was driven to enact with me this scene of love and hate? I need time to think of it.

"Dr. Buchanan, the cab is here. I'll go now if you give me my keys."

I snap the two silver segments apart, handing him his house keys.

"No," he says engagingly, "give me the car keys, too. I'll send someone from the office over tomorrow morning to pick it up."

I see into his head and know he plans to leave, that he will not come back to the office, that he will not finish his therapy. He feels he has disrupted the treatment by touching my skin, by seeing my imperfect body. And maybe that was his plan in part. The cab driver gives a discreet honk. I go to the front door and flash the light to signal our awareness of his presence.

I shake my head. "No, Mr. Harrington. I'll keep your car keys. It's imperative that we discuss what has happened this evening. You owe it to yourself to understand all the feelings that led up to it, plus those you may have about me and yourself, now that you've seen my . . . my condition."

I am nonplussed. The speech that started out so firmly, so analytically, has bogged down in the muddy waters of my own feelings.

"Besides," I smile up at him, "you wouldn't rob me of the opportunity to drive that Mercedes, would you?"

Humor succeeds where reason fails. He gives a mock salute and heads out the door.

"See you tomorrow," I remind him.

He nods, walks briskly down the porch steps, then turns on his heel and looks me straight in the eyes for the first time all evening. "Thanks," he says. And he is gone.

I flick off the porch light, double-lock the front door, and turn to survey the living room. The tea things need putting away, the bath towel lying on the floor has to go into the laundry, the spill on the coffee table needs mopping up. I straighten things as needed, noticing Harrington's jacket on the sofa. It is a nice jacket—casual, yet sophisticated. The smell of his cologne passes over me as I hang it in the closet. For the moment I am amused, as I wonder what the neighbors will think: husband out of town, doorbells ringing at 11:00 P.M., strange sports car parked in front of the house all night. I can't decide whether it will be good or bad for my image.

Everything is in order in my house. I ascend the stairs. All at once I feel cold, and I begin to tremble again. It is a hot July night, but I am shivering and my feet are like ice. I turn off the air conditioner in the bedroom, pull back the curtains, and throw open two windows to let the warm, moist air in. I am too tired to brush my teeth, dry my hair. I lie on the lightweight cotton bedspread, listening to the night insects, trying to remember their names. They buzz and stop, buzz and stop, as if waiting for an answer. I am still cold. I get up, throw off the damp bathrobe and crawl under the covers of the bed. I pull my knees up to my chest and place my hands between my thighs to warm them. If only

Daniel were here to mock me as he rubbed my feet, "Christ, your feet are cold. Haven't you got any blood?"

My trembling grows more violent and I feel the shock of the experience envelop me, now that I have finished with all my responsibilities to Mark Harrington's psyche and the order of my house. The look on Harrington's face as my bathrobe fell open flashes in front of my eyes over and over again, and I hear his voice saying, "Oh no, oh my God, oh no."

"Oh no" to the diagnosis of cancer and "oh my God" to the loss of the breast and "oh no" when the dressings finally come off and I see myself in all my hideousness.

"I want a mirror," I raged at the nurse in the hospital. "I must have a mirror."

But all the mirrors in the house are covered. Someone has shrouded them, according to the old Jewish custom. Against demons? Spirits? Do the dead dwell in mirrors? I do not know, for I am only a child. But the mirrors are covered, and the house is crowded with wooden folding chairs marked with the name of the funeral home. My mother arrives from the cemetery, where I have not been allowed to go ("No, no, my babies are too young to see him in the ground," she had wailed). She is leaning on her brother's arm. She is very small and frail, so thin I am sure she will shatter if I hug her too tight. The look on her face is blurry and dazed, but she finally raises her head as she enters the room. Her face comes into focus as she spots the mirrors: "Who draped my mirrors?" she says angrily, dropping my uncle's arm.

Her voice grows in volume, and she is suddenly very tall. She walks purposefully to the mantel piece and standing on tiptoe, jerks the white sheet down onto the floor. "There will be no superstition in my house. Not as long as I am alive."

And then she fades back out of the spotlight and into my uncle's arms. He supports her until they reach the couch where she collapses and remains. It is a week before I see her rise. I stand in the corner watching, with wide myopic eyes covered by glasses too big for my face. I am fiercely proud of her. And though she is very, very small and very, very alone, I know that I and my brothers and sister will be safe.

My hands are warm now, and I pull them out from between my

29

thighs. Tentatively, I place the left one on the place where my right breast used to be. My fingers are shocked by the grisly hardness, the concave quality to that once soft and fleshy spot. I see with my hand what he saw with his eyes downstairs, what I saw when the nurse finally brought the mirror, what I see every time I take a bath. It is ugly. It bears no resemblance to a woman. It bears no resemblance to anything human. It is scar tissue and damaged skin. It is not the way my body was before I grew breasts, and it is not the way it was before the surgery. It is something altogether new, altogether wrong, altogether hideous. No wonder Harrington was sick. I feel slightly sick myself. Poor Harrington. Poor me.

I roll over on my back and stare out the window at the old pin oak tree with its branches etched by the moon. I remember when we had the dead branches pruned away by the fearless young men from the forestry department at the university. I watched them from this very window as they climbed sixty feet up the tree trunk, then, with their portable power saws, clambered out on the more precarious lateral branches and began to buzz away. All the limbs were tied with ropes before they were cut, then lowered gently, almost lovingly to the ground. They painted the raw places with an orange sticky substance, sawed up the dead wood and stacked it alongside the garage. For weeks the tree looked awkward to me; its outline against the sky seemed too bony and angular. Finally my eye adjusted. And, in the spring when the first green leaves came out softening its silhouette, the stately old tree seemed quite handsome again, quite fine. I wish that I could grow leaves to camouflage my losses.

There was no camouflage when Mr. Harrington's eyes saw my white skin against the midnight blue corduroy. How shocking it must have been for him. I wonder what implications it will have for him in terms of castration anxiety, nurturance, other important issues. I must be on the alert. If he doesn't bring anything up, I may have to bring it up for him . After all, it fairly stares him in the face.

I turn over on my right side but cannot get comfortable, until I pull a pillow over to nestle under my shoulder and my chest as the woman from Reach for Recovery suggested.

Yes, castration is a theme that should be uncovered by this unfortunate episode. The beheaded Medusa, her coiffure a tangle of snakes, the bleeding phallic woman. No one may look upon her except with mirrors, backwards. Mark Harrington will have to face his feelings about that now. And so will Leah Bronstein Buchanan. Again.

I hear Daniel's nautical clock strike four bells downstairs. The first watch is half over, it is 2:00 A.M. I readjust my pillow, and I sleep.

In my dream I am walking down an unfamiliar street wearing a nondescript, beige suit. I step into a stall shower and then whirl out, ripping off my blouse and proudly exposing my chest like Superman. I am dazzling in silver sequins. Passersby on the street shield their eyes with raised elbows. Those who don't are blinded by the rays emanating from my shining torso. I spread my arms, and I am far above them doing an elegant breast stroke through the air, oddly graceful, like a porpoise or a pelican. Floating out behind me is a brilliant blue corduroy cape emblazoned with blood red serpents. My heart soars.

2

FRIDAY MORNING——

I AWAKE next morning, very early, the sun streaming through my window. There is a terrible taste in my mouth, from not brushing my teeth perhaps, or from the events of the night before. I sit up abruptly, trying to convince myself that all of it has been a bad, but readily interpretable, dream. Yet the memory clings, assuming more and more reality in the light of day, rather than sliding away and receding, in the way of dreams. I force myself to focus on it, and he is there before me. Harrington.

Mark Harrington. Young (yes, thirty-four looks young to me now), handsome, self-assured, plenty of money. He strides into my office twice a week as if he were on his tennis courts graciously proffering a warm handshake and a word of praise to his (always) losing opponent. With his rugged good looks and his beautifully tailored clothes, his warm smile and hearty laugh, it is at first hard to imagine why he should be sitting across from me in my office, rather than on one of his polo ponies or in a lounge chair by the country club pool.

As his saga unfolds, the aching void beneath the seeming perfect surface of his life begins to appear. Over the months I have watched him try to fill that void with sports cars, alcohol, and women, only to reappear in my office each Tuesday and Friday, still smiling, but with a quizzical expression in his too bright eyes.

Something haunts this man, something I have glimpsed but not yet seen. He presents to me the details of his life like a child unwrapping the Mother's Day present he has made in school, and I try to hear the strange song he sings: The words are there, but the melody is missing. It is a strain to listen, and I find my mind wandering sometimes to his handsome face, more often to the muscular thighs displayed in well-fitting winter twills, or in summer seersucker, which I fancy I can see through. He has large tanned hands with long tapering fingers, which frequently twist his wedding band, exposing a pale brand of flesh on the third finger of his left hand. Absentmindedly, I look at the gold and the diamonds lying in my own lap. Looking up, I see his lips moving, and slowly the words shape themselves, first in my eyes, then my ears and brain. He is talking about his wife, a slim, cool looking, elegant blond I have seen on his arm at the symphony, and about his betrayals of her with various secretaries and stewardesses. I feel excited as he recounts his exploits in great detail and cross my legs as if to hide from him the invisible pulse that throbs between them.

Is he unconsciously attempting to seduce me with his words? If so, to what extent am I complicit in this act? His unconscious reaches out to me like a caress, and for the thousandth time, I thrill and shudder to the nakedness of need that sits across from me in that slightly worn chair. I feel it, a palpable third presence in the room, pulling me inward and downward to merge with its selfish self.

In years gone by I resisted this symbiosis so violently that I frequently found myself forced to speak, even changing the subject, to break the spell. I would redirect the patients' attention to a statement made a minute before the swelling of this mysterious and clutching love, pretending interest in a dream, a slip, or making a facile interpretation. Like the fencing I did in college, thrust and parry, parry and thrust. I could not bear the claustrophobia that enveloped me in those moments, as I felt myself being sucked out of my chair or, worse still, as I felt the breath of their naked need reach out to envelop me where I sat. Persistent, like the waves leading up to an orgasm, is their longing, the sound of their silence. Hypnotic and terrible and hauntingly seductive.

It was my old supervisor, Saul Rabinowitz, who helped me work it out. Saul, with his quiet wisdom and his ready smile.

"So let it happen. So what if it happens? It's the hardest thing in our work, really. What you're talking about is the crux of the transference. Why do you keep warding it off? What are you afraid of? Let's find out so you can get on with your work."

He probably knew all along what I was afraid of, just as I know now: It was the nakedness of my own need staring back at me from the eyes of my patients. Their terrible wish, their terrible fear of merging with me, reflected in part my own terrible wishes and fears: to merge, not just physically, not just sexually, but to feel another being blend with yourself, his mind, if you will, his soul. How utterly terrible. How awful, in the Biblical sense: how full of awe. How exquisite! The end of struggle, the end of longing, the end of conflict. Merger, symbiosis, death, rebirth. What some people experience as God, as the call, as being born again, I experience in the sanctity of my office, when I allow the ebb and flow of the tides between my unconscious and the patients', when at last I see them, as Moses saw God, face to face, and I know them, and myself.

With some patients it never happens. Perhaps their need is not so great, or it is hidden in a place I cannot find. Perhaps I do not see in them enough of myself to allow it to happen.

But with handsome young Mark Harrington, I knew from the first it was there, waiting. The throb between my legs is only the beginning, the first sign. Superficially he signals me with sex, the language he thinks he understands. And I hear him because he is attractive and because Daniel is in Spain and because I am missing one breast and because I want to be young and desirable. And I do

35

not feel guilty for that. What bothers me is when I sit there letting his words wash over me until my pants are slightly wet, dreaming of opening my legs to him instead of working at opening my mind, which is, after all, what he is paying me for. To feel aroused by a patient during psychotherapy is one thing, not unusual, not even harmful. But to stop at that and learn nothing from it about the patient or yourself, that reflects a loss of control, a slippage in technique that bodes ill for the treatment.

My errant thoughts about Harrington make me wonder if I should be going to the office at all, let alone practicing psychotherapy there. Maybe Saul isn't the one I need to talk to . Maybe Dr. Isaacson is the one. Perhaps the five years I spent in his office and the three in Dr. Edwards's weren't enough. Maybe I need another three or five years, or eight, or even ten, to straighten myself out—if I have three or five or eight or ten years left, that is. But I do not want to think about that. Better to think about the intricacies of my profession and my ability to pursue it. Have I chosen it as a form of self-indulgence? How much unreconstructed narcissism is left in me, anyway, threatening to inflate itself and insidiously crowd out my patients' needs in favor of my own?

I gave up the idea of becoming an actress early on, having realized—maybe even before I met Frank—that my talent wasn't great enough to suit me to the starring roles I would have preferred. But now, now I play all the roles. I am at the same time hero, supporting actor, villain, director, co-author, audience, and even the stage itself. Or, to switch the metaphor to cinema and psychoanalysis, I am the screen on which is projected by the patient the drama of his life. All I have to do is sit in my chair and the story begins to unfold. The plots vary a bit, yet, in essence, are always the same. Grand passion, high tragedy, low comedy, and, God knows, much melodrama, all are enacted in my office. I do not move a muscle. I rarely speak. Yet the patient sees me as Sarah Bernhardt, Laurence Olivier combined. At last my *femme fatale* dream comes true: I am all things to all men. And although I have no memorable speeches or gestures, still I am never upstaged. Even though the spotlight is usually on the patient, I am in every scene.

What an unfair advantage I have over every other person in that poor patient's life! Altough I may be older or younger, richer or poorer, more attractive or more plain than his or her mother, father, boss, teacher, lover, or spouse, in the end (actually the middle) it is I who will triumph. In the blush of the positive transference it is I who am the most loved, and in the fury of the negative transference, it is I who am most hated. Just thinking about it I am drunk with power. The temptation to abuse this power is so great at times that I fear I won't control it. Yet I always do. I gaze levelly across the room, suppressing the frown, smile, or blink that might devastate, seduce, or confuse them.

What can't I achieve in my office to gratify my bloated ego, to inflate my self-esteem? Merely by crossing my legs, or changing the inflection in my voice, I can make or break the patient's day, sending his mood soaring or crashing as he leaves my office. If I choose to do so, I can. I can do it consciously, thanks to Dr. Isaacson, Dr. Edwards, and Saul, and, thanks to them, I won't. But there are therapists who do it unconsciously, and others who do it consciously, calling it part of the treatment, when in reality they are manipulating the transference in a most unscrupulous way.

Still there are times when I do not blame them, times when my own life feels so sad, so empty, that I long to live vicariously as part of somebody else's. To be so loved, to have no peer, it is part of everyone's dream. But I do not traffic in dreams anymore, except to analyze them. In my office, in my world, only reality holds sway. Or does it?

Lately, I worry not so much about my influencing or controlling the patients' lives, but about their influencing mine. They make their statements, gestures, complaints, and suddenly I do not hear them anymore. I am swept back into my own past to a time when I had no control. And I am frightened. For, if I have no control, then my office has become a ship without a rudder, and everyone in it may be swept along by the too-strong and dangerous current of emotion, into the sea of heaven knows what. I am the captain. I must have control at least of myself, if not of the complicated theory and technique of this treatment process that so many people mock and so few understand.

Perhaps it's the surgery, and I'm not dealing with it. It was

37

majory surgery. It was cancer. They removed my breast. There, I've said it. God, I'm tired.

How can I be so tired? I wish Daniel were here to put his arms around me. But he wouldn't put his arms around me. He'd tell me, "Snap out of it, for God's sake. Of course I still love you. I didn't marry your breast, dammit, I married you. So for Christ's sake stop your moaning. It's really self-indulgent and very like you to want to rehash the whole experience. It's over, Leah. You're here. I'm here. The kids are here. It's over. Enough."

I can hear him say it just as if he were standing across the room about to go out the door to the university. How many times did I look up at him just before he left to say, "Can you really still love me, now that I'm so ugly?".

And how many times did he put his arms around me and reassure me before he finally got fed up and began this other speech? I almost wish Jacob and Hannah were here so that I would have to come out of myself and begin to respond to them. No, I wish somebody were here to put his arms around me. But what would I do with those arms around me? Whatever would I do?

So I go to my office, and I listen to my patients, and I try to make sense out of the sporadic bursts of words, the sometime silences, the nervous gestures, the barely audible sighs, the almost tears. I listen for the theme, I wait for the thread to appear. And from time to time I hear it, that elusive melody, or I see it, that narrow twisted filament, which, if I can only grab hold of it, will pull things together. I sit in my chair and lean back, eyes half-closed, waiting. And, as I wait, I begin to hear other voices murmuring persistently beneath the drone or wail of whoever happens to be sitting across from me, and I see other images drift in front of my half-closed eyes, different ones from those being painted by my patient.

I know it is common for something a patient says to trigger the analyst's own memories and feelings. And from my training and my own analysis, I have learned to use these unbidden thoughts as a part of the treatment. For frequently, the therapist's unconscious responds to that of the patient before there is any clear, conscious understanding of the needs, fears, or longings being expressed.

I am no longer afraid of these responses to my patients. I trust my ability to interpret my own unanswered needs as well as theirs, and I can moderate the process and make use of it. But I do not trust these recurrent flights of fancy that remove me from my office and set me drifting in the faraway world of the past, or the unknown one of some fantasied future.

At first, I tried dealing with these fugues psychoanalytically. When did they take place? Was it with any particular patient at any particular time? Was there some type of material being produced by the patient that disturbed me? Homosexual themes perhaps. Strong transference feelings. Or was countertransference raising its ugly head? Did I care too much or too little about one patient or another? Did he or she remind me of someone in my past: father, mother, husband, self? I traveled down each of these paths, turning over every rock, pulling aside every shrub, hoping to find some hidden nest of worms or insects in my own head, that—once confronted—would allow me to move on in the patient's therapy. Finding no solution I turned to other paths. Could I be bringing too much to the office from home? Was there something in my current life that made it impossible to listen, that forced me to turn inward?

I am at a dead end again. I pull myself out of bed. A dull headache is already gathering strength somewhere behind my left eye. As I force myself to wash and dress, I mentally tick off the hours that confront me.

9:00 A.M.: Sandra Drake, twice divorced, a nurse who made a serious suicide attempt two months ago; she lives and works in a coal town some seventy miles distant and comes to see me once a week.

10:00 A.M.: Eric Johanson, biochemistry professor at the university, a frozen little man whose life is governed by test tubes and computers; he sees that his world is crumbling since his wife and child have left him, but hopes to win them back through one act of faith, psychotherapy.

11:00 A.M.: Fran Matthews, housewife and mother of three, bewildered that her plan to be a perfect wife and mother has been hampered by the fact that she is frigid toward her husband and rigid toward her children; she is overburdened by guilt, which makes her more rigid, more frigid.

12:00 noon: Ilana Fromer, rebellious twenty-year-old student who seems to feel her duty in life is to seduce every man she meets, especially Daniel, whose classes she has defiantly enrolled in for two semesters running, despite my frequent interpretations of this acting-out behavior; she is young, blonde, and pretty. He tells me that she has not succeeded in her seduction but has managed to write one terrible and one quite decent paper. She came into treatment reluctantly at the urging of her parents, who could not understand why a girl with an IQ of well over 130 should be flunking out of school.

After a tempestuous hour with Ilana (her given name was Elaine, but she romanticized it), I have a well-deserved lunch break. And then Mark Harrington at 2:00 P.M.

The events of the night before wash over me again, leaving me weak and dizzy. Gone is my sense of myself as a competent, professional woman ready to start another day. I grip the banister hard as I descend the stairs to the too-small kitchen that has been the bane of my remodeling plans since we bought the house eight years before. There in the sink, neatly rinsed and stacked, but not yet washed, are the tea things from the night before. I look at my wristwatch and, seeing seven, an hour at which I know at least one real restaurant that serves breakfast, I flee.

I walk out the back door and into the garage where our station wagon is housed. I carefully back out of the drive, wary of early morning joggers, and as I pull into the street, I see a flash of dark green in my rearview mirror: Harrington's Mercedes, resplendent in the morning sun! So, I am not to be allowed to have my coffee before I deal with this matter. Sighing, I drive back up the gravelly drive (Daniel keeps saying we have to have it paved, and I keep finding other priorities for the money), park the car, fish in my purse for the proper keys, and then head resolutely for the sports car, which, I am sure, cost Harrington very nearly what our house cost us.

I walk towards the front yard, noting as I cross the dewy lawn that the grass needs cutting, and then stand for a moment admiring Harrington's elegant machine. The doors are unlocked, and

40

the driver's window rolled down. I wonder if this is typical of his careless, carefree ways or a symptom of the stress he had been under when he arrived at my door last night. I have to bend low to get into the front seat, but once there I find plenty of room for my long legs.

The smell of the soft, tan leather is the first thing that hits me, then the luster of the polished hardwoods on the dashboard. The car fairly reeks of luxury and good taste. I note with satisfaction the leather cover on the steering wheel and the inconspicuously placed, but easily reached, am-fm radio, stereo tapedeck, and air conditioning.

I put the key in the ignition and as I turn it on feel the car come alive around me: the engine doesn't so much throb as hum, and the whole automobile seems to tremble gently, like a blooded horse at the starting gate. I think of Daniel and his old MG, which finally gave up the ghost during the first years of our marriage, and I feel how much a car like this might have meant to him, might still mean to him.

Mentally, I calculate how many patient hours it would take—before taxes—to buy such an extravagance. Then, sighing at the stupidity of it, I shift into first, let up on the clutch, and roll toward the corner. Although I haven't driven a shift car in years, this one fairly tells me which gear it wants to be in as it glides from first to third with the barest attention of my right hand and left foot.

I begin to get a sense of Harrington and his fascination with these expensive toys. It feels good to drive the damned car down the street. Years ago when Daniel and I would get dressed up to go to a party, we'd stand in front of a full-length mirror admiring how nice we looked, what a handsome couple we were, as if each of us were the perfect accessory to the other. This car makes me feel like that.

I speed along for a few tranquil minutes, letting the wind play its mindless games with my hair. Then, remembering whose car it is and why I am driving it, I become quite sober, shift down to turn a corner, and pull into the parking lot of Robertson's. I carefully roll up the window and lock the door, tuck the stray hairs back into place, and stride into the dining room of this

41

family-style restaurant well known for its down-home country cooking.

Once inside the door, I head for an inconspicuous booth, grateful that the place, though busy, is not too crowded. All around me I hear the clatter of knives and forks attacking ham and spoons stirring endless cups of coffee. A parade of platters comes out of the kitchen, each plate garnished by its obligatory dollop of grits. The waitress comes promptly, calling me "honey" as she repeats my order of one soft-boiled egg, toast, and coffee. I don't really want anything to eat but feel I have to justify my sitting here with something more than coffee. As an afterthought I add, "and a large tomato juice." The waitress's face brightens as she notes this respectable addition to my order; then she shoves the pencil into her elaborate hairdo and ambles off toward the kitchen.

I settle into the booth and begin to turn over in my mind the events of the evening before. I know I am badly shaken and admit to myself that the prospect of seeing Harrington today does not thrill me. I would, at the moment, cheerfully turn him over to any of my colleagues. Then I think of the many months of work behind us, the burgeoning transference, the violence of his acting out when things finally bubbled to the surface, and the horror-stricken look on his face when he saw me. What to do, what to do? If I send him to someone else it might mean rejection to him, as if his act were too terrible for forgiveness. Besides, it might well cost him a year to work through his relationship with me and develop another with someone else. I have to keep him in treatment with me, at least until he (we) have worked through the experience of the night before, and beyond that if possible.

I stir the coffee the waitress slapped down a minute before and wonder whether Harrington will show up today. Is the lure of the Mercedes sufficient, or will his shame, fear, pride, and confusion prompt him to cancel and send someone else for the car?

My egg and toast appear, the juice apparently forgotten, and I stare at them wondering if I can get them down my partially closed throat. I spoon up some of the egg, trying to disguise the fact that it is too runny by eating large bites of toast with it. That is hard enough to swallow, but the thoughts that follow are even more unpalatable.

Am I in some way responsible for Harrington's bizarre behavior? Have I given out signals to him that have drawn him to my door just as surely as a light aircraft in fog is pulled in on a radio beam? Has my need to have him find me as appealing as I find him made me neglect an analytic stance in favor of something more seductive?

I mentally scan the last several therapy hours, seeking subtle encouragement I might have given by smiling too readily or crossing my knees too conspicuously. When have I gazed at him too hard, talked too much, paused too long before offering an interpretation? I look around for the waitress, and, catching her eye, mouth the words, "more coffee please."

She gives me the "O" sign with her thumb and forefinger, and as she comes to my table to fill my cup, I wonder if a sub-rosa message from me to Harrington has been so clearly understood. Has he answered my need to be found sexually attractive just as readily as the waitress has fulfilled my wish for more coffee?

I hold my head in my hands and stare at the newly filled cup as if the answer might be found in that gently undulating blackness. I feel as exposed and ashamed as I had the night before when Daniel's robe slipped off my shoulder.

Maybe I should have gone up to Cincinnati to see Saul weeks ago. Maybe I should even be calling him now. I feel the need to address my thoughts to someone: Saul, Dr. Isaacson, Dr. Edwards. But all of them are gone. I think of Daniel. He doesn't approve of my recurrent wish to "bare the innermost trappings of my soul," as he calls it. "Honest to God, Leah, it's obscene the way you have no desire for privacy."

But there is no one to bare it to now, so no matter.

I finish my coffee and pay the check, not bothering to question the charge for the unfulfilled promise of tomato juice. I didn't want it. (Is there a philosophical point in that somewhere? Are we always bound to pay for those things we ask for but do not really want?)

I leave the restaurant and drive Harrington's car the short distance to my office, parking it in a far corner of the lot to avoid Nellie's curiosity and possibly to make it difficult for Harrington to find it should he decide to come and sneak it away with an extra

43

set of keys, thus avoiding our appointment. I laugh at the futility of that plan. As if anyone would have difficulty spotting that car anywhere. I let myself in the back door of the office and am surprised to be greeted by the smell of freshly brewed coffee. Nellie is frequently late for one reason or another and, as often as not, I start the coffee.

"Mornin'," she greets me, and immediately fills my mug from the steaming pot.

I don't dare to refuse this peace offering (I snapped at her about mislaying a file the day before), even though I know that this third jolt of caffeine could be fatal. It is hard enough for me to sit still in a chair for four hours running, especially with my bad back, without being hyped up on too much coffee. I drink from the proffered cup, gossiping idly with Nellie about slightly stale items from yesterday's newspaper. She fills me in on recent developments (the morning paper is her lifeline), carefully documenting useful bits of information she has learned about births, deaths, transfers of property, and divorce applications, especially as they apply to any of our patients.

I listen, nodding occasionally, and make certain to express interest as required. Then I ask her about her children, knowing that that will precipitate a long soliloquy requiring only the minimum of response.

As she rambles on and I absentmindedly sip at the hot coffee, I feel a twinge of longing for the twins. I want to look at their animated faces and touch the softness of their hair, to see Hannah's crinkled nose as she good-humoredly tells a story about a trick played on one of the camp counselors, or Jacob's solemn eyes as he recounts in detail all the things he has seen on a nature hike. They both seem so terribly far away. I know they'd throw my arms off if I tried to encircle them and hug them. "Oh Mom," they'd say with exasperation, "don't be so mushy." (Mushiness has been much deplored in the past six months, especially by Jacob. But even he forgets himself sometimes at bedtime and cuddles in as I read to him or we talk about the day's doings.) I hear the door to the outer office click shut and know that the always punctual Sandra Drake has arrived.

"Well, Nellie," I sigh, "time for work," and I carry the half-full cup down the hall toward the patients' waiting room.

Nellie's voice follows me in a stage whisper, "Almost forgot to tell you, your three o'clock canceled."

For a second I feel defeated. I am that sure it is Harrington. But he is 2:00. It is poor Orville Wheeler and his wife Alma. He must have had a bad time with his chemotherapy this month. Thirty-two years old and dying of a malignant brain tumor. And I am supposed to show him how. I am not up to the task. Yet he and his mouselike little wife seem to derive some satisfaction from their visits while I feel more and more ashamed when I compare the ill grace with which I have accepted the surgery that robbed me of my breast to the stoical, rustic dignity with which they have come to grips with slow and painful death. A 3:00 cancellation. But the Klinefelters are due in at 4:00. Damn! No rest for the weary. I don't really like working with couples and am only doing it as a favor to my psychiatrist colleague, Doug Prentiss, with whom I share office space. He has been seeing Mrs. Klinefelter for two years and is at an impasse: "Something has to be done about that rigid, anal, obsessive-compulsive, passive-aggressive, bastard of a husband of hers," Doug says.

But Mr. Klinefelter refused to be seen alone; so I took them on as a couple while poor Doug continued to work with Mrs. Klinefelter. I find it almost impossible to relate to two people at once, at least in any meaningful way, and have often wondered whether Providence handed me a set of high-strung twins as a test of character. So I doggedly pursue the mists and miasmas of the Klinefelters' miserable marriage hoping that something good will come of it. Doug tells me that Mrs. Klinefelter gets some grim satisfaction out of seeing hubby on the hook one hour a week, hardly a proper reason for treatment to continue. And I have in all honesty told them I don't think we are getting anywhere, but they want to continue.

I flip a mental coin in my head before I walk the rest of the way down the hall. Heads. I win. "Cancel the Klinefelters," I tell Nellie, already feeling guilty at this unprecedented act.

She looks up from her paper in amazement, "Well, aren't you a regular go-to-hell today!" she chuckles. "That's the smartest thing you've done in a long time."

Feeling strangely lighthearted that my work day will end at three, I walk down the hall, preparing a proper face for the greeting of Miss Drake.

Sandra Drake sits across from me, unheeded tears rolling quietly down her face, a catch in her voice as she tells me how hard it is for her to work, to converse with people, to live, since her hospitalization the month before. "I just know they're all starin' at me and thinkin' and wonderin' and tryin' to get a glimpse of those ugly red scars on my wrist. I once heard that people who try to kill themselves are only tryin' to attract attention, and maybe that's true, but I sure don't like the attention I'm gettin'. And I know you were right that I had to leave the hospital and go back to my job and I like my work, really I do, but I just can't stand to be around people and yet I'm afraid to be alone. Why, I walked into the general store last Saturday just to see another human face, to hear people talk, and I stood there for five full minutes fingerin' some cans of tomato soup and tryin' to work up enough courage to say 'Nice day today, isn't it?' or 'Have you got the time?' I wanted so bad to hear the sound of my own voice talkin' to someone because, well, you know how alone I am up there. But I'm afraid of them, I really am. I'm afraid of everyone, and when they looked over at me I didn't know what to say or do, so I took some money out of my pocket and bought two cans of soup without sayin' a word and, Dr. Buchanan, I don't even like tomato soup, and then I just sort of backed out the door and sort of slunk down the street and I heard the door slam. . . ."

The door on yet another train crashes shut, and I am quivering from head to toe. It is the third train that has rushed by me, the third one I should have boarded, and now I know I'll be late to school for sure. And I'll miss my English class, the only one I was looking forward to even a little. But the Park Street station is so crowded in the early morning, and I already used up what courage I had boarding at Charles and riding to Park. The train was packed the whole way, and I could feel people's bodies pressing up against me, and I felt sick and could hardly breathe. I probably wouldn't even have been able to get off at Park, except that so many other people were getting off they just sort of swept me out with them. And now I am standing here shivering in my too-thin skirt and unlined ski jacket. As each train barrels past, it leaves a whooshing tunnel of November wind behind it, and the cold outside air wraps itself around my bare legs, until I feel them ache. I clutch my green book bag tighter to me, hugging it for warmth, for safety.

Now the station is emptying out, and it is quieter and doesn't smell so much of people. Soon, soon, if I am able, I will board the train and ride it all the way to the end of the line at Route 128, just as I did yesterday. And maybe the MTA driver will be nice, as the one yesterday was, and bid me sit near him and smoke if I like after the train empties itself somewhere near Newton.

I feel in my ski jacket for cigarettes, and my fingers close gratefully over the squat, almost-square packet that is such a pretty shade of blue. Gauloise. They smell terrible and taste worse, but when I light one, I can feel the smoke biting into my throat and lungs, and I know I am at least alive. The crinkle of the cellophane is somehow reassuring, and I feel a bit better and think that, yes, I will board the next train.

And as I wait for it, I wonder what I will do when I get off the train. Will I sit in the station and smoke until I run out of cigarettes as I did yesterday, or will I take a bus or hitch a ride to school? My doctor may be disappointed if I don't go to school again today. I don't think he gave me a pass just to sit smoking in the station. But the station is quiet in the middle of the morning, and the wooden benches feel real against my back, and school is so very far away and so filled with people. Not anonymous people, like the ones pressing up against me from Charles Street to Park. They are hateful enough. But at least I never had to feel their eyes burning into me or hear their kindly, curious questions. The people at school will want to look me in the face. They'll want to talk, and they'll expect me to talk too.

In my other pocket, I feel the now dog-eared edge of the note my doctor arranged for with the dean, and I know its contents by heart from having read and reread it as I smoked and swung my legs in the station yesterday: "Please consider Miss Bronstein's absence from classes from November 1, 1957, to November 28, 1957, as excused absences." Nothing more. At the top of the note there is the discreet heading bearing the name of the small, northeastern liberal arts institution: Brandeis University. Just below it, the additional information, Office of the Dean of Undergraduate Studies. And in the lower right hand corner, now looking a little worse for wear, the signature of that somewhat bewildered and rather kindly man who found himself in the unenviable position of driving me to the hospital on November 1.

It was touching, indeed, when he showed up some days later, clearly ill at ease in this setting, with a gift of books and magazines for me. And maybe someday, when I'm able to read a paragraph without holding my head between my hands and forcing my eyes to see the words and my brain to comprehend them, maybe someday I'll read them. But for today, my task is more straightforward: I must climb the hill that winds up from the road to the university; I must present Dean Jackson's note to my professors; I must return to school.

". . . return to school." I am momentarily confused as to whether the last words are hers or mine. I refocus my eyes and see Miss Drake fidgeting in her chair, tracing the still-reddish scars on her left wrist with her right forefinger. I glance at my own left arm; the whitish lines there are barely visible now. Instinctively, I try to rearrange the expression on my face from one of confusion to one of concern. Miss Drake glances hesitantly at me and then quickly looks away. It is always difficult for her to look me in the eye. I am safe. My reverie has gone undetected. I reach for my coffee in an effort to wash away the acrid taste in my mouth and notice that it is quite cold. So my daydream has gone on for some minutes, and once again I have robbed Miss Drake, who conscientiously pays my fee the first week of every month. She can barely afford it. I become more active for the remainder of the hour, asking questions, even proffering some advice, in the hope that this will keep me with her. As I walk her to the door, I silently pray that the antidepressant Doug has prescribed for Miss Drake will prop her up while I let her down. Maybe I'll do better next time.

48

I close the door behind me and lean against its cool weight gratefully. Pulling off my glasses, I rub the bridge of my nose between my left thumb and forefinger and wonder how this headache could have gotten such an early start. I have ten minutes before Johanson, probably already in the waiting room, must be admitted to the holy of the holies. Ten minutes to figure out why I spent part of the last hour in my own past rather than Miss Drake's.

How can I go on with this charade? It isn't fair to them to give them only that part of me that is left in my chair, while my mind ranges somewhere else. Where? Why?

I glance around my office at the books in the bookcases, the recent journals laid out neatly on my desk. Is the answer somewhere there? If I open the right book, the most esoteric journal, if I turn to the proper page, find the most erudite article, will it tell me what I need to know? Or must I travel north some eighty miles to Saul's office? Could he, with his quiet good humor and gentle ways, could he give the answer?

But something in me refuses to look into my books or go up to Saul's office. The answers lie in me, I know, and in the work I did so many years ago. For the first time in years, I see Dr. Edwards looking at me with his patient eyes. He is listening, waiting, maybe even allowing himself the luxury of hoping that I will move ahead, that somehow I will stumble over or burrow through whatever blocks my path, single-mindedly seeking after the truth that he is teaching me to prize, like a germinating seed pushing up through the earth on its quest for light.

Eric Johanson slips into my office carrying his ubiquitous umbrella. He is a slightly built man whose face, physique, and way of moving give him the appearance of an adolescent. Sometimes it is hard for me to believe that he is three years older than I. To my greeting of "good morning" he has replied with his usual curt nod. Now he is seating himself carefully in the chair, adjusting the bicycle clips that encircle the calves of his legs. He lays his umbrella on my bookcase and glances at me expectantly. I wait. He is wearing what I call his summer uniform: a blue cord suit, white shirt (short-sleeved, I presume, for one day when the air conditioner wasn't functioning he actually removed his suit coat), and a red and blue rep tie. His winter uniform consists of a tan corduroy suit, white shirt with long sleeves (I can see the cuffs), a brown and green rep tie. I have often wondered, as I wait futilely for him to start the hour, whether these are his only clothes or whether he alternates them with other uniforms, which he wears on days when he is not in my office.

"What do you want to talk about?" he starts in his usual way.

I recognize it for what it is, a mildly aggressive ploy designed to shift the burden of the treatment to me, to thwart the cardinal rule that he say whatever comes into his mind, to underline the fact that he is not in control here (something he very much resents), while at the same time he maintains control by putting me on the defensive. I wait. He shifts in his chair. Sometimes I have answered him with "say whatever comes to mind" or "I see you're having difficulty getting started this morning." Today I feel sadistic; I let him squirm a little. It probably makes more sense therapeutically to be silent anyway. I hope the look on my face is properly empathic. But it is hard to reflect his feelings since his feelings are almost impossible for him, or me, to detect. He shifts again. There is a tight quality to his face.

For a second, I intuit anger. Should I identify it for him ("You seem angry this morning.")? No, I'll follow the old comma rule: when in doubt, leave it out. Saul always liked that one. He gave me in exchange this piece of wisdom from one of his teachers: in psychotherapy, when you are the therapist, don't just do something, sit there. I sit.

Outside, a mockingbird goes through his varied repertoire. I lose myself in the pleasure of his music, then wrench myself back to the cold discomfort of Johanson's fidgety silence. He seems even more uneasy than usual. I wonder what is bothering him. If I ask him what has taken place since he left my office three days ago, he will give me a recitation of every event. ("I left your office and bicycled down the highway toward the university. The traffic was heavy, and it was quite warm that day. Nearly 36 degrees Celsius, if I recall correctly. I chained my bicycle to a tree in front of the biochemistry building, because all the bicycle racks were taken. I rode the elevator to the fourth floor and stopped in at the lab.

Jenkins was there, washing out Erlenmeyer flasks . . .") He will go on and on with this dull history of the dull mechanics of his dull life, never once shedding a glimmer of light on what he feels, what he thinks, who he is.

I let my attention hover and wonder when he will speak, what he will say. He mumbles something. It is almost inaudible.

"I can't hear you," I state simply.

"I said my wife called me last night," he fairly shouts.

Bingo! His wife called him and he is angry all at one fell swoop. I reiterate his statement, pointing out his angry tone, hoping to encourage him to proceed. He does. At last the hour is under way. Heaving a mental sigh of relief, I settle back in my chair and begin the process of sifting through the material he presents, looking for that elusive golden nugget that will illuminate Johanson's shadowy world.

When the hour draws to a close some minutes later, I am satisfied that I have done my job. Nothing brilliant, mind you, but at least I stayed with him, helped him to stay with himself. He leaves the office aware of the anger he has felt toward me, toward his wife, toward the women, the betrayals he has known.

10:50. Fifty minutes gone, and I have not once thought of Mark Harrington's visit to me last night. Perhaps the caffeine has done me more good than harm. I leave my chair and move about my narrow office, stretching my arms to nearly touch the walls. I rise on tiptoe and try to see the bird whose serenade so cheered me during Johanson's soliloquy of silence. But he is gone. Or else his grayness hides him among the branches of the parking lot's lone tree, and he will remain invisible until a flash of white wing bars quickens him in flight. I salute the skillful songster and go out to use the bathroom before Fran Matthews's arrival. I am pleased with myself that I stuck with Johanson during the whole hour. No flights of fancy, no unremembered reveries. And he is one of my most difficult patients.

On the way out of the bathroom I note that I have eaten off all my lipstick, as I usually do. I apply more, give myself a smile, and return to my office, stopping on the way to offer a word of encouragement to Nellie, who is now engaged in her least-favorite task, filling out insurance forms. I wonder what time it is in Spain. Four in the afternoon or six in the morning? Daniel is the one who always understands such things. He knows where the sun is and where it is going. He can always tell me when the picnic table I have set on the patio will be in shadow. I push it into the shade of the pin oak and go in to finish preparing supper. I come out to find him moving it.

"We won't eat for nearly an hour," he reminds me, "and," giving the table a final shove, "by then, the shade will be right here."

Sometimes I try to play the game with him. "Look," I say, pointing out an ominous cloud, "we'll have rain before the afternoon is out."

He shades his sailor's eyes with his left hand, scanning the sky. "You'll never make it as a meteorologist, goose," he chides me affectionately, "the weather comes from over there," and, with his right hand, he points to a patch of brilliant blue sky.

It is a mystery to me and will always remain one how he can predict rain, wind, the path of the sun, the rising of the moon, the location of constellations, no matter what hemisphere we are in. I hope it is sunny in Spain. But not hot. Daniel doesn't like hot weather.

Fran Matthews is a tall, nervous brunette of thirty-five with doe's eyes and hands that are never still. Though we are not at all alike, she reminds me of myself, and, narcissistic as it may seem after that admission, I am especially fond of her. I think she knows that she is a favored child, though I try to keep it from interfering with the treatment. There is, however, a spontaneous rapport between us that cannot be hidden, as if we had known each other since childhood. Fran recognizes this and, in her sensitive, straightforward way, has said on more than one occasion, "if you were not my therapist, we would be good friends, I think."

Her therapy is going rather well, and the sincere affection we feel for one another, an affection that I believe transcends transference issues, seems to serve as ballast when the treatment leads us into stormy seas. For example, during the past weeks Fran has been embroiled in the issue of letting me go away from her this summer. She has become alternately cajoling, demanding, petulant, effusive, and angry.

I have been waiting for this because I know that her intense but unhappy relationship with her mother lies at the root of her inability to respond sexually to her husband, maternally to her children. She cannot accept her womanness; she cannot accept herself. The negative feelings she has begun to experience toward me at first depressed and then astonished her. Now that they are coming out into the open, I hope to help her reexperience, through her relationship with me, the vicissitudes of her relationship with her mother.

These are troubled waters for anyone to traverse, but particularly for Fran, who shies away from anger and unpleasantness at all costs. If it were not for the positive warmth of what some analysts call the "real relationship" between us, I doubt that she would venture to cross this frightening body of water.

The hour is going along well enough this morning when suddenly Fran is silent for a moment. She clutches at her throat with nervous fingers and says in a choked voice, "You're leaving in two weeks!"

I blink and wait. The emotion seems disproportionate to the statement although I know she is deeply affected by all of my comings and goings at this phase of the treatment. She has pulled her long legs up under her on the wing chair, and tears are beginning to spill down her cheeks. "I feel so lost, so, so alone," she whimpers.

I let her sob for a moment or two, then push the box of tissues closer to her. She accepts one and quietly blows her nose. I sit with my fingers intertwined, chin resting on them, and wait some more. Nothing. "Perhaps you've felt like this before," I suggest, feeling very certain that she has.

Will the suggestion take her where she needs to go, or will I lose her as I have so many other times? Is it premature? A glimmer of recognition passes across her streaky face, then a shadow, then another glimmer.

"Y-yes," she says in wonder, "when I was very small."

She is with me, willing to pursue the memory, though it is clear it is elusive and painful. She knits her dark brows and wipes wet mascara off her cheeks.

"Yes, I do remember," she says unfolding her legs and sitting a little straighter. "I was six, no seven, and I had to have my tonsils out. You know, all of us had our tonsils out back in the forties, didn't we?"

It is the style of her transference for Fran to include me in all of her rememberings. I don't answer but, rather, smile my encouragement.

"Well, my mother took me to the hospital, but she never said she was going to leave me there, and she didn't tell me what was going to happen to me. It was going to be a surprise, an adventure, with ice cream at the end, and a big storybook doll for me, too."

Fran continues with her story of loss and abandonment, fear and pain, anger and reconciliation, but I cannot hear her. She is receding from me, and I am helpless to stop her. She grows smaller and smaller, like an object seen through the wrong end of a telescope, until she is so far away that I can no longer see her lips moving. I want to reach out to her with my hand, to call out and tell her "don't go."

I know her story is an important step in her therapy. Almost spontaneously, she is tying together her feelings about my leaving with the sense of loss and anger she had felt toward her mother so many years ago. I want desperately to keep her with me, but then I realize that it is not she, but I, who am going, falling faster and faster, just as surely as Alice, down the rabbit hole. Helpless to stop myself, I don my observer's mask and see at the far end of the telescope, but now coming closer to me, a girl of eighteen or nineteen sitting in a shabby wooden chair at a long wooden table. She is looking down at something in front of her. There is a fork in her right hand. A voice says, "Please try to eat something, dear," and the girl looks up. It is me.

I look pleadingly at the nurse, but she is firm; so I dip the fork into the mashed potatoes. They are swimming in margarine, but even if it were butter, I would gag. I cannot do it. I shake my head and beg to be excused. The nurse nods her permission, and I escape to the day room where other patients sit in isolated islands, some actually knitting or playing cards. I look longingly at my own little room, just off the dayroom, but I know if I retreat to it the nurse will pull me out. I sit down and pretend to read one of the magazines that the dean brought me, but I cannot remember one sentence as my eyes slide to the next. I hope the magazine will shield me from the forced conviviality of some of the others. One or two of them look at me, about to talk, but they respect my ruse, and I am left alone.

The scene changes. I hear the tap tap of stiletto heels on the cold bare floors. The nurses' shoes are silent. I look up from my bed and out the open door (they have permitted me to "read" in here for half an hour at a time, provided I leave the door open), and I see a burst of color coming toward me. Her suit is camel-colored, actually, but there is a bright silk paisley scarf tied smartly at her throat, and her patent leather purse and shoes flash me a greeting. Warm arms are around me and the smell of Estée Lauder perfume. I am overcome with love and shame before this soft, sweet-smelling, shining woman who embraces me, and I wish that the tears I felt on my face as she kisses me were mine. But I cannot cry.

They have sent for my mother although I have expressly asked them not to. I am glad they overrode my protests although I am ashamed for her to see me here. I hang my head as she strokes my hair. I sense her pain and would do anything to spare her. In a spasm of gratitude, I reach for her one ungloved hand and kiss it fervently. She pulls away as if burned, "Leah, please, I've told you before, don't kiss my hands, it's so, so servile."

I am dumb.

Another scene. In the day room again. I am wearing a black skirt with stitched-down pleats and a white "sissy" blouse. My hair is combed, and I, too, smell of Estée Lauder perfume (one of mother's gifts). I asked permission for my razor this morning, and they let me shave my legs. My hands shook so hard that I cut myself in three places, but they are scabbed over and hardly show through the Hanes Barely Black stockings Mother has given me.

"It's very new," she told me as she helped me dress. "Colored stockings are in this year."

Moments before she had loudly asked the day nurse, "What's the best restaurant in town? I'm taking my daughter to lunch!"

I love her for her forced gaiety, all of it for my benefit. But I do not know how to thank her or to tell her that I am afraid to leave the hospital, even with her. Still, the doctor said yes to Mother's request for a three-hour pass; so for the first time in a week, I will breathe the outside air. She is with the doctor now, has been for over an hour, just as she was yesterday. They are talking about me. The doctor told me they would talk about me.

"We have to tell her something, Leah, what shall we tell her? We don't have to tell her everything."

I look at him bewildered, he had promised all was confidential.

"Don't you see, Leah, she has a right to understand some of this."

I nod, and look down. What is there to tell? That her National Merit Scholar is flunking out of school? That her valedictorian of the Hebrew High School class drinks a fifth of rotgut rum every Friday and Saturday night? That her virginal daughter, never even kissed until she was sixteen, does obscene things with boys she barely knows, sometimes with two or three at a time?

"Tell her what you have to tell her," I whisper.

He nods. "I'll tell her how depressed you are, about the over-doses of aspirins that preceded your slashing your arm, and about how you can't concentrate on your schoolwork, and maybe a little about your drinking."

I sigh, relieved. He hasn't mentioned the boys.

"That will be enough to help her understand you need some help."

I look at him gratefully. He hasn't betrayed me. And now she is with him and all her hopes about me are crumbling. I am just another disappointment in a life full of disappointments. I have let her down, and she is taking me to the most expensive restaurant in town for lunch.

She comes out of the conference room with the doctor. It is clear that she has just freshened her make-up. I see the two shake hands. He waves a greeting to me and starts down the hall in the other direction while she walks toward me.

Suddenly, she spins on one spike heel, draws herself up to her full five feet and says, so all can hear, "Just one more thing, doctor . . ."

He turns accommodatingly and says, "Yes, Mrs. Bronstein?"

A dramatic hand indicates the dismal dayroom, with its shabby furniture and unappetizing aura, "Are the flies part of the therapy?"

She is magnificent, and she knows it. The next morning, a crew of painters appears on the ward. To this day, I do not know when its arrival was scheduled.

At Lockober's, I sit in awe watching the elegant waiters and dishes with silver covers whirl by me. I know we can't afford this. My thick steak comes covered with mushrooms. I eat one and try to swallow a bite of the pink meat, which barely needs chewing. My mother carries on the conversation brilliantly, as if the two of us were really talking. Years later, I will wonder what it cost her. Not the meal, but the effort at festivity.

When the waiter regretfully removes my nearly untouched plate, I am overwhelmed with guilt. I had been taught by a thrifty father to eat everything in front of me. Adding to the sacrilege, my mother orders dessert for me. It is creamy, smooth, and rich. I eat a little, looking at her with large thankful eyes. She hasn't asked me a single question. I drink a second cup of coffee, mostly so I can use the cup to warm my hands. She offers me endless chains of cigarettes though she disapproves of my smoking.

Later she returns me to the hospital and makes a sad goodbye. She has other children to think about. She has a business to run. I clutch at her hand and stare into her cheerful face, her troubled eyes. She will write. She will call. I am to eat more, smoke fewer cigarettes, comb my hair. She and the hospital together will find a good doctor for me here in Boston since I refuse to leave school permanently and return home. No, the hospital doctor is just a resident, I cannot continue seeing him. He is leaving the city in a matter of weeks. Another embrace. My hands are cold.

I lay my face on the fur collar of her coat, not caring how strange it looks. I have to bend over, for she is six inches shorter than I am. A nurse comes to disentangle my arms from my mother's neck. Momma is crying, but she has to go to the plane.

As the heavy door clicks shut and is locked behind her, I hear a familiar whistling noise. I know that it emanates from that hollow place between my stomach and my throat. A heavy weight goes off

57

my shoulders and settles in the empty spot where my heart used to be. I am lighter, freer, but there is a stone between my ribs. I am bereaved.

". . . it really is amazing how much lighter and freer I feel, now that I've told you that. It was just like you told me a long time ago. All these feelings of sadness and anger are a heavy burden to carry, like a big stone on my back. It feels good to put it down. I never realized until today how out of proportion some of my feelings about your going were, and all along they were trying to tell me something about feelings I felt long ago. I've resisted so much drawing any parallels between you and mother, because I hate her, and I love you, but, this morning, I see, I feel there is a connection . . . "

Fran rambles on in her halting quest for truth, and once again I am amazed at the intricacy of the human mind. I have taken the very words of her monologue (part of me must have been listening) and have woven them into my memories, just as in a dream we take the ringing of an alarm clock, or the crying of a baby, and translate it into some similar sound that is an integral part of what we are dreaming, thus preserving our sleep.

I look at Fran and see that she is continuing to explore and interpret her feelings, and I am thankful that two years of slow and plodding analysis have left her able to do so on her own without any help from me. For I have been no help to her this hour, that is certain. I have barely even heard her words. The betrayal of her trust sticks in my throat. I feel ashamed, guilty; I want to make amends. And yet, at the same time, I can't wait to get her out of my office.

I feel I should make some kind of comment, give some closure to the hour. But I am lost in a world of my own and can find no way of getting back to hers. I see her looking at me expectantly as she pauses in her ruminations, and I desperately search for something intelligent to say. The threads of her speech dangle loosely before me, but I am afraid to reach out and pull one, lest I unravel the very fabric of her new understanding.

She smiles. "You're not going to say anything, are you. Well, I'm glad. Because I know why. You're not saying anything because you want me to do it myself, because you know I can do it myself. Oh, Dr. Buchanan," she hugs herself, "I feel so good. I know you're proud of me. I can feel it, and I'm proud of myself."

I let her continue with her projections. They seem harmless enough, and they make more sense than anything I can think of in my bewildered state. I glance at my watch. She sees the glance.

"I know the hour is up. And I'm ready to leave for once. Because I know I'll be back, and that you'll be here. You're not like mother in that way. You'd never leave without saying goodbye. Because you're not afraid to face my sadness, or your own."

I rise with her, returning her warm smile. "See you Monday," I murmur.

"Yes," she whispers, as she heads down the hall.

When the door to the waiting room closes gently behind her, I have a minute to ponder the last words she has spoken in my office "... you're not afraid to face my sadness, or your own ... " and to wish that were true. Is that what it boils down to ? Am I hiding from my own feelings? I feel emotionally drained and so tired that I am unsure how to face my next patient. I have to do something. I tell Nellie to get Dr. Rabinowitz for me in Cincinnati. Then I return to my office to wait for the buzzer that will tell me the call has gone through.

Minutes later, Nellie buzzes to tell me that Dr. Rabinowitz's secretary has told her that he is out of town for two weeks, and can she take a message. No, that is all right. I'll call him later in the summer.

I still have nearly five minutes before I have to see Ilana, née Elaine, Fromer. I really don't feel like grappling with her this morning. She is going through a particularly snotty, delayed adolescence and can be vituperative toward anyone who smells remotely of "mother." I, fortunately for the treatment, but unfortunately for the state I am in today, have a very maternal scent in Ilana's slightly flaring nostrils (the result of an overemphatic nasal plastic).

I pick up the telephone and dial Jeanne in Cincinnati. She is a good friend, and I always come away from my chats with her feeling at least temporarily lighthearted. We have complementary senses of humor. I dial her at home but get no answer. Then I remember that no doubt she will be at the boutique that she opened shortly after she moved to Cincinnati. Jeanne has a shrewd business head, something she discovered soon after her husband died. Her marriage had left her childless, and so she poured all of her endless energy into her shop, just as she pours all of her abundant affection into her friendships.

I wait impatiently for her to answer the phone, already picturing the nice little French restaurant we will eat dinner in tonight. But it is not Jeanne's voice that answers.

"Gee, I'm sorry, Leah," says Margaret, Jeanne's store manager, "but Jeanne has gone to New York on a buying trip. Do you want me to give you the telephone number at her hotel? I know she'd love to hear from you."

For a minute, I think that I will go to New York, too. I'll meet Jeanne there, share her hotel room, go shopping or visit with my kid brother, Samuel, while Jeanne is out doing whatever buyers do. But New York is out of the question. I have a seminar to give Saturday morning at the University of Cincinnati, the last one I'll be giving before I go to Spain. I can't let the students down.

"No," I tell Margaret, "that's all right. I'll speak to Jeanne when she gets back. Actually, I spoke to her only a few days ago. She told me she was going on this trip, but I completely forgot. It must be a sign of encroaching middle age."

"Oh, don't be silly Leah," says the twenty-eight-year-old Margaret, "you're still young. You and Jeanne both."

"Yes, well, thanks for the thought. Tell Jeanne I'll be in touch. I bet the clothes that she orders will be knockouts. I'll have to come up to Cincinnati as soon as the stock comes in so we can play dress-up."

"You do that, Leah. Jeanne would love to see you."

"Thanks, Margaret. Take it easy. Bye." I hang up the phone and I am alone again. I lay my head down on my arms and try to think what to do.

I have to see Miss Fromer. And, God help me, Mr. Harrington. And then the long afternoon stretches out before me. I want to get away from the office, away from my house. And I don't want to be alone. I think of calling Anna in Cleveland. She is just loyal enough to drive down to Columbus and meet me for dinner and a long talk. Maybe Max would come with her. He is fond of me, too. But they have a four-year-old daughter, their long-awaited joy, and they'd have to find a baby-sitter and then face that long drive back, late at night.

It is a rare friendship I have with Anna, made even deeper by the fact that Max and Daniel respect and like each other. All four of us are friends, something you dare not hope for after marriage. But I am really too tired to drive all the way to Columbus. And I don't feel like imposing my mood on two of the people I love best.

I lift my head and crane my neck to look out the ceiling-hung window. I wonder where my friend the mockingbird has gone. Does he ever tire of singing everyone else's song? Does he long for a tune of his own?

12:08. Time to see Miss Fromer. The eight-minute wait will no doubt have put her in a surlier mood than usual. Why do I feel so antagonistic toward her this morning?

Ilana Fromer floats into my office on a cloud of Intimate perfume. She is wearing, from the bottom up, toeless high heels with ankle straps, a pair of jeans that, from their appearance, have been spray-painted onto her tough little body, a hot pink tube top made of some type of jersey material, a pair of theatrical-looking sunglasses that cover her best feature (violet blue eyes), and silver hoop earrings that are big enough to be worn as bracelets. I admit to myself that though her garb borders on the ridiculous, she looks sensational.

Then the analyst in me overcomes the jealous woman groping toward middle age, and I remember that behind the large sun-glasses and the sullen expression she affects, Ilana's eyes are childlike and sad. The course of her therapy has not been smooth. She is addicted to adolescent acting-out behavior. She smokes too much marijuana, pops uppers too often, and is promiscuous beyond most people's most lurid fantasies. She has no hope for the future, so she says, and no interest in the past. She is a child of today and, as such, is miserably aware of the futility of all her tomorrows.

On the surface, it is odd that I so often feel antipathetic towards Ilana, for at nineteen I was very like her, albeit not so sure of myself to flaunt myself sexually the way she does. Our costumes were different, true, she in her revealing outfits and I in my long black stockings and jerseys, but underneath was the same frightened child rebelliously masquerading as something else. And certainly Ilana and I (or the I that I used to be) are more alike than I and the perfect, conforming, conventional Fran.

But I never really approved of myself during my beatnik or bohemian period, and I suppose some of that disapproval manifests itself with Ilana. At Brandeis, I jeered and scoffed at people like Fran who consistently made Dean's List and wore engagement rings from Yalies. I scoffed from my superior stance as one of that theatrical crowd who didn't deign to go to the senior prom. (They sent a delegation to us, the class president and some of his ilk. Please come, they said, it's so important to have class unity. We let them plead for a while, then finally nodded our agreement. At the country club, where the dance was held, we showed up in stylish but short dresses—all the other girls wore long gowns—accompanied by boys who were juniors and sophomores, many of them homosexual—after all, those of us who dated were involved with older men, far off campus—and we drank so much that we eventually ended up in the swimming pool in our undies and were unceremoniously thrown out. The delegation from the class council regretted its benign invitation.)

But there was always a part of me that looked wistfully at those published Dean's Lists, those shining rings. I knew how happy it would make my mother if I brought her such precious prizes. For years I had watched the gleam in her eyes as she stood on tiptoe to add yet another of my trophies to the uppermost shelf of her china cabinet. They still stare down at me whenever I visit her in Cleveland. All those years, I reached ever higher for the prizes I prayed would satisfy her or myself, the prizes that would finally make me feel worthy. But all along, something inside me was stifling, choking, gasping, dying. And it was only with Dr. Edwards's and Dr. Isaacson's help that I could learn to breathe again.

The pendulum swung and I with it—Leah the achiever, Leah the rebel—until, at last, I took control of all of myself, and I was free. More than 15 years have passed since all of that turmoil. But Ilana Fromer often makes me angry. Is it her sullen attitude, her openly hostile way? Or is there a part of me that is nostalgic for, jealous of, those wild, abandoned, but sometimes lyrical days?

Ilana darts me a nasty look from under her oversized sunglasses.

"Shit," she snarls. "You won't even let me smoke in this damn office."

She looks around the room with a smirk, drapes her long legs over the arm of her chair, and launches into a by-now-familiar attack.

"Look at this place! It's so goddam tasteful and nondescript it's disgusting. Beige carpeting, subdued lighting, the obligatory potted plants, leather chairs, walnut desk, prints on the wall, books on the bookcase. La de da. It's so fucking perfect. Just like you. Middle class, non-descript, and perfect."

She pauses in her tirade to check it's effect on me. I am noncommittal.

"You won't even fight back, will you? You haven't got any guts. You're empty inside. All worn out, worn down, worn smooth. No rough edges on the great Dr. Buchanan."

She is gathering steam again.

"And don't think I don't know. You and your perfect life. Married to Daniel Buchanan, the brilliant, handsome, cold, goddam rock. He never cracks a smile. I'll bet his goddam skin is made of plastic. What does it feel like to go to bed with a stone? Can he get it up for you, or does he only get off on his books?"

She is defiant as she spits this last at me. I let her go on. I am not sure where all this has come from. My memory scans the previous hours, looking for a clue. She has attacked before, but this is by far the worst.

"But he's perfect for you, because you're just like him. You, with your tasteful suits and decorator office. You're like a goddam machine. Career, husband, two children—a boy and a girl—twins, no less! What's the matter, couldn't you fit childbirth into your busy schedule more than once?"

(I am in the cold emergency room of that distant hospital and a strange doctor is holding my hand as I writhe with the far-too-early pains. "It's no use, Mrs. Buchanan. There's no heartbeat. Your baby is already dead. I'm going to give you something now. You'll sleep. It may take hours—there's no point in your being awake . . . ")

"What are you anyway? You must feel so smug and superior sitting there all day in that damned chair like some kind of goddess. You're not even alive."

This last is said with contempt, but there is a slight quaver in her voice, and I realize she is near tears. I am undecided what to do. My opening is weak: "You're very angry this morning."

She explodes into another tirade.

"Well, isn't that sensational? Is that what I pay you fifty goddam dollars an hour for? The brilliant Dr. Leah Buchanan has deigned to come down from her throne and actually sully her hands by identifying one of little Ilana's emotions. Fantastic, Doctor. You're a fucking wonder, you really are. You'll probably be elected president of the American Psychologists for that brilliant insight."

I am silent. I don't know where to go from here. Something has happened, that is clear. But she is too angry, I cannot ask what. I wait, thinking of Saul: "Don't just do something, sit there." This has always been the hardest thing for me.

Funny, I don't feel angry with her this morning. I feel like going to her where she sits and petting her a bit, soothing her like the frightened child she is. Her attack has been too transparent; it is clearly a defense.

She sighs, puts her legs out in front of her, and slumps back in the chair. Long seconds pass. I watch them flash by on the clock perched on the bookcase behind Ilana. She is twisting her long blonde hair with one finger of her left hand. She looks about twelve years old. She reaches for a tissue and daubs at her eyes behind the glasses. She finally removes the glasses, and I see from the puffy redness of her eyes that these are not the first tears she has shed today.

"OK, so now you know. I've been crying. What of it?"

She is trying to affect the defiance and rage of the moment before, but she has lost her momentum. The anger has been replaced by some terrible sorrow. I wonder if she knows? She always runs away from her unhappy feelings. I choose my next words carefully, rejecting my first notion, which was to ask "How do you feel now?" Instead, I point out quietly, "You seem very sad just now."

More tears spill out, blazing trails of mascara down her cheeks.

"What of it?" she mutters, trying to sound tough. Then she abandons herself to her tears. After awhile she mops up, sniffles a little, and then she says quietly, "I've been awful to you this morning, just awful. And it isn't even your fault."

She is ready to go to work.

"Sometimes it's easier to feel angry than to feel sad," I point out to her.

She nods. "But I said really awful things. I have a terrible temper. The funny part of it is that I believed them when I said them, but I honestly don't believe them now."

She gives me a kind of quizzical smile. I look at her and wait for her to go on.

"It's just that your life is so orderly and mine is so chaotic. Sometimes I hate you for it. You can't know what it's like to be me. Do you know what happened last night? I went out on a real date with a very nice guy. Remember that one I told you about, the one my aunt kept trying to fix me up with? And I wouldn't go because he was a doctor, of all things. I mean, really. But I finally did go, and it turned out he was really all right. I mean, he's nice looking and he's not stupid, the way most doctors are."

She glances at me to see whether I've taken offense.

"I'm not trying to be nasty. Besides, you're not that kind of doctor. I mean the ones who've never read a book other than *Gray's Anatomy*, or whatever they read now. But this guy, he knew about the plays I do and the movies I like and the music and everything. And he didn't treat me like a baby just because he's twenty-six and I'm twenty. It turned out that he hadn't wanted to call me either but had to because his mother and my aunt are like best friends back in Pittsburgh, and his mother kept bugging him.

Well, we went out for pizza and beer, and then I invited him back to my apartment, and he came, and well, then I started acting crazy, and I don't even know why. First I rolled a joint but he didn't want any, and then I got stoned, and then I tried to get him to screw me, but he wouldn't. I mean, I could tell he wanted me by his eyes and the way he kissed me and everything, but he just kept sort of pushing my hands away gently and saying, 'No, not tonight, honey, not when you're high.' "

(The backs of Daniel's fingers caress my cheek like butterfly wings and my head leans toward his gentleness. "No, Leah," he is saying, "not tonight. When we make love, let's not be in a hurry.")

"And then he left. He said he'd call, but I know he won't, he just left. I was really mad when he did that, so I smoked some more and then I turned on some music real loud and started dancing by myself. And that's when this guy who lives down the hall knocked. I don't even know his name. I've seen him before and everything, but I don't know him. Well, he saw Richard, that's the doctor's name, sort of square but nice, he saw him leaving when he was coming in, and he heard my music go on higher, so he knocked. He said he thought it was a party and was he invited, and he just sort of stood there, grinning at me. So I let him in and offered him a joint, but he prefers to drink, so he went back down to his apartment and got a bottle of bourbon, and he drank and I smoked, and then we danced for awhile, and then we balled all night. When I woke up this morning he was gone."

Her head is hanging down, but she raises it abruptly.

"I don't even know why I'm telling you any of this. There's no way you could ever understand. And if you think for one fucking minute I'm sorry, you're out of your mind. And you and Richard can both go to hell."

I am spinning back through nearly two decades to my own apartment in Cleveland. It has been a jittery night, and I have walked around Shaker Square three times, looking in darkened shop windows. Coffee at the Rapid Stop hasn't helped. At last I go home, avoiding the bars I sometimes stop in, pleased with myself for avoiding them. It is eleven o'clock. I am too tired to wash my hair. I take a bath, hoping to calm myself down, put some Clear-asil on the two ugly pimples that are harbingers of my period, brush my teeth, and go to bed. By midnight I am asleep. The telephone rings me awake, and I fight my way out of an un-pleasant dream to get to it. I hear music and many voices in the background, then a voice repeating, "Hello, Leah, this is Mike," then a Greek sounding name, and then more noise. "Leah, do you remember me?" says Mike Sombodyopoulis.

I reach for my glasses, as if that will somehow help me clarify the fuzzy image I have in my head of a pair of dark eyes and some strong white teeth. I think I remember.

"I'm a friend of Bob's. You know, I was at that party at his apartment."

I remember the party, but the image of Mike is still unclear. Bob, I remember. Teacher at a local private school, trying to avoid Viet Nam, former Peace Corps in Africa somewhere, very good on the classical guitar, not so good in bed. (It had been such a disappointment to me to find that those fingers, which had hyp-notized me as they caressed the strings, could be so clumsy on my body.) Mike and Bob. Yes, now I remember. Mike was one of Bob's friends, a teacher, too, no doubt.

"I know it's late to be calling, but I thought you might be up and, um, I mean, I'd like to stop by and chat awhile if you are."

I am tired, but it is not in me to say no. I cannot think of a reason why he has chosen Thursday night at midnight to try to fuck me, but it doesn't matter. I tell him to come right over. I pull myself out of bed reluctantly as I used to when I was six on cold winter mornings when my brother Al let me help him with his paper route. Al is not here now to pull layers of sweaters and jeans over my flannel pajamas, so I slip off my nylon nighty and don a green velour caftan.

I wash the Clearasil off my face but decide against makeup. I will be too tired to wash again. I put on perfume, brush my hair, and insert my diaphragm. All of my movements are automatic, and I can offer no explanation for them. It is something that I have to do. There is no other way.

Within thirty minutes, he is humping me drunkenly on my

living room sofa. (I do not want the smell of him on my clean sheets.) I play with his hair where it curls around his ears while he reaches his fast and grateful climax, murmuring another girl's name. I feel charitable, so I do not laugh.

I lie there for half an hour, planning what I will wear to work the next morning and how I will rise early to douche so I will not have to carry any trace of this Mike Somebody with me into the anonymous world of the publishing firm where I edit copy. When I judge that he has slept long enough, I rouse him gently and urge him into his clothes. He has a dazed look and seems very young. He kisses me dutifully, tells me how terrific I am, promises to call soon, and leaves. I collapse back on to the sofa (I do not want him in my bed, even once removed) and into sleep, counting on the morning traffic to wake me. I am glad he will not call again. His silly gratitude makes me feel vulnerable.

These memories have not taken me far from Ilana and her tears, and I do not feel lost or confused as I had when memories of Massachusetts General Hospital invaded my hours with Sandra Drake and Fran Matthews. The incident with Mike had woven itself in counterpoint to the main theme of Ilana's story of Richard and her bourbon-drinking neighbor. I had been able to hear the simple melody of Ilana's plaint, elaborated by the tune of my own past.

Perfectly good psychoanalytic technique, that. Nothing to worry about. As long as I do not identify too closely with Miss Fromer, as long as I do not mistake my feelings for hers, or worse still, hers for mine. I look at her sympathetically as she recovers from yet more tears, and I wonder where to begin. Her tirade when she first came in was clearly precipitated by her anger at me for keeping her waiting in the outer office and by her fury over her rejection by Richard. Her sexual acting out with the unknown neighbor also stemmed from Richard's rejection. As for her wild need to seduce Richard and spoil what had been in her own estimation a nice evening, that stemmed from a hornet's nest of transference issues and from confusion about her role as a woman, her feelings about herself, and men in general.

I realize I am shakey. Maybe the coffee, maybe the experience with Harrington last night. Ilana has stopped sobbing and will soon be ready to go on. I am suddenly tired and not sure I can go on with her. She sees my life as orderly and is undecided as yet whether or not she wants hers to be that way. I understand her perfectly and cannot help her with her choice.

Orderly? Isn't that the very label I used to pin on Dr. Isaacson and Dr. Edwards, the one I still pin on Daniel? It's a hateful-sounding word and yet somehow comforting. Orderly. All at once, I remember a poem I memorized years ago:

> I came upon the order of my life
> One evening in a sensual mood
> While reading in an ancient author
> I have never understood.
> I came upon the order of my life
> As one would meet a madman with a knife
> In a familiar but strangely darkened wood.
> Surely to be worthy is to know.
> Could it then have been another way?
> More dignified or more bizarre,
> Leaving me more changed?

For a moment I think I will share the poem with Miss Fromer. But I reject the idea. She must find her own mottoes.

I live through the rest of the hour with Ilana, trying to help her grope her way from anger to sadness, from tirade to tears, and on through both to understanding. She is a bright girl, if stubborn, and I don't need to hit her over the head with an interpretation for her to understand it. Acceptance is another matter. She rails at me when I try to get her to deal with her angry feelings toward me and what they mean, but after another outburst and a blanket rejection of even the beginning of an idea that I matter enough to her to influence her behavior, her good mind takes over and she allows as how when she accepted the date with Richard she couldn't help thinking how much it would please me that she was going out with a nice doctor, and then how that very thought had rankled in her, making her decide to spoil his impression of her and, thus, obliquely, she hoped, disappoint me.

I listen as she wends her way down a tunnel of transference

69

issues, and, occasionally, I hold the lamp of my own understanding up high enough to help her with her difficult passage. I know that her mother lurks around the next bend, but the hour is almost over, and I am almost spent, so I leave that for another time.

The work is difficult for Ilana and for me. I have gratified neither her, by telling her that I care about her, nor myself, by revealing to her some of my past escapades in an effort to show her I am neither a goddess nor a machine. Some of my colleagues think that would be the better way. But I am devout. I know that Freud's way—my way—is best. Ilana doesn't need a chum. She needs to grow up. And she needs, ultimately, to feel responsible for her own growth; not to think that I have done it for her.

I will continue to accept her tirades, projections, acting out, until she is ready, through understanding, to give them up. I will never be her mother or her friend. What can I be but a Virgil to guide her through the paths of her own particular hell? She leaves, sunglasses carefully replaced, with a mumbled apology and a slightly louder "see ya next time."

I watch her as she regains her composure midway down the long hallway, and I retain an image of her swaying, impertinent, dungaree-clad fanny for seconds after the door has closed behind her. Goodbye, Ilana Fromer. *Ma semblable, ma soeur.*

It's nearly one when Ilana leaves my office. No one to see until Harrington's (supposed) arrival at two and then nothing beyond that. I am grateful not to have another patient at the moment and at the same time sorry that nothing definite occupies me for the next hour. I know that reading is out of the question.

On impulse, ignoring the cost of a daytime call, I pick up the phone and dial Daniel in Spain, marveling at the mechanical intricacy that allows me to sit at my desk and, with one index finger, cause a small black object to ring in his apartment, 3,000 miles away. An imperious voice answers almost immediately, "*Diga.*"

For a moment I am startled by the odd Spanish telephone response, so much more formidable than the cheerful Argentine "*Hola,*" or the curt, but friendly, Mexican "*Bueno.*"

"*Diga* yourself, *viejo,*" I reply.

"Leah, why are you calling, are the children all right?"

Daniel came to fatherhood late and with a passionate involvement a younger man could not imagine. I reassure him that both Jacob and Hannah are fine and ask if he has had any mail. We regale each other for expensive minutes with stories about postcards signed "Your son, Jacob" or "Love, Hannah Elisabeth Buchanan." I cradle the phone next to my ear, trying to get closer to Daniel, grateful that he isn't angry about the call. He can be quite peevish about any change in plan, and we were due to converse on Sunday when the rates would be down.

The conversation meanders around his current research, a recounting of a fabulous *paella valenciana* that he had eaten two afternoons before, and on through a recapitulation of the twins' and my travel plans, including flight number and arrival time. Daniel finally says, "Why did you call, Leah? It's not like you to phone midday." (He knows what time it is in Kentucky!)

Falteringly, I begin to tell him that I had some difficulty with one of my patients and need a little reassurance.

"Leah," he interrupts, "we've been over this before. I've asked you NOT to talk to me about your patients. That's between you and them. Or you and Saul. But don't involve me. It's unprofessional."

I know this is a sore point with him, and in all our years together I have never been able to get around it, even when I suffered so terribly over the suicide of a former patient. But he refuses to budge. I never have known whether his stance is just another instance of the many rigidities of his personality, or whether it reflects whatever resentments he harbors about my career. It doesn't matter. He is adamant.

Weakly, I counter that Saul is out of town and that I need to talk to someone about it.

"You know my feelings on this topic," he interrupts fiercely. "I'm sorry, but you'll just have to work it out yourself."

I sigh audibly.

"Or maybe Doug can help you with it," he adds as a peace offering.

"Never mind," I say as cheerfully as possible, "it's not that important. The main thing is that you're fine and I'm fine and both the kids are A-1. I'm really glad your research is coming along so well."

"Yes. And I'm glad you called. It's good to hear your voice."

"Yes, Daniel, I miss you too."

"Well, then," he goes on skirting the emotional issues, "should we talk again on Sunday as planned, or what?"

"I'm going up to Cincinnati for that Saturday lecture to the psychiatric residents," I tell him, and, thinking of it only as I say it, "I may stay over."

"Good idea, you can see Jeanne."

For some reason I don't bother telling him that she is in New York. "Let's cut this short, Daniel, it was an extravagance on my part."

"Forget it, it was a nice surprise."

"I love you, honey," I whisper.

"And I love you."

Then we both hang up. The call leaves me unsatisfied and teary. I make the decision right then and there to drive up that very afternoon and stay over Friday night. My watch says 1:15 P.M. as I head down the hall to ask Nellie to make a reservation for me at the Terrace Hilton, a downtown hotel located five minutes from the medical school where I will lecture. I decide to drive over to the mall and windowshop during my lunch hour.

I falter a minute when I remember I have Harrington's car instead of my own, but figure he owes me that much, at least, and I make the three-minute hop in the sporty grandeur of his Mercedes.

Once in the mall, my mood improves. The fall stock is already coming in to the stores, and I like the look, smell, and feel of wool. Tweeds, plaids, herringbones, or solids—all give me a sense of vitality. Even corduroy uplifts my spirits. I appraise the mannequins, delighting in the rich color and textures of their costumes.

I have always felt more comfortable in winter and in winter clothes. Although I suffer terribly from the cold, I would prefer two weeks snowbound in Vermont to a month at Copa Cabana beach.

I walk through the store, fingering camel hair coats and mohair scarves. I feel like buying something. I squelch an extravagant desire for a cashmere blazer in favor of a small bottle of Femme cologne, on special at the Madame Rochas counter. I had worn that scent for awhile in college, discarding it later when Frank said it reminded him of his wife. I spray myself generously from the sample bottle on the counter, take the small package the salesclerk hands to me, and return abruptly to my office.

At 1:55 I sit in my office eating a container of yogurt, waiting for Harrington's arrival and staring at the diplomas on my wall. *Bachelor of Arts.* That was the hardest. The first year and a half dominated by cheap liquor, plentiful pot, and faceless boys with hot hands. The last two and a half years dominated by Dr. Edwards. Faithfully, three times a week, by hitching, MTA, commuter train, buses, I traversed the distance between the outlying western suburb of my campus to downtown Boston. Three hours in transit, one hour in his office. Twelve hours a week, back and forth; Park Street, Charles Street, North Station.

I sat in Dr. Edwards's office not knowing what connections he expected me to make, knowing only that for some odd reason he valued me and meant to keep me alive. He had names for all the feelings I could not yet verbally express, names like sadness and anger and grief. He made interpretations that I tossed aside with a shake of my head, but he stared at me solemnly and never let me off the hook.

"How sad for you to lose your father and your grandfather, the two men you've loved most in your life, all in the same year," he pointed out empathetically.

"Lots of people lose parents and grandparents," I parried, "it happens every day."

"We're not talking about lots of people," he pressed on, "we're talking about you."

Slowly the pieces fell into place, began to fit together, the shape of the puzzle emerged. With Daddy and Grampa Bronstein dead and Al soon to go away to college, there was a terrible emptiness in the house, and there were no men at all. Ruthie and Sammy were both still little, babies really. And Momma, though she cooked and cleaned and worked and walked and talked, was never really the same. But maybe I, a precocious ten-year-old, could somehow make it right. If I just worked harder, behaved better, got even more prizes at school and Hebrew school, then Momma would smile again, and everything would be okay. The self-imposed burden was incredibly heavy; the goal was unattainable, but I pursued it relentlessly, only to wake up one morning at Brandeis University, separated from the last vestige of support in my life, a thousand miles from hearth and home, from the mother who was my rock as well as my responsibility—only to wake up that morning and feel the bottom drop out of my heart.

Cut loose from every restraining tie, set adrift in a world where freedom was a fancy name for rebelliousness, I soon discovered that the pervasive emptiness could not be filled with whiskey, drugs, or boys, which objects I came to pursue as relentlessly as the trophies and blue ribbons that had preceded them. Guilt and shame rushed in to fill the void where grief and sadness used to be. And an incredibly powerful feeling I could not yet name, but which Dr. Edwards would one day label anger. There was nothing left to do but die. But Dr. Edwards had other plans for me.

Master of Arts. My return to Cleveland, the apartment on Shaker Square, the job that mother had arranged for me at the publishing firm—a job that was supposed to become a career. Trips back and forth to New York, to Frank, hoping, always hoping, that he would ask me to stay forever. The growing night terrors, the series of faceless strangers. Clearly, my work was not yet done.

So, back into therapy, this time with Dr. Isaacson. I fought him for so long, knowing in my heart that he would win, just as I wanted him to win, planned for him to win. He would win and rob me of Frank, of the one man who had made me feel alive in the way I used to feel, alive the way I was before Daddy and Grampa Bronstein died.

I fought Dr. Isaacson with all my soul, at the same time that I

74

compliantly appeared at his office for every appointment, knowing that this work had to be completed before I could allow myself to become the woman he seemed to recognize, sitting across from him in that overstuffed chair.

More night terrors and confusion, countless trips to bars, where nameless steelworkers bought me boilermakers and then pawed me in the quasi-privacy of the parking lot. I remember only one of them, John, who worked the three-to-eleven shift at Republic. He paid me tender tribute as he held me in his bear-like arms: "I don't know who you are, babe, but you sure got a lot of class."

Dr. Isaacson waited, watched and waited, and taught me to be patient with myself. Pride came at being on my own, at finding the job at the school for disturbed children, at being good at it. Then graduate school and a series of desperate dates with eligible stockbrokers, doctors, and attorneys, whom I dangled in front of Frank on my New York visits, praying it might make him jealous enough to marry me.

And still I stayed in treatment, and I came to learn that it would not be enough to free myself from fantasies of Frank and of my father. My enmeshment with my mother, my inability to separate—to know, at last, where she left off and I began—that, too, had to be addressed. Dr. Isaacson was relentless, relentless but kind. And ever so reliable, just as his predecessor had been. I led him, me, us, a merry chase, but at long last, the night terrors diminished, replaced by feelings I could name: anger, sadness, more anger, and anger again.

Then came Daniel; and then, *Doctor of Philosophy.*

I stare at the diploma: *Leah Bronstein Buchanan.* A childhood jingle flashes through my brain: *Change the name and not the letter, change for worse and not for better.* I shake it off, wondering where such a disloyal thought could have come from. I think of Daniel, so far away in Spain, and how he does not deserve my unconscious betrayals. Then I remember the phone call, and I realize I am angry with him. I needed him. He let me down. It made me mad. My bewilderment and guilt slide away. The work with Dr. Edwards and Dr. Isaacson was not in vain.

I look at my watch: 2:25. I sigh. Harrington isn't coming. I realize, with a combination of amusement and dismay, that my disappointment goes beyond therapeutic considerations. I am hurt, like a seventeen-year-old who has been stood up for a date. What is this ridiculous infatuation I have with Harrington? Surely, after last night, I can harbor no illusions about the degree of his disturbance. Why do I persist in these blushing schoolgirl emotions? What does he mean to me? Does he remind me of someone? Or am I that desperate for sexual reassurance, male attention, whatever, that I am blind to everything I know about transference, countertransference, or even men and women in general? My mind turns over all the information I have about him, and I see that my adolescent feelings are a perfect reflection of his. He is the teenager, not I! My heart and mind are saying for him what he has not been able to say directly. All of it fits: the fast, fancy cars, his need to make it with every pretty woman he meets, even his crush on me.

He is an overgrown adolescent responding to the push of his hormones and the pull of an unresolved Oedipal conflict. He is still acting out because he has not been able to resolve conflicts that should have been laid to rest fifteen or twenty years before. His charm, his brains, his good looks, and his wealth have allowed him to slip this sad but selfish schoolboy nearly unnoticed into the adult world. And now he, and those who are closest to him, are paying the consequences.

I feel charged with energy, as I always do when I have an insight about a patient. The murky waters begin to clear. Harrington's clumsy attempt to strip me has left him standing naked. Is that what he was doing, showing me the way, making graphic for me what I had not clearly understood? Have my own attempts at analysis seemed equally clumsy and brutal to him?

My mind is racing so fast that I am breathless where I sit in my chair. His actions of the night before, like an atypical response on Card IX of the Rorschach, will clinch the diagnosis, uncover the true dynamics, and point to the future course of the therapy. I know I will be able to put it all together soon. I feel as smug and self-satisfied as Daniel is when, eighty pages into an Agatha Christie or a Simenon, he announces, "I've got it!"

I am so wrapped up in working out the details of my new

understanding of Mr. Harrington that I jump when Nellie peers around the jamb of my office door to tell me Mr. Harrington has arrived. She adds in her usual conspiratorial tone, "He looks terrible."

Nellie's appraisal of Harrington's appearance is accurate, if impertinent. As I open the door to the waiting room, I see him pacing back and forth, smoking. His eyes are bloodshot, and he is unshaven. He is wearing the same clothes he had on the night before, but his badly wrinkled shirt is open at the neck, and his tie is gone. I remember his jacket is still hanging in my closet. I can't catch his eye, and he apparently hasn't heard the door open, so I quietly ask him to come in. He looks up at me, then away, stubs out his cigarette in an ashtray on the table, and, forgetting his usual polite insistence on holding the door open and following me, he brushes past me and precedes me down the hall to my office door. Once there, he regains a part of his composure, smooths his hair, and waits for me to enter the office while he holds the door courteously.

As I walk in, I notice with some annoyance that Ilana's heavy scent still lingers in the air, masking, but not entirely covering, my own subtler perfume. I hope that Harrington realizes that I am Femme but not Intimate, then smile at the implications. (Did I buy the cologne for him, because of him? Do I need to reassure myself—and him—that I am indeed a woman?)

I sit down, but he remains standing at the door. He cannot seem to decide whether to sit or bolt and run. I get up, walk over to him, indicate the chair, close the door, and lay his car keys on the table beside him. He mutters his thanks and puts them into his pocket. A glance at the clock tells me it is 2:45. He has left us exactly five minutes, but perhaps I will let him go until 3:00. It would be tempting to give him the 3:00, but all my training tells me not to. I look at his haggard, but still-handsome face, with the shadows under the bloodshot eyes, and I wait.

"I'm sorry I'm late," he ventures.

I look at him and wait for him to go on.

"But, I didn't want to come. I, I was afraid, ashamed . . ." His voice tapers off, and he hangs his head.

"Afraid?" I echo.

He shakes his head and makes a gesture of dismay with his hands. "You know," he pleads, "don't make me say it—it's cruel. Last night, I mean," his hands are over his face now, elbows resting on his knees as he sags into the chair, "it was so awful, I mean, I was so awful." He stops.

"It was so awful," I repeat with a slightly questioning tone. The slip has some importance in my view, but I am uncertain how far to pursue it.

"No, I meant I was awful. I should never have, I had no right to, to come to your house like that and, and force myself on you. I can't understand . . . I don't believe . . . oh, what's the use? I was abominable to you. You have the right to hate me."

He lets his hands fall away from his face, but his eyes still stare at the floor.

"Is that what you were afraid of," I question, "that I would hate you?"

He shakes his head in agreement and whispers, "I don't want you to hate me. I, I wanted you to like, to, to—yes, I will say it—I wanted you to love me."

I hear his use of the past tense, and part of me longs to reassure him. I watch a shadow of myself go to him and take his hand. She is saying: "Don't be sad, my dear, dear boy, of course I like, of course I love you. Nothing that you do or say will ever change that."

She is soothing his forehead with a cool, white hand, as she vanishes, and I say nothing.

Harrington clears his throat. "I came here today to tell you that I'm sorry, really sorry."

I gaze at him sympathetically and feel my head give him a gentle nod, almost of its own accord. He goes on, gaining courage and volume as he does. His back straightens. "I realize that I had to be pretty crazy to do what I did last night. And, and the fact of your operation," he blurts it out, "is immaterial. I don't mean it's immaterial for you," he adds apologetically, "I mean it has nothing to do with the fact that I actually tried to, well, almost rape you. Except, I guess seeing you like that, well, it was like a slap in the face; it brought me to my senses."

It certainly cooled your ardor, I think cynically. When a man slips a lady's robe off her shoulders, he isn't looking for that grisly sight. I keep silent.

"All night long I thought about you, and how I must have hurt you, and how I never wanted to hurt you. You're just about the only person in the world I care anything about. Except Kelly Ann, and maybe Monica. I couldn't go back to the house. So I had the cab take me to a hotel. And I just lay on the bed, smoking and thinking all night. Oh, I guess I dozed off toward morning, but not for very long.

"I decided I would go home, get an extra set of car keys, slip over to your office, and steal my car back, without ever seeing you or saying a word. But something in me said no. I ate some breakfast at the hotel, and then decided I still couldn't go home—and I certainly couldn't go to the office—so I started walking. And would you believe, I've been walking and walking, on and off, for nearly four hours? I covered a lot of ground, let me tell you.

"Anyhow, I came, even though I knew it was too late to come, and maybe I did that on purpose, too. But I came to tell you that I'm not quitting therapy, that is, if you're still willing to work with me, after last night. And, also to say how very much it hurts me to think that I must have hurt you."

He looks at me with the shy pleading eyes of a chastened lover, and I look back at him. For a moment I feel his strong hands gripping my shoulders, his breath on the back of my bare neck. I shiver in spite of myself, with fear, with excitement. I look at him again, and it is as if I am in my ophthalmologist's office and he has just slipped another lens in place, saying "better or worse, one or two."

The image of Harrington is clear: my bashful, ardent lover is just another little boy. I sigh for my lost love, my found understanding. I say, "It must have been a very difficult decision for you to make," and I am home free.

It is a dialogue now, me pointing out his fears, he confirming that he felt them. The clock throws 3:02 at me, and I realize we must stop. I make the decision to point out the "it was awful" slip to him once again, in order to convince myself, as well as him, that

I am not afraid to deal with his terror of my damaged body. He acknowledges how disturbing it was for him to see my scar, but insists that what made it awful was his realization that he had hurt and embarrassed me. I suggest that he must have had some other feelings, too, and that we will have plenty of time to deal with them in future appointments.

I point out that the hour is up, then decide to add that I realize what a tough decision it must have been for him to come in today, face me, and plan to continue treatment. I tell him that whatever feelings I may have about the events of the night before are not germane·to his treatment. They are mine to deal with, not his.

We rise almost simultaneously. He looks at me and says, "Dr. Buchanan, will you let me shake your hand?"

This is no time for interpretations. I hold out a hand to him, and he takes it in both of his.

"You're an extraordinary woman, you know," he tells me, and then we are both in the hall. I watch him as he walks out, thinking how tired he looks. A voice inside me reminds him to go home, take a shower, be sure and get some rest. But I am silent. He doesn't need another mother any more than he needs another bed partner.

"See you Tuesday," I add as an afterthought to his departing back.

He turns and echoes, "Tuesday," and he is gone.

3

FRIDAY AFTERNOON——

WHEN Daniel and I moved to Kentucky, he drove a van with all our household goods, and I followed in his old MG. I-75 wends its way through gently rolling, green, green hills, up out of the Ohio River Valley and over to the Blue Grass plateau of Kentucky. I never really understood what a plateau was until there, after rounding the last curve, climbing the last ridge, I saw it stretching out before me like a dream of heaven, some sixty miles south of the Ohio River: velvety grass in every direction, interrupted only by white streaks of fence rail, and the rich, brown, curving lines of tall, blooded horses. Impossible that I once hated it so, that my heart sank every time we crossed the bridge out of my native Ohio into the alien, alien south.

Kentucky cars carry license plates only in the rear, and I used to feel almost terrified by the signs I saw in front: proud confederate flags and those hideously cute slogans reading, "If your [picture of a heart] is not in Dixie, get your [picture of the hind quarters of a donkey] across the Ohio River." How I longed to do just that! I have walked through the ghettos of Cleveland and the Arab Quarter of East Jerusalem feeling less ill at ease than on Main Street here in this town.

And I don't think I will ever get used to the narrow-minded provincialism of so many people here. They have no use for, no interest in, any other way of life. They are that sure that their own is superior. Perhaps on some level I envy them their certainty.

In any case, a subtle change began to take place within me some five years ago: I found that my heart felt lighter when the compass on my dashboard pointed south. It felt good to leave the noisy, dirty city behind me and to head for the clean air and slow pace of Kentucky, to head for home.

But today, I am glad enough to be headed north. It is not that Cincinnati holds so much charm for me, although I've always found it a fascinating town; it is that I am glad to be putting distance between myself and the confusion at home. I have no illusions about escaping my own depression or outdistancing the vivid memories that more and more invade my waking life: I just want to get away. I want to get out of the arena of responsibility, to lay down the burden of being Dr. Buchanan. Leaving off being Daniel's wife, Hannah and Jacob's mother, hasn't eased me enough. I need to shake everything off, like a dog emerging from a muddy pond. And I need to be far enough out of everyone's reach that they think twice before they intrude on me.

The rain begins as I make the turn north onto I-75. The first few minutes of the storm are frightening, as only a summer thunderstorm can be. The sky is a dark curtain, except where brief bursts of electricity tear it open and light darts across the rip, as if to mend it with long bony fingers. My windshield wipers, even at top speed, are no match for the sheets of water that flood over the dam of my car. Ordinarily, I am a cautious driver, and good sense tells me to pull over to the shoulder of the highway as some of my more prudent fellows do, but something in me pushes me on, headlamps reaching out helplessly toward an occasional glimpse of taillight some yards ahead. I am one with the car as we crawl along. The tires are paws at the ends of my limbs, and the metal body is a shell to protect my skin from the wet.

82

Then, as suddenly as it began, the storm stops, moves off, leaving in its wake a gentle rain and the timid arrival of some sunshine. I am just another driver again, seated in an ordinary-looking Chevrolet station wagon. The farms on either side of the road are incredibly green, and herds of foolish cattle huddle gratefully around a few tall trees. No horses are in sight. Has the storm driven them back to their barns? Or are they so valuable that a hired hand has led them in before the first thunderbolt could frighten some high-strung beast into hurling itself against a wooden fence?

I feel especially calm and in control, as I sometimes do after a violent argument with Daniel or a good cry. I relax my hands on the wheel, sit back and depress the accelerator to a safe sixty, only five miles above the limit, and a safe distance from the usually driven seventy.

No point in hurrying, I tell myself, no matter what I do I will cross the Ohio River during rush hour, for it is now just past four. At least I will be heading toward Cincinnati, rather than south over the bridge like most of the commuters racing home to northern Kentucky for the weekend. And the Terrace Hilton is only five minutes from the junction of I-75 and I-71, so I won't fight the traffic long.

Thank goodness Daniel isn't with me! He rails so against inefficient drivers, poorly designed cloverleafs, noisy traffic jams. His own intelligence is so great and his reflexes are so fast that he finds the stupidity and slowness of his fellows a constant irritant. It is incomprehensible to him that others are neither as quick nor as well-organized as he.

I am hardly a happy-go-lucky person myself, but I can sit quietly behind another car, even if its driver has no real awareness that a red light has turned green. ("They're like dinosaurs," Daniel moans in exasperation. "It takes a full minute for their brains to send an impulse to their right foot.") Besides, for some reason, I can think in a car, just as I can in the bath. Perhaps I feel safe in enclosures. Or perhaps the bathtub and the car are the only two places where I can escape the constant chatter of two boisterous children.

I drive on, thinking a little of Harrington, and of my damaged

83

body, and of Daniel and his refusal to hold out a hand to me from far away, even though I said please as my parents had taught me to, and of Frank who schooled me in the sad, important lesson that just because you love a person does not mean he has to love you in return, and of the twins, who have suffered through too many scenes of anger and of tears, despite Daniel's and my two-in-the-morning pledges to each other that never again will we fight in front of Hannah and Jacob; and yes, even of the nameless girl child who died before she was born, and who would have been nearly twelve years old by now.

I think of my father, who didn't want to die at forty-six, and of my mother, who didn't plan to be a widow at forty, and of my grandfather, nearly ninety, wearing a gray cardigan sweater and sitting in the growing darkness of a winter Saturday afternoon, too religious to turn on a light on the Sabbath.

"What are you doing, Grampa?" I ask him. (Even at the age of eight, I cannot understand that someone might not be doing anything.)

I look at him with his patient, catlike face, his old, wrinkled powdery skin, his wiry white goatee, and his still alert blue eyes.

"I am waiting, *na-arla*," he tells me tenderly, and I wonder why he, who has always thought me so clever, has called me a little fool.

And I wonder what he is waiting for in the semidarkness, and why he is not afraid. I wish he would take me on his lap, chuck me under the chin, and say, *"nu, mammala,"*—I am named for his dead wife, and he cannot bear to call me Leah—"are you still going to *cheder?*"

Then I could proudly tell him that I am, indeed, still in Hebrew school and that I am the first one in my class to be able to recite the *Adon Olam* prayer without mistakes. And maybe he would reach into his sweater pocket for one of the slightly fuzzy lemon drops he always seemed to find there, and I would say "thank you, Grampa" and plant a kiss on his soft, familiar-smelling cheek.

My own cheeks are wet with all these recollections, and I feel the tears continue to slide easily out of the corners of my eyes. So, I am still looking for a lap to sit on, eh? And now that I have finally learned that it cannot be my former analysts' or Daniel's or my father's or any of the strange men who thought my lap-sitting and cuddling meant I wanted to be laid, now that all of those lessons have been thoroughly learned, I resurrect my grandfather, dead these thirty years.

I wipe my eyes with the crumpled tissue I have rummaged for with a nervous right hand and finally found in the bottom of my purse. If Daniel were here, he would be saying "Christ, Leah, why don't you carry a packet of tissues with you, or at least fold the ones you plan to use instead of grabbing a handful and stuffing them into your purse, where you can never find them."

I sniff back my tears, then blow my nose loudly. Daniel would criticize me for sniffing back. All at once I am fed up with Daniel, his criticisms, and his smug superior sense that his way is best. The arguments began before the honeymoon was over. Nothing I did was right: I made the bed with hospital corners, he preferred navy corners; I rolled his socks, he preferred them folded flat; I used margarine or safflower oil wherever possible (no husband of mine would drop from a coronary at forty-six), he insisted on butter (his background of poverty makes him proud on certain points).

It all sounds so trivial, but it drove me crazy then, and now that we have compromised on the early issues, now, every month, every week, there are new issues. The grocery shopping: I never stock up on what Daniel considers the important items. I must admit that it is true that I can live in a house where we run out of peanuts from time to time, or where the backlog of toilet tissue in the closet isn't sufficient to last a month. But Daniel can't. So he does most of the grocery shopping.

Pretty cagey, the way I abdicate all responsibility in the face of criticism? Well, it doesn't work, anyway. It's like that Greek myth where you try to slay the monster with a thousand heads, but every time you cut one off, another appears in its place. There are days when it reduces me to tears. Like the time we were planting our spring vegetable garden with the children, and Daniel screamed at me because I put in a row of beets where he wanted the lettuce to go. The children stared in terror as he stood there railing at me and brandishing a hoe in his hands: I had ruined *everything*; I didn't give a *damn* about the garden; I did it on *purpose*, just to upset him. I am kneeling in the dirt, foolishly cupping the few remaining beet seeds in my left palm. I look up at him and know for the thousandth hopeless time that I am married to a madman, a lunatic; that I am doomed to a life of misery and terror.

But there are other days, other Daniels. And for every caviling quarrel over toilet tissue, there is also the benefit of having an orderly husband. I hear other women complain about carrying out the garbage, and I can smugly say I haven't so much as emptied a wastebasket in fifteen years. He is helpful in the house, devoted to the children, and, I think, faithful to me (despite the fact that since my surgery I fear I disappoint him sexually). He doesn't drink too much, he is a hard and steady worker, and he has never hit me.

I know it's childish for me to ask for more, but I long for a day when he will voluntarily put his arms around me and tell me he loves me—and not on the way to the bedroom. He is generous about money, urging me to buy clothing or household items that I hesitate over, encouraging me to count on restaurant meals when I'm too busy to cook, and surprising me with jewelry or a cashmere sweater that I would never get for myself. But he is stingy with words and touches. He doesn't like to talk much, unless he is lecturing on some historical topic, and it is beyond his capacity to walk up to me and say, "Hey, I missed you today" or "Gee, you look good to me right now."

He doesn't like to hug or kiss, except in the act of lovemaking, and although I find that hard enough to accept, it is even worse for me that he neither likes to be hugged nor kissed himself. When either one of us returns from work, we give each other a ritual peck, more for the sake of Hannah and Jacob than anything else, but the children have probably never seen him put his arm around me while we watch TV or stare into the fire, nor has he ever touched my face, my hair, in passing, nor held my hand, not since the earliest days of courtship, and even then, I realize, it was almost all instigated by me.

I used to try to rub up against him, like a cat, demanding to be petted. But that only angered him. Then I tried ignoring him, but he never noticed, unless I refused him in bed. Then he would say,

"Two can play at that game," and refuse to have anything to do with me sexually for weeks, or even months, at a time.

Sometimes I feel like one of those infants in the early psychological studies of deprivation, the poor little babes in orphan homes who were fed and changed and kept warm, but who failed to thrive anyway or even died from lack of human contact. Their skin begged for a caress, their little bodies beseeched the world at large to cuddle them. And, in large measure, isn't that what I used to do?

So how is it I chose this man to be my husband? This brilliant, handsome, arrogant, and detached man. It seems petty to admit it, but sometimes I feel jealous because he is ever so tender with the children, especially Hannah. They can climb on him, cuddle with him, romp over him, like frisky puppies, and he never tires of ruffling Jacob's hair, squeezing Hannah's chunky little body. I look on with a mixture of joy and envy, delighting in their love for each other, wishing there were some left for me. But perhaps my ideas about love are adolescent. For Daniel has always stood by me.

And now, as I drive up the interstate away from the manicured horse farms of the plateau and into the less glamorous, but more interesting and varied, landscape of ridges and hills, now other Daniels leap into mind. There is the Daniel of the beginning, holding me, telling me, "You're a fool, Leah, to think it some kind of miracle that men desire you, to throw yourself at them and count it a victory when they catch. You're young and you're beautiful. They'd be idiots to refuse you, or saints, maybe. Don't waste yourself like that. Let someone love you, let me love you."

There is the Daniel who held my hand in the recovery room after we lost our baby. I hear his voice as it fades in and out of my half-conscious brain, see the tears streaming unashamed down his ashen face. He is stroking my cheeks, my forehead, my hair.

"It's all right, it's all right. We lost the baby, it's true, but you're all right, Leah, and I'm here, and if you want to, we'll try again."

And I see for the first time that he is getting old, that he is tired, that he is doing it all for me. Then there is a more youthful Daniel, tall and proud and excited. He cannot contain himself.

"You did it, Leah, you did it," he congratulates me, kissing my hands, my face. "You're beautiful and oh my God there are two of them, two of them. Christ, Leah, how did you do it? They're both perfect, they're beautiful, they're just like you. A boy and a girl. All at once. Who says I'm an old man?"

And he picks up the processed cheese sandwich off the tray they have just brought me and tenderly feeds it to me, absentmindedly taking every second bite himself.

And yet another Daniel, again in a hospital room, holding my hand, whispering in my ear, "You're safe, Leah, you're safe. The doctors are quite sure. The tumor was encapsulated, it hadn't spread. You'll live to be a hundred, and you'll have to put up with me for all those years."

And later, as I weep mute tears, he pats my arm and sits quietly beside me, breaking his empathic silence only once to tell me, "Leah, I love you."

On balance, I know, he is a good man, if a difficult one. Irritable, hot-tempered, high-strung, he is apt to be unfair to me and the children, if the days are hot or his work is not going well. But on Sunday morning, it is he who reads the funny papers with Jacob, teaches Hannah to tie her knots for Camp Fire girls. In the winter it is Daniel who splits the kindling and patiently lays the fire in the grate, just because he knows we love it so, even though it means he will have shovelfuls of ashes to deal with the next day. And who always thinks of going out into the country to picnic, look for the first autumn leaves, or feed the ducks in a hidden pond? Or remembers to throw a handful of salted nuts in the bowl of hot popcorn, just to surprise the children? Who dances Jacob and Hannah around exuberantly to the finale of the Jupiter Symphony or slides with them fearlessly down icy snowbanks or stands them up in front of the Miró print in our living room, saying, "Now what do you see, children, horses? Cockroaches? Flashes of red and blue?" or tucks them into bed at night with long stories about rainbow trout and moose and elk in the wild Wyoming mountains of his boyhood. Daniel, Daniel, always Daniel.

And when I think I can bear no more of his moodiness, his criticism, his solitary nature, when I am convinced that I cannot live another day without tenderness, love, or at least a kind word, who turns to me in the night and whispers, "Leah, Leah, why am I so hard on you, the children, myself?" or catches me in his arms after the children head off to school and says, "How about it, we're not too old to do it in the morning, are we?"

Daniel, looking so handsome in his Burberry raincoat; Daniel, being charming and brilliant at yet another dinner party; Daniel, emptying the pocketful of buckeyes he has gathered on campus and solemnly polishing them for the twins; Daniel, returning to our Mexico City hotel room with a bouquet of flowers and excitedly telling me of the glamour of the Zona Rosa as I wait for Hannah and Jacob to finish their nap.

I remember a time when I was so exasperated with him after a winter of his depression and withdrawal that I flew to Cleveland with the children, ostensibly to visit my mother, but really just to get away from him and to talk to Anna and Max. Max listened to my tearful complaints and my ruminations about divorce, all the time puffing on a long cigar. Anna murmured sympathetic words from time to time.

Finally Max said quietly, "Look, Leah, when you married Daniel, didn't they say something about for better or for worse?"

I nodded.

"Well," he summed up brilliantly, "this is worse."

And so it goes. There is the worse, but there is also always, just around the next curve, the better.

That stretch of I-75 from central Kentucky to Cincinnati is so familiar to me that I am able to engage in this long reverie and still remain aware of the road. As I conclude my thoughts about Daniel, I round the curve that reveals the peaceful beauty of the reservoir at Corinth and Owenton and note with satisfaction that I am making good time. Although it is Friday afternoon, I have beaten the traffic out of town and am still too far from Cincinnati to be affected by the volume of cars that always crosses the river in one direction or another.

I stretch a bit, sigh, and turn on the radio. It is easy to pick up most of the Cincinnati stations from this distance, but I am still too far out for the university station on FM, and I am not in any mood for raucous music and loud disc jockeys hawking cars, beer, and acne remedies from their echo chambers. I switch the radio off again and look around me.

The country is a shade less green here than it was thirty miles south, but I like the play of shadow against hill, tree, and water, and the feel of the road as it arches its back over the ridges. I think of Freud's likening of landscapes to the human body, as I note with amusement the cleavages, deltas, and mounds of the surrounding country. And then I remember my own body, no longer smooth and gently rolling like these pleasant landscapes, but abrupt, stark and embarrassed like the barren hills to the east, where strip miners have defaced the earth as surely as my surgeon has done to me.

A body, a hillside should be molded by the patient voluptuous hands of a sculptor or a god, not chopped and cleaved by the educated brutality of bulldozers or knives. Harrington's look of horror flashes before me once again and then, superimposed on that image, the awe, reverence, and tenderness on his face as he said, "You're an extraordinary woman, Dr. Buchanan."

I wallow in his praise for a moment, letting the words roll over my skin, my brain, like some soothing lotion or balm. Then I shake it off and confront my hunger for such extravagant approval. Is that really what I am seeking everywhere, from Daniel, from the patients in my office? Is my life no more than a noble pose contrived to evoke comments like Harrington's from the world at large? I feel diminished, ashamed, worse still, exposed. I drive northward contrite, a child who has been caught in a lie.

The road climbs gently onto whatever plateau it is that opens up just before the Cincinnati airport—still in Kentucky—and I prepare myself for the rapid descent and tight curves that mark the plunge into the Ohio River Valley. I slow the car to the speed limit, aware of the traps the highway patrol always lays at this junction in an effort, perhaps, to slow the heavy traffic before it reaches the city limits, or to catch the wrongdoers on a patch of level highway before they plummet out of reach toward the river, or, maybe, just to gather up some revenue from the travelers prior to their escape from Dixie into the North.

The traffic is thicker now anyway: no doubt the bridge is clogged with cars some miles ahead. I glance across the highway to the lanes traveling south and take pity on the trapped creatures who creep along the crowded road, eager for whatever welcome wives, children, or television can give them at home. They are at a virtual standstill; I, at least, am making progress. Some animal sense alerts me that something is behind me, and I glance in the rearview mirror in time to see the ugly, powerful muzzle of a huge Mack truck bearing down on me. I look for my opportunity to change lanes and let him pass, unwilling to speed up and outrun him, like a frightened antelope before a lion. I have always been convinced, despite the good press truckers seem to enjoy, that any one of these monsters would happily swallow or crush me, rather than slow down, lay back, or change lanes. I have spent too many days wearily dodging them on this very highway, especially in the rain, when they seem to take a special delight in passing my little compact wagon, cutting in too soon, and flooding my windshield with the volumes of water their immense tires kick up rudely in my face.

Seeing an opening between a fast passenger car and a slower camper, I dart to the right and watch the red truck gobble up the spot where I had been only seconds before. I pace myself to the passenger car ahead of me and relax for a few minutes before the mill race down to the river begins. Then, tightening my hands on the steering wheel, and leaning slightly forward, I am all attention to the final dangerous miles that end so abruptly with a surprising glimpse of the tall buildings of Cincinnati emerging suddenly, like the Land of Oz, from behind a final hill. With the car, I lean now left, now right, as the curves press me one way, then another. I hug the left hand lane, which ends in a rail, too claustrophobic to allow myself to be sandwiched between cars on both sides.

With each curve I take, my mind fastens on the memories that have obsessed me: my father's death, the hospital, the confusion of my college years, my mother, the meaningless sexual encounters. I can't sort any of them out as the highway draws me downward to the river, but I seem to glimpse a meaning hidden somewhere behind the tangle of images and feelings. I feel, as I often do in my work with patients, when I watch in fascination as they weave what at first seems the web of a drugged or drunken spider. Then, suddenly, emerging from a background of dull and broken strands, shining, as if with dewdrops in the morning sun, suddenly appear the main threads, the very filaments that lead relentlessly to the center, to the precise spot that the satisfied spider had so artfully hidden and thus unconsciously displayed.

The bridge jumps out at me, and I push to the right to avoid being swept onto the continuation of I-75 that would land me somewhere in Michigan. I need, instead, to move toward I-71 as I cross the bridge, then dart left off the highway and into the downtown area. Minutes later, I hand my car keys to the proper attendant, who promises to return them to me after locking my car in some nearby garage. Then, smoothing my hair and beckoning to the anxious bellhop in one unbroken motion, I go to the desk and register: Dr. Leah B. Buchanan.

I always use my title in hotels, restaurants, or with airline companies. Women are frequently ignored by the officious underlings who rule in such places. Doctors never are.

The man at the desk solicitously confides in me that due to some special problems having to do with remodeling on certain floors and a meeting of Procter and Gamble salesmen, the hotel is unable to give me the single room I requested. I can, however, have a suite—one of their smaller suites, he apologizes. Naturally, it will be at the same price as the single. He is sorry for the inconvenience. Behaving with what I hope is the proper mixture of understanding and disdain, I wave aside his apologies and his wishes that I enjoy a most pleasant stay at the Terrace, and follow the waiting bellhop into the elevator.

I would prefer to carry the one small suitcase myself but have always been afraid to assert myself on this point when arriving at hotels, though I am adamant at airports.

The bellhop makes the usual production about opening curtains, indicating closet and bathroom, and hoisting my suitcase (which I can lift with one hand) on to the luggage rack at the foot of one of the two immense beds that dominate the room. I fold a dollar bill into his hand, and he salutes me with the usual "if I can be of any service etceteras" as he backs out the door.

Alone. I look around me. The room is a pleasant surprise. It is spacious and does have a sort of sitting room, complete with armchairs, coffee table, writing desk. The furniture is modern, the colors are subdued, and the prints on the wall are unobtrusive. The whole suite gives off an air of tranquil anonymity, and I feel soothed just standing in it.

I am grateful that Jacob and Hannah are not here bouncing on the beds and that Daniel is not irritably pacing up and down in front of the door, eager to go out and buy a newspaper. (He cannot orient himself in a strange city without a map and a local paper. Two hours in any town and he knows it as well as I would in two years.)

My sense of relief at being away from my family makes me feel guilty, and I am ashamed of my selfishness. A decent wife, a good mother would prefer to be with her husband and children. Or at least she would stay home where she belongs, rather than carelessly spending money on luxuries like weekends in hotels.

My self-chastisement does not dampen my delight in the room and in being able to enjoy it alone. I strip off my wrinkled suit, intending to take a long bath, then open my suitcase to reach for a robe and decide to unpack first. If Daniel were here, he would be annoyed. He can't stand it when I start one thing and end up doing another or try to do two things at once.

"Why do you allow yourself to be distracted?" he questions me, exasperated. "It's so disorganized."

In three minutes, my few clothes are either on hangers or in drawers, my shoes and suitcase are in the closet, and my cosmetics and jewelry are on top of one of the dressers. I slip on the robe my mother brought me in the hospital. It is edged with champagne lace, very elegant, very feminine.

"Stop hiding under those sheets and that ugly hospital *schmatta* you're wearing," she ordered. "Put this on. You'll feel better when you do."

And she helped me slip it over my aching, bandaged body. It zipped up all the way and ended in a flattering mandarin collar, which she tugged at smartly. "There, now you look pretty again," and she idly began to smooth my hair with the brush she found on the bedside table.

I felt like a little girl, grateful and mute; every brush stroke was a caress. Momma was here. She would make it better.

The metallic sound of the zipper closing disrupts my thoughts. Weak and angry from these futile memories, I rip off my earrings and head for the bathroom, knowing the water will revive me. But, when I get there, what I see fills me with dread: no welcoming pink-porcelain bathtub awaits me, but instead, an oversized enclosed stall shower. The glass on one side of the enclosure is not frosted, but sparkling and clear. And the wall facing that side of the enclosure is one, vast mirror.

I run from the bathroom and throw myself, sobbing, down on the cool blue bedspread. My exhaustion is so complete that within minutes, contact lenses still in place, I fall asleep.

I wake up with a bad taste in my mouth and a scratchy feeling in my eyes. There is a damp circle on the bedspread near my mouth, made by the saliva I had drooled in my semistuporous sleep. I feel disoriented, as you do when you wake in strange surroundings the first time. I am disgusted by the wetness under my cheek, by the unclean feeling in my mouth and eyes, and by myself. It is like waking from the heavy dreams that sometimes follow masturbation: the unbearable tension has been relieved, and there is nothing left but shame.

I roll over, pull myself to a sitting position, and stand up. Mirrored wall or no, I am headed for the shower. Only water, clean, merciful water, can give me back to myself. I gather up the kit that contains my toilet articles, take clean underwear out of the dresser drawer, and walk into the enormous bathroom. ("Christ," I hear Daniel saying, "I've stayed in hotel rooms smaller than this.")

I turn on the hot water before entering the shower, so that my skin will not be shocked by the initial frigid streams that burst from the shower head, and, back to the mirror, I slip off my robe. In a moment, clouds of steam rise into the air-conditioned room, and the enemy at my back is misted over.

I step into the foggy enclosure and sigh for the warmth and wetness that envelop me. For long blissful moments, I stand there letting my body merge with its favorite element. Then I begin to scrub myself with soap and washcloth and emerge from the mindless state the shower has given me. I plan what I will do. After I dress I will look over some notes for my lecture tomorrow, slip downstairs to the coffee shop for supper, maybe watch a little television, and go to bed.

I turn off the water and reach for one of the towels on the rack outside the shower door. I like to dry myself inside the shower, where it's warmer. As I rub myself all over the steam begins to clear, and I catch a glimpse of my back in the mirror. My own back, even after all these years, is, of course, still somewhat unfamiliar to me, and, as I note my long neck and legs, the indentation of my spine as it curves down toward my flat buttocks and slender thighs, I am pleased with what I see. Not bad for an old woman, I smile to myself.

Then, daring a half-turn, I examine my left side—the smallish, well-shaped if not uplifted breast, the too-prominent rib cage I have always hated (at age eighteen I would have traded thirty IQ points to be long waisted), the stomach that is gently rounded with maturity and childbirth but still flat enough to pass muster in a knit suit without a girdle.

I take a breath, turn once more, and finish my inspection. This, then, is my reality: I will never be asked to pose as Playmate of the Month; Daniel won't groan in anticipation when he unhooks my bra (he hasn't groaned in anticipation, or unhooked my bra for that matter, in more than ten years); I can no longer raise eyebrows at university dinner parties with the daring decolletage of my dinner dress. My body is ugly.

I am very sad about it. I do not like the way I look when my clothes are off. But, I am alive and have every hope to remain that way. *Fertig, bastante*, enough. Thus, I try to lay to rest my fears and griefs and disappointments. And, mentally reciting all of my good fortune like a litany—husband, children, career, friends, house, silver flatware—I dress myself and make myself look whole again.

95

4

SATURDAY——

DRIVING back I think about the seminar I have just completed with the psychiatric residents. I am satisfied that they now have a basic understanding of the Rorschach and about the valuable role its interpretations can play in understanding patients' dynamics. I have elevated the inkblots in their eyes from the private hocus-pocus and mumbo jumbo of their psychologist colleagues, only one step up from tea leaf reading, to a respected diagnostic tool that can aid them and their patients in their quest for clarity.

Yes, it went well. All the residents but one seemed eager enough to learn more, to see the Rorschach in action. As for the Doubting Thomas, him I will convince when I return from Spain. I have asked him to choose one of his patients at random and have him or her tested by a staff psychologist. The next time I am in Cincinnati, I will read that Rorschach blind, and, with only the sex and age of the patient known to me, will give some interpretations.

This parlor trick I have done before, and while I do not endorse it as a method, it is clearly convincing. If the Rorschach responses of the patient are numerous enough to be interpreted, I will be able to judge a great deal about the person's cognitive and emotional functioning.

Of course, in my own office I would support those findings with other tests, a clinical interview, social, educational, and occupational history. But for the purpose of converting the unenlightened, a blind interpretation should do nicely.

I smile and feel slightly smug as I near my turnoff. OK, hotshot, I remind myself, if you're so smart, how come you haven't a clue as to what's going on with Harrington? But I do have a clue, really, many clues. If I can just get enough distance from the whole mess to sort things out.

At home I find things unchanged. What can change in less than twenty-four hours? (I think of my lost child, my lost breast, my dead father: now you see it, now you don't. Now you have it, now you don't. Presto change-o. But in life's disappearing act, what is gone never reappears.)

On the front porch I find the morning paper and mail in the mailbox. Something to come home to. I sort through the mail and find, surprise of surprises, among the circulars and bills, a letter from Hannah. Not a postcard, but an honest-to-goodness letter. Her childish scrawl lifts my spirits and for a moment, my little sunshine girl is with me:

"Dear Mother," I read. My eyes slide down to the body of the letter. I start, then shift back to the salutation.When did she start to call me Mother? Where did Mommy go, or even Mom? I don't remember her calling me "Mother." Is this a letter writing convention, or has she already grown so far from me after only two weeks at camp? I read on. "I am writing a letter instead of a postcard," she tells me conspiratorially, "because some things are just too private. Can you believe that two girls in my bunk have hair under their arms and you-know-where-else? One of them is so big chested that she actually wears a bra! She really needs to! She says everyone in her family matures early. I bet before the month is up we'll know for sure. It is possible she could have her

98

periods already. Do you believe this? I look at myself all the time, but I don't see any sign. Not even a hair. Do you think I'll ever grow up? How old were you, Mom,"—ah, I'm Mom again—"when you got boobs? Do you think I ever will? Carla, she's my consilor (sp?)," (I learn this for the sixth time,) "says I'm the best rider in the bunk. She says Alec, the riding teacher, told her I have real potenshul (sp?). I wish you and Daddy," Daniel's status never changes, "could buy me my own horse. Will we ever be that rich? Oh well, I don't mean to be greedy. I'm very happy that you sent me to this camp. We ride every day. Except Saturdays. I guess because this is a Jewish camp. They must think that even the horses are Jewish and have to rest on the Sabbath. I love it here. I see Jacob every day, and when he isn't being silly or mean, he's nice. You should see how tan he is. He swims all the time. I called him fish-face at lunch yesterday, and he didn't even get mad. I hope you're having a sort of vacation even though you have to go to your office. At least you don't have to put up with Jacob and me! Ha Ha. Daddy must love all the peace and quiet in Spain. I can't wait to see him. And you. My bunkmates are jealous that I get to go to Spain after camp. It is kind of neat (but not as neat as having your own horse! Just kidding). I love you. Please try to answer my questions. Write soon. I love camp. Love, Hannah," and she is gone.

I stand staring at her letter with tears in my eyes and a smile on my lips. This irrepressible child has welcomed me home. But, the price of that welcome is high. She wants me to talk to her, to tell her about breasts, not my favorite topic this summer. I walk slowly into the living room and seat myself on the sofa, raising my hands to my chest as I do so. I start to cup myself, left hand on left breast, right hand on my prosthesis, then lower my hands to my lap. I think about breasts. My breasts as they used to be.

They never caused me any real trouble, except perhaps by emerging late, like shy, nocturnal animals from the still-enchanted forest of my body. I arrived at junior high school, virginal in a white cotton undershirt. My mother had no older daughters. She did not know the social mores dictating bras, even for the flat chested. Training bras, they called them. Even when I reported to

99

her, months later in my embarrassment, the impressive enormity of those fleshy child-women sporting Bali's with underwires, even then her compromise was a camisole with eyelet.

I daringly let the strap slip out from one of my sleeveless dresses that spring, hoping as I sat in my Algebra class that someone would see it. At gym time I changed into my royal blue gym suit behind the closed lavatory door, and I cringed when the teachers herded our hot, sweating bodies into stall-less, curtainless showers after field hockey.

I never really needed a bra until I was past nineteen. Something happened then, hormones began to flow, and within a matter of months I went from a 36A, which I couldn't quite fill, to a respectable B, without gaining any weight. I longed to return, if only for one afternoon, to the eleventh grade in Shaker Heights, when Noreen and Lindsey and I would hop the bus for Cedar Center and the mysteries of Solomon's Corset Shop. There I would obediently "lean in" as the matronly corsetiere passed her hands deftly over satin, cotton, and nylon spandex while I turned crimson from embarrassment as she pronounced for all to hear that I definitely still needed a "molded cup." How I envied Noreen (32D! her bras always cost more than anyone else's) and Lindsey (34C, the most popular size at school). Both girls were slighter and shorter than I, but their rounded bodies were graced by well-developed breasts and neat, flirty fannies that jutted and swayed proudly under pleated plaid skirts. I stood two inches taller than Noreen, four inches over Lindsey, broad shouldered, long legged, flat in front and back.

Years later I learned to appreciate my narrow hips and my height, for I found that, miracle of miracles, sophisticated clothes looked better on me. And, when my breasts did at last develop they were high and firm, not requiring help from Bali or Olga or anyone else. My mirror told me they were shapely, even though my college boy friend did not confirm that view. He once said he didn't like them, that they were shaped like bananas. I peered at myself inquisitively, wondering how he had come to that conclusion. Bananas? Horizontal bananas or vertical? I squinted at my naked reflection as I emerged from the dorm showers. Myopic as I was, I couldn't trust my own judgment. Still, what I saw were oranges, or, perhaps, small melons. Never bananas, I prayed.

Of course, that same boy friend also told me he hated the smell of the jellies and creams I used with my diaphragm. I switched brands compulsively, only to realize months later that the problem was his, not mine. My breasts, the Ortho and Koromex jellies and creams, all were convenient excuses for his impotence, premature ejaculation, whatever.

But I had had no real experience when I met him, and it was long before the days of women's lib, so I trained cold jets of water on my breasts after my shower, in an effort to firm them; I did special exercises, and I switched to the pill, all in the hopes of pleasing him. With even more hormones racing through my hyped-up system, my breasts grew larger, fuller (36C), but his penis did not receive similar benefits. We settled into a pragmatic routine of oral sex between classes in the basement of the library, with occasional clumsy couplings on weekends at his off-campus apartment. He equated penetration with success, wriggled his rapid climax, then drifted quickly off to sleep. I took to wandering into the kitchen of the apartment late on Saturday nights to share warm milk and cinnamon toast with Roger, the only one of the five rommates who did not have a girl friend. Sometimes, as we sat there dunking our toast and discussing Antonin Artaud, I wondered sheepishly how much Roger could hear through the plywood partition that separated his room from Steven's.

Back to my breasts. I went off the pill. (Can one year on the pill cause cancer?) But my breasts stayed big. I expanded my horizons, found newer, more appreciative audiences. They all admired my breasts. At first it was a shock, then a thrill, finally I took it for granted that, when I disrobed, my body would be met with sighs of appreciation. One of my lovers vowed that the mole near my left nipple drove him wild with passion. I checked it in the mirror and decided it really was quite attractive. But, to me my breasts were not objects of passion. From masturbation, long before intercourse, I learned there were far more direct routes to ecstasy. I took pleasure in having my breasts stroked and caressed, but what I felt was a warm, comfortable feeling—enjoyable, but hardly orgasmic. I liked men to play with my breasts, much as I liked them to rub my back or stroke my hair; it felt good and besides it pleased me to know that doing so pleased them.

Time passed and I came to understand just what attractive playthings breasts were for men. I practiced shrugging my bra straps off my shoulders and pushing them together, creating cleavage with my arms held tightly against my sides. Like my long mane of auburn hair, which I tossed majestically or played with coquettishly, my breasts were designed to attract. Long before the mid-sixties when bra-burning became fashionable, I frequently went without underwear, (panties as well as bras), brazenly flaunting erected nipples under clinging jerseys and titillating myself as well as my boy friends, as their hands crept up to stroke my thighs between my stockings and garter belt.

My breasts continued to surprise me for a long time after they fully developed. I frequently found myself absentmindedly cupping them with curious hands as I strode across campus or sat cross-legged on my narrow bed reading Strindberg. They were strange to me, new, and I had some trouble adjusting to the upheaval in my body. Those fleshy protuberances on my chest were like nothing I had ever known. I had to keep checking on them to reassure myself in the face of a dozen questions: were they really mine? were they still there?

By the time I met Daniel, I was oblivious to them. I had grown accustomed to their friendly flopping when I ran from the shower to answer a ringing phone, to their obedient forward thrust when I wore an uplift bra, to their swelling tenderness just before my period, and to their odd, lethargic responsiveness to the tongues, teeth, lips, and fingers that prodded, probed, and played with them. I owned them. They were mine.

Their function did not become clear to me, though, until the twins. The second night after Hannah and Jacob were born I felt the rush of milk tingling under the taut skin near my nipples, and by morning I knew what engorgement meant. Large? I was mountainous! And hard as a rock. Every node was palpable. I was awed by this almost grotesque evidence of maternity. I couldn't wait for Hannah and Jacob to open their eyes, to cry for their feeding.

Impatiently, I lifted them from the isolettes where they slept beside me. Then I lay back gratefully in the marvelous symbiotic perfection that only nursing brings: each of us blissfully content in the simultaneousness of giving, taking, giving, taking, an endless circle that leaves the emptied mother as full as the satisfied nursling.

Within thirty-six hours, the engorgement was manageable and I settled into a routine of seemingly endless feedings. My breasts never failed me. They produced more milk than I needed even for two lusty babies. They leaked milk right through the pads I stuffed into my nursing bras so that near feeding times, when I sat in my office, I often crossed my arms over my chest to hide from my patients the stains I felt spreading from bra to blouse to suit jacket.

My breasts let down at Jacob's or Hannah's slightest cry, pouring milky tears down my skin where I stood in the shower, leaving puddles on the bathroom floor as I rushed into my bathrobe to get to whichever babe had awakened earlier, hungrier than I had anticipated.

Once my left breast caused me considerable discomfort due to a plugged duct. For some reason, neither Jacob nor Hannah was able to empty that one, sore, swollen area. It grew hot and tender and I feared an abcess. I laid on hot compresses and timidly pushed at it, but without result.

Daniel found me that evening, standing in front of the bathroom sink, a towel wrapped around my waist, grimacing at my image in the mirror as I tried to press the painful spot where the milk was clogged.

"Let me do that, Leah, you're being too gentle. The Herefords we broke for milk on the ranch in Wyoming were always having the same problem. And if the calf couldn't take care of it, I could. Give an experienced hand a chance."

I stood embarrassed and amazed, mute as the dumb animals he had tended so many years before, while my husband concentrated his attention and his fingertips on a small spot on the outside of my left breast. Applying more pressure than I had dared, he worked it loose, and I watched in awe as something the

103

consistency of cottage cheese finally oozed out of my nipple. My other breast leaked in sympathy, leaving wet patches on Daniel's shirt where I embraced him in naked gratitude.

"The Herefords were less effusive in their thanks," he muttered into my hair.

No, I never expected betrayal from my breasts. They did proud service whenever called upon, and if they shrank a little, sagged a little, after the twins, well so what, they still lay obediently on my chest, soft and friendly, filling out the contours of my clothes, cushioning my children's heads, comforting my husband in the night. If betrayal were to come, I once thought, surely it would come from below.

My cervix I never trusted. It plagued me for years with all its secretions, sending monthly blood and frequent yellow discharges into my pristine white panties, reminding me of my womanness with telltale odors, cursing me in a dozen different ways.

And, that place between my thighs never looked nice to me after puberty when the labia swelled and the hair sprouted. Mysterious, dark, and damp, it harbored microorganisms like monilia that caused me to itch and burn, served as a breeding ground for the cystitis that made urinary frequency into a painful nightmare, and worst of all, throbbed mysteriously when I manipulated it myself but frequently refused to do so when some important other party was involved.

My breasts annually submitted themselves with stoical grace to their examination by the gynecologist, and monthly (when I remembered) to my own. Never once did the doctor suggest that they be burned (cauterized), frozen (cryotherapy), douched, suppositoried, or painted purple (with gentian violet).

My untrustworthy cervix, on the other hand, submitted me to all those indignities and then had the temerity to continue to frighten me with occasional "iffy" Pap reports. But that wasn't the worst of it. The worst came with pregnancy, when I suffered from the threat of a thousand different diagnoses, all of which pointed out the ultimate inadequacy of my body: miscarriage (how could I be so careless with something so important?), spontaneous abortion (vaguely illegal), incomplete abortion (can't I do anything right?), suspected septum of the uterus (deviate?), possible placenta previa (must I always be impulsive?), cervical incompetence (doesn't even require a comment), all of it adding up to tears and pain and blood and emptiness, the false hope of yet another pregnancy, the all-too-real despair of loss, and so on, until finally, with hormones, and bed rest, and semiweekly internal pelvic exams, and furtively muttered atheistic prayers, finally Jacob and Hannah appeared for Daniel and me and the doctors and all the world to see. The verdict was in: not guilty to all the previous charges. My body did it. I was a woman after all, a real woman, with all the proper working parts.

Still, if the cancer had been cervical I wouldn't have been surprised, not after all the warnings and treatments and the tests. And I don't think I would have minded really, for who needs a cervix anyway, after childbearing is complete? I wouldn't have missed a cervix; I've never even known mine really well. Oh, I have touched it on occasion through a thin veil of rubber, while making sure my diaphragm was in place, and I have felt it as it dilated to accommodate catheters for various X-ray studies or for the heads and bodies of my babies. But I have no real sense of my cervix. My gynecologist knows it better than I do.

My breasts, on the other hand, my breasts at once so public and so personal, my breasts were not supposed to get cancer. No. They were meant for pleasure and for beauty and for sustenance. For them to hold inside themselves no longer the lovely, warm, life-giving milk but instead, the ugly threat of slow, insidious death, that was the ultimate betrayal.

I should have been glad when the surgeon lopped the cancerous one off. Traitor! Murderer! If thine eye offends thee pluck it out, if thy breast offends thee . . .

5

SUNDAY——

I HAVE finished letters to Jacob and Daniel and am working on one to Hannah when the telephone rings. It is not easy for me to find the right way to reassure my daughter that her breasts will emerge according to their own schedule. I wonder, too, if some of Hannah's anxiety stems from the fact of my mastectomy. Not everything can be handled in a letter. Mother and daughter will have to have a long talk in Spain.

The telephone is persistent. I resent being interrupted and know that there is irritation in my voice when I answer.

"Dr. Buchanan?" I hear the soft breathy accents of Miss Drake. This is the first time she has ever called me at home.

"This is Sandy Drake," she goes on. She is Sandy, not Sandra, a bad sign.

"I'm sorry to bother you at home on a Sunday, but, Dr. Buchanan . . . " her voice catches on a sob, "I, I, I, I felt like I just had to talk to you."

"I'm here," I reassure her and wait for her to go on.

She is crying in earnest now, staccato phrases choking out when she catches her breath. I can make little sense of what she is saying, so I listen for the tone. She sounds sad, frightened. I throw out a line to her there where she is drowning in a sea of unnamed feelings. "You sound scared," I tell her.

She pauses between sobs, "Y-yes," I hear her whisper. "I am scared. Scared and alone."

"That's a terrible way to feel," I tell her.

"Terrible," she echoes. "Anyway," she goes on, apologizing, "I'm sorry to bother you, it's just that today I, I kept feeling so alone, and like it didn't matter, that no matter how hard I tried, it would never change, and, that, maybe I should just give up trying, and, you know . . . " her voice trails off.

"Your feelings do matter, Miss Drake, and you matter. It's my job to remind you of that."

She cries some more, but quietly.

These calls are always awful for me. This woman is seriously suicidal. How can I keep her safe? Does she belong back in the hospital? Or dare I trust to the fragile relationship I am trying to build with her? Will that be enough at least for today? Did my lapse into daydream during her last appointment on Friday precipitate her need to make contact with me now? Can what damage has been done be repaired over the telephone?

"I'm sorry to bother you," she reiterates.

"I'm glad you called," I tell her. "Please remember that I asked you to do just that whenever you are feeling this way."

"Yes, you did ask me to call, didn't you?"

"Yes, I did. I did because as long as we can talk about things, then there's hope that you can feel better again. I can't help you if I'm the only one left. That really would be sad."

Her sobs are less violent now. "I, I wanted to call you, to talk to you."

"That's good," I reassure her.

Is she all right now? Do I dare let the conversation end? I allow her to cling onto me for a few more reassuring minutes.

"You're not mad that I called?" she asks again.

"On the contrary, I'm glad. You're keeping your side of the bargain we struck: you promised you'd get in touch with me when your feelings were too much for you to handle alone."

108

"I did say that, didn't I?" she remembers.

"Yes, you said it and you did it," I remind her.

"You really are glad I called, aren't you?"

"Yes."

"Well, I feel a little better now."

"Good."

"Sometimes I just don't think I can go it all alone."

"You don't have to. I'm here."

"You are, aren't you?"

"Yes."

"And if I needed to call you later on, that would be OK?"

"That would be fine. I'll be right here."

"Even at night?"

"Yes. My telephone works at night too, all night."

She sighs. "You must think I'm a real baby, Dr. Buchanan. A baby and a coward."

"To the contrary," I tell her. "It takes considerable courage to face the kinds of feelings you're facing."

"Well . . . " she is winding down now. I can tell it is all right to let her go. I wait for her to be able to sever the connection that she has made. "I guess I'll hang up now."

"Fine."

"I'll see you Friday."

"Good."

"I'll, I'll be there Friday."

"Good, because I'll be waiting for you."

Another sigh. "Bye, Dr. Buchanan."

"Goodbye, Miss Drake."

I hear the click and she is gone.

After the phone call I feel as if I have run three miles. I sit down and go over the conversation in my mind. I am relatively satisfied. Worried, yes, but also fairly certain that Miss Drake will call me rather than act out against herself. This is Sunday. Friday is not too far away. She knows I will answer her calls for help. I think it will be all right.

My letter writing mood has been dispelled. There is no way to get back to Hannah and her prepubescent questions about boobs. I am robbed of my quiet, solitary Sunday. My patients have

109

intruded themselves again into my life. I cover the typewriter and think of Sandra Drake, with her soft voice, her trusting eyes, her scarred wrists. And then of Ilana Fromer and Fran Matthews and of Johanson and Harrington. I think of the twice-a-week patients and then the twice-a-month patients. I think about them all.

My patients. I love them. They are so helpless, so unhappy, so weak. They look to me with sad frightened eyes and trust in me to solace and to heal them. They are willing, hard working, faithful. They come to my office when they are told to and leave when I tell them the hour is up. For the most part, they are punctual and predictable in their appointment keeping. They struggle to share with me their innermost secrets, they reveal to me their little deceits, they forsake old habits and defenses, all because I ask them to. And in return, what do I give them? My time? A sizeable monthly bill? An occasional sympathetic smile? The implied promise of better things to come?

My patients. I hate them. They are willful, stubborn, and demanding. They blame their parents, spouses, bosses, children, friends, and ultimately me for all the problems that stem from faults within themselves. They are blind and stupid, angry and selfish. Oh yes, most of all selfish. I am weary of their whining and complaining. I am sick of their self-centered ways. Their child-ishness, their narcissism know no bounds. Will they never grow up? Will they never change? I give them all I have to give. I deliver up to them (along with my professional knowledge, my theoreti-cal expertise) the very center of my being, my soul. Even when it means that I rob my husband, my children, I do not stint. I give and give, and even when it seems I am not giving it is a gift because I then demarcate for them, with them, their depletedness and the unreasonableness of their demands. I give until I fear that I myself will become as empty and depleted as they are, and they negate it all, denying me with a shrug, a blink, a muttered "I already knew that."

I hate them. I love them. I am them.

Oh, how I long to talk to Saul, but he is gone, on his holiday, not available to me. And Daniel is gone. And Dr. Edwards and Dr. Isaacson, gone, all of them gone. So here I am at last, at the age of forty, with my children at summer camp, my husband in Spain, my former supervisor out of reach, my old therapists a memory rather than a living presence. I, Leah Bronstein Buchanan, am on my own.

At this very moment an image flashes through my mind. It is Dr. Isaacson, I think, at his desk, reading over some papers, making a note here and there. He shifts in his chair as if he is at last aware of my presence, for I am floating far above him, like some Chagall bride. As he raises his head and looks up over his shoulder at me, I see his face for the first time, but I am not sure it is his face; it could be Dr. Edwards's, or no, I think perhaps my father's. He raises his left hand in a gesture of greeting, of goodbye, as I float past him, both of us smiling, on our way somewhere else.

Sleep does not come easily to me anymore. Not since my surgery. I am afraid to abandon myself to it so I fight it, as I did the anesthesia, swimming up again and again from the drowning sensations of loss of consciousness, seeking yet one more gulp of the air of reality and control. But I always lose in the end. Is it death I fear? Perhaps. And yet, once I succumb to sleep, I luxuriate in it, reluctant to rise in the morning.

Before Daniel and the children left, I read late at night, wrote letters, sipped warm milk, sometimes laced with cognac, then, when morning came, I lingered too long in bed until conscience demanded that I rise and prepare a decent breakfast for my family.

Tonight none of these methods has worked. The books on my nightstand are useless as soporifics: the mystery story is so badly written that it jars me; the esoteric tome on analyzing the border-line personality is certainly boring enough, but its breadth, depth, and scope make me feel hopelessly provincial and untrained.

I turn on the TV but can't imagine why I would want to listen to people in my bedroom whom I would not consider inviting into my living room. I get up and begin to walk into the hallway to check on the children. Then I remember they are not here. I walk into Hannah's room anyway, flip on the light switch, and look around at the neatly made bed heaped with bright pillows and stuffed animals, the oversized poster of mare and foal, purchased from her allowance money at the Horse Park two weeks before she left for camp, the shelf of books so crowded that it overflows into a careless stack on the desk, the Mexican rug slightly askew on the floor. I walk to her closet and open it, stare at the dresses she has no use for at camp, then back out of her room, feeling as though I have somehow intruded on her privacy.

I walk down to the end of the hall to Jacob's long, narrow room, which lies transverse across the front of the house, up under the dormer. With the light turned on it is as bright as day, for he has chosen to have his ceiling painted yellow and to add a bright yellow graphic to his otherwise-austere white walls. His bed is also neatly made, but barren of pillows and animals. His desk is orderly and clean, with his stamp album centered on it and his pencils standing at attention in the Dundee marmalade jar he liberated from his father's desk three years before.

On his bulletin board are a few snapshots he has taken of trees, rocks, flowers, and even friends and family, with the birthday camera he is learning to use. And on his nightstand is a carefully constructed model of a space station, accurate to the last detail. I stand staring at it for a moment, then flick out the light and leave. I walk down the hall between Hannah's room and Daniel's study and resignedly return to my own.

I turn out my lamp but cannot get settled. I toss, turn, sigh, then turn again. My mind begins to fill with my patients and their problems, which I see stretching out like a caravan in an endless desert. I consider them individually for a moment, their faces, their voices; then the actual people fade out of the picture and I am left with the long stream of their personal agonies: the failed marriages, the lost loves, the dead children, the academic setbacks, the promised promotions, the automobile accidents, the long hospitalizations, the brain tumors, the unsuccessful spouses, the financial disasters, the unforgiving fathers, the overbearing mothers, the unwanted babies, the guilt-producing abortions, the sexual inadequacies, the awful infertility, the broken hopes, the buried dreams, the barrenness—the burden of their lives. They travel across the desert landscape seeking an oasis and I sit there, beside a tiny puddle of water, one lonely fig tree, too old to give fruit, too broken to give much shade.

But my job is not to quench their thirst, to shelter them, I remind myself, but merely to teach them to lay their burdens down or to help them learn to carry them more smartly. The caravan rests by me for a minute or a year then divides and moves on in many different directions.

In my dream I am approached by a tall handsome sheikh, his robes and *keffiyah* long and flowing, but they are black. He sidles up to me, like a crab, then silently begins to dance with me. As we dance I feel light and cool despite the fact that he is holding me very tight. His breath smells oddly sweet, like ether, and his arms encircle my waist, my neck, my knees.

"Who are you?" I ask as I feel the breath being squeezed gently but persistently out of me. "Who are you and what is your name?"

He, very tall, seraphlike, envelops me in long black robes that might be wings, as he leans over, and in Arab accents murmurs, "Leah is weary and I am here for her. My name is . . . " But in the morning I do not remember the ineffable name he whispered in my ear.

6

MONDAY——

I STAND in the tiny bathroom at my office waiting for the tepid tap water to run cooler so I can fill my empty coffee mug and swallow down another two aspirins. I have taken more aspirins in the last seventy-two hours than I usually take in a year. The headache, which formed itself behind my eyes on Friday morning, grew worse as that day went on, but it faded to a dull throb over the weekend. Today it is back, as if on Saturday and Sunday it had only been lying low, crouching for a leap, as Daniel would say. Every movement of my head is torture. I can neither sleep nor eat. Yet here I am at my office with a full day of patients behind me and Fran Matthews yet to see.

I hold my hand under the running water. It is still lukewarm. I give up on its getting any cooler, after all, it is July, and I swallow the aspirins down with the water. This process leaves an acrid taste in my mouth. I head back to my office, sit down in my chair, and allow myself the luxury of closing my eyes and putting my feet up on the hassock in front of the patients' chair. I have ten minutes until Mrs. Matthews arrives. Maybe if I rest a bit the aspirins will work their magic.

It has been a terrible day. Mondays are always difficult. I wonder what kind of stubborn masochism has made me schedule so many borderlines for Monday? Doug sees his least-well-put-together patients on Friday, ten of them, back to back. He says by Fridays he is so tired it doesn't matter. He can't practice meaningful psychotherapy, so he dispenses kind words and medication. I can't work with borderlines when I'm tired; I can barely do it when I'm rested. So somehow it has evolved that Mondays are filled with my most difficult, least productive hours: a barren landscape of emptiness dotted wih occasional outcroppings of rage. My last appointment, Fran Matthews, with her relatively intact ego and eagerness to please, is like a ray of sunshine at the end of a gloomy day.

When I usher Mrs. Matthews into my office less than five minutes later, she does not look like a ray of sunshine. She sits down heavily in the chair and does not look at me. She plays with a crumpled tissue in her hands, then throws it in the wastebasket and looks up at me.

"Is that a new suit?" she begins.

I look back at her and say nothing. The suit is three-years-old, a simple, khaki-colored affair. Surely she has seen it before.

"Well, it looks very nice on you. Very crisp and businesslike. Professional."

Too crisp? Too businesslike, I wonder? Cold, maybe? Is that what she's trying to tell me?

"If I wore a suit like that it would be all wrinkled by this time of day, but you look as fresh as a daisy," she goes on.

I feel the wetness under my armpits and think of the irony of her remark. What has precipitated this? And where is it taking us? She sighs and shifts in her chair.

Apropos of nothing she tells me, "My mother called last night."

Mrs. Matthews's mother is a very successful stockbroker and financial expert in Chicago, one of the first women to achieve

116

prominence in that field. So my suit is a reminder of mother . . .

"It must be part polyester," she adds, taking me down a peg.

"Polyester?" I echo, in spite of myself.

"Your suit, I mean. Because it isn't wrinkled at all. But it doesn't look like polyester," she reassures me, "it looks like linen."

"Your mother called last night," I remind her, recovering my line of thought.

"Yes, she's on her way to San Francisco with Jack and she said she just wanted to see how the children were and say goodbye. They'll be in California for two weeks."

And I'm leaving on my vacation soon. Hmmm . . . "How did the call make you feel?" I start to ask, but she interrupts me with "Where did you get it?"

I am confused.

"The suit, I mean. Oh, I know you won't tell me. And it doesn't even matter, really. There's no way I could ever look like you. So cool, and efficient, and professional."

"Like me, or like your mother?" I question, and the tears begin to flow.

Mrs. Matthews stares at me with wet eyes, then shakes her head, and looks down at her lap. "Like either of you," she mutters, "what difference does it make? No matter how hard I try I can never get it right. But you, she, you're both just perfect. Sometimes when I'm at home, you know, and I'm trying to clean out my closets, and the kids are fighting and we're having tuna noodle casserole for dinner for the third time in two weeks, sometimes I can just picture the way it must be at your house. I can see you walking in calmly at the end of the day and kissing your husband and children and . . . and, serving up a perfect supper of crabmeat bisque and quiche lorraine, or something. I bet it's always like that at your house. You probably even have candles on the table, even when you don't have company. And nice conversations, and nobody quarrels or spills milk."

As she goes on with her fantasies I remember my own, the ones I formulated about Dr. Isaacson's wife when I was in treatment with him and that continued to plague me for years thereafter.

Although I had actually seen her a half-a-dozen times (with him at the theater, in a shopping mall, a parking lot), I could never retain a clear mental picture of her. It was always distorted by my projections and the nature of my transference. So at times she was a tall, square-faced blonde with a silk scarf tied modishly in her hair. Other times she was a tiny, mousey, nondescript brunette, wearing glasses. For all I knew she might have been both: she might have had two heads! Usually I made her a school teacher.

Did Dr. Isaacson actually tell me that or did I make it up. Or are all psychiatrists' wives former school teachers? In my patient's mind, Mrs. Isaacson no longer worked. She tended the good doctor's house and children. I saw her as a perfect mother, a perfect wife, who took interest in draperies and could cook beef Wellington without batting an eye. She collected antiques and did volunteer work for some important charitable or even political causes. She was content to sit in Dr. Isaacson's shadow, never demanding that the light shine full upon her face. I hated her. I admired her. I wished she would teach me how to be a woman.

I imagined she never raised her voice at her husband or told him that he let her down. She didn't irrationally spank her children one minute and smother them with kisses the next. She was a consistent mother who would brook no neurosis in her, his children. She did not scream like a banshee two days before her period and was undoubtedly too graceful to break out in pimples even in middle age. Her hair was never oily.

She had orgasms in bed at will and never masturbated or fantasized about strange men or lesbian lovers. She was receptive, always, to Dr. Isaacson's advances and just aggressive enough to make his life interesting. She could never be called castrating nor by any stretch of the imagination, dull. She was intelligent, articulate, well read, but she did not feel the need to pursue her own career or outshine her husband. She was utterly satisfied with being a woman and positively gloried in the dual role of wife and mother.

She may have had that one obligatory affair in college, prior to meeting her husband, but after that there were no other men. She never went through that Curious George phase where everything has to be seen, tasted, touched, no matter how dangerous the outcome. She was a good woman, right out of the Psalm: "A virtuous woman who can find? Her price is above rubies . . ."

I laughed at her behind her back, mocked her, derided her, and envied her. Was there ever a time, I wondered, when I could have been like that? Would I have been happier? Would I have been me?

Mrs. Matthews is still talking, but though my mind has wandered, it has not hindered my understanding of her. I have heard what she is saying and have elucidated her words with some of my own remembered feelings. Yes, I know how it is to compare oneself to the Great Phantom Wife and Mother and find oneself lacking. I listen carefully for a minute more.

Mrs. Matthews has left the imagined Buchanan dining room and is making her way through the rest of our perfect household. I wonder if she will reach the bedroom. When she hits the study, which she describes as a sort of holy of holies where no child's hand, foot or voice is ever welcome, I judge that it is time for an intervention.

"Is that the way it was at your house?" I ask her, and the earnest work begins.

We spend the remaining minutes interpreting her fantasies and her projections. How she thinks I look, dress, keep house, treat my husband and my children, gives us clues as to what she thought about her mother, what she thinks about herself. We are right on target. It is a good hour. But my headache still throbs behind my eyes.

I am washing the supper dishes when the doorbell rings. Supper dish, actually. One lone soup bowl, and, of course, the pot I heated it in. I haven't used the dishwasher since Daniel and the twins left. Haven't needed to. I haven't prepared a proper meal since then. This is a sort of vacation for me, after all. I wipe my hands on the dish towel and head for the front door. Who could it be?

I hestitate a moment before undoing the latch, unprepared for any further uninvited guests. Nonsense, I tell myself, it's still broad daylight, not even six-thirty, a clear summer evening.

119

"Flowers for Dr. Leah Buchanan," says the young man standing on my porch.

He hands me a large, elongated white box, tied with green ribbons. Through the cellophane window I see masses of yellow roses. My heart leaps like a schoolgirl's. Daniel, I think, as I accept the box from the delivery man. He's surprising me with flowers to make up for that curt telephone call! Even as I formulate the thought, I realize how ridiculous it is. This is not a Daniel-like gesture.

The florist's boy tips his cap and trots toward his truck. I stand there holding my prize awkwardly, like a maiden aunt with somebody else's new baby, then I back into the house. Yellow roses! The only other time I have ever received them was opening night of my senior play, when Frank sent them from New York, with the little card I still have in a box of old letters in my bottom desk drawer, "For Miss Julie, my leading lady, Love, Frank."

But that was twenty years ago. What will this card reveal? "These roses are less extraordinary than you are. Forgive me, Mark." I lean back against the living room wall, the same wall that Harrington pinned me against four nights ago, and I bite my lips to keep from crying. Why couldn't the flowers have been from Daniel, I think, as I bury my face in their delicate fragrance?

The headache I have been fighting throbs dully behind my left eye, diminished by the codeine my colleague Doug gave me at the office.

"Take this when you get home," he had advised me. "You look as if you haven't slept in a week."

"You know I don't like to take medicine. I rarely even take an aspirin," I reminded him. "This is some kind of tension headache, it'll leave when I deal with whatever's bothering me."

"You haven't got another eight years to spend on the couch, Leah. Take this tonight. Get some rest. You owe it to your patients, if not to yourself."

"All right," I had acquiesced at last and swallowed it along with my vegetable soup, half an hour since. The pain is definitely less now.

I feel oddly light-headed as I move toward the kitchen in quest of a vase for my flowers. Though I hate the thought of being reminded of Harrington every time I look at them, it is not in me to throw them away. I fill the vase with water and arrange the long-stemmed flowers in it, stepping back to admire the finished result. They really are lovely! Twenty-five perfect beauties, just getting ready to bloom.

I carry them back into the living room and put them on the corner table near the fireplace. Before I lie down on the sofa, I turn on the FM stereo. They are playing Spanish guitar music on my favorite station. I pull a pillow behind my head and wait for the headache to succumb to the codeine.

As I stare at the roses I think of Harrington and of the message he has sent me. He thinks I am extraordinary. How will I get that notion out of his mind? Or, more important, why does he need to think that? I close my eyes for a moment. The codeine is definitely beginning to work. When I open them it seems that the roses have also opened a little. Is it possible that I have slept? Their scent is beginning to pervade the room, or at least I think it is.

The guitar music thrums in the background, making me think of Daniel in Spain. I wish he were here holding me. I wish someone were here. As if in answer to my unspoken thought, Harrington appears beside me. He is stroking my face, my fore- head, my neck, with the back of his elegant hand. I banish him, but he returns and begins touching me anew. Gently, but insis- tently, as he did the other night. I close my eyes and let myself imagine: he is there. I force him out of my mind again: he is gone. At last I sink into my drug-induced slumber. Harrington reap- pears. This time I welcome him with open arms.

He pulls me up off the sofa and dances me around the room. We tango languidly to the strains of the Spanish guitar. His breath on my neck is hot and he whispers provocatively in my ear, all the while continuing to stroke me. I am half-faint in his arms. The scent and color of yellow roses are everywhere as we slowly circle the room. Dizzy, nearly breathless, I sink against him, stumble, and he carries me to the sofa where he arranges me against him, limp like a rag doll. I lie there staring, now at his dark eyes, his white teeth, then past them to the yellow flowers opening before me. What difference does it make? He is giving me what I have always wanted, what Daniel cannot afford to give. At long last I have a lap to sit on, a shoulder to lean on, a hand to wipe away my tears. What matter the cost? I will have it. I must. So what if it is only for a day or an hour or a minute?

My skin breathes in his caresses, and I sigh. Is it wrong for me to want this so much? Do I harm him, Daniel, myself, by resting here in his arms? Because I am an adult, analyzed, a psychotherapist, a wife, a mother, because of these facts must I always turn my back on my own needs? Are those needs so infantile, dangerous, threatening, destructive that they must forever be submerged beneath the facade of my competence and strength? Is there never a time to rest in someone's arms, a child again at last, to abandon all responsibility, to abandon all thought, to be, simply to be, at rest?

My body feels strangely light. Roses are everywhere. I am no longer resting as much as floating in this phantom's arms. I trust him implicitly, completely. I abandon myself to his care as I once abandoned my soul to God's keeping every night when I dutifully recited the *Shema:* Hear O Israel, the Lord Our God, the Lord is One.

But who is my lord? This handsome phantom humming a familiar melody somewhere near my left ear? Daniel, perhaps already eating *medias lunas* for breakfast in his pension in Seville? Saul? Dr. Isaacson? Dr. Edwards? My father? No. I will banish all of these thoughts. I reject you, renounce you, all of you. I want my peace. I want Harrington to hold me. Such a sensitive, intelligent man. He knows I am extraordinary. He said so at the office. He wrote it on the card. He whispered it in my ear, only moments ago.

Extraordinary Leah, with her long auburn ponytail and her green myopic eyes, saying *Kaddish* for her father at the synagogue. Extraordinary Leah winning first prize in the Hebrew School oratorical contest. Extraordinary Leah graduating as high school valedictorian and going off on scholarship to such a demanding university. Extraordinary Leah drinking a fifth of rum every Friday, Saturday, and Sunday night, until finally she smashes one of the bottles and with the jagged pieces and her own right hand slashes the sorry saga of her imagined failures into the flesh of her left arm. Extraordinary Leah sitting, endlessly sitting, staring, forever staring, waiting, restlessly waiting, in the day room of the psychiatric ward of Massachusetts General Hospital.

And now he has come at last, after all my long, lonely, empty, futile patience. He has come to heal me with sweet-smelling yellow roses and with warm, soothing caresses that require nothing from me but faith and trust and my head resting lightly on his shoulder.

The guitars are still strumming in the background. My eyes are so heavy. I know I am not a very good dancer. But he is such a strong leader, he makes it seem easy. I really should lift my head up. It's time to make an interpretation. Or at least to ask a question about Monica or Kelly Ann. But I am so tired and the music is so insistent and the scent of the roses is making me dizzy all over again. Ah, Harrington, you're not as bright as Daniel, and your motives are unclear to you. But you sure know how to help a girl relax. What is that melody that you or the guitars are humming? It seems I used to know the words. A lullabye or something. La la la la la la la la la la la la, *que bonita quando duerme. Ah que bonita,* la la la la, *que bonita quando duerme. Ah que bonita, es mi hija, que bonita quando duerme, Como una amopola entre los trigales verdes.*

7

TUESDAY——

HALF the day already gone and my headache, held in abeyance by the codeine only for a few hours, is still with me. I have seen three patients already, watched their faces, listened to their voices, as I drifted back and forth between them and my memories and an image of a living room full of roses.

Now Ilana Fromer is before me, looking particularly provocative in a very low-cut sundress. I can see the tops of her high, rounded breasts. I can even see the perspiration in her cleavage. She is a girl whose juices flow freely: perspiration, tears, saliva. When excited in my office, she has to swallow frequently as she talks. When she cries, she goes through stacks of tissue, making most unladylike gulps in her throat and loud, honking noises as she unabashedly blows her nose. She throws her body about in the chair, revealing large wet patches under her arms and, on very warm days, down her back. Everything about this girl-woman flows.

Nothing is clicking for me this session. Miss Fromer presents material I know must be analyzed, but I am dumb. Perhaps she does not sense the change in me but takes for granted my long, ostensibly analytic, silences. I listen to her words, but I do not hear what she is saying. The words, yes, but, ah, the melody! I try hard to pay closer attention, repeating to myself inside my head her every sentence. I find myself blue-penciling her remarks, annoyed with her grammatical inconsistencies. She says, "The reason is because . . . " I strike *because* mentally and pencil in *that*, but she does not learn from my telepathic tutelage. She is careless with subject-verb agreement, saying "each one of them are" instead of "each one of them is." She habitually uses *they* when she could and should use *he* or *she,* and she says *their* when she means *his* or *her.* Does her usage reflect some liberationist view, or merely ignorance?

I shake my head and listen some more, appalled now by problems of style, as well as grammar. How can she hope to learn to live well when she cannot even speak well? Her awkwardness and imprecision are linguistically unforgiveable. I wonder if I should purchase for her a copy of Strunk and White's *Elements of Style,* explaining that one cannot behave clearly unless one thinks clearly, and that sloppy syntax is the hallmark of a sloppy mind.

This reverie alternately amuses and depresses me. I analyze it, recognizing the distance I place between myself and Miss Fromer by assuming my dry grammarian's role. Her suffering is no longer real when I edit it. I have fallen back on the old habits of my days at World Publishing. Perhaps I should have stayed there among my dictionaries, thesaureses, and dull, technical manuscripts. No one was ever harmed by my reveries in those days.

Fromer is telling me something about a party she went to the night before, the usual drugged-up brawl that ended in the usual smutty embraces. I am not listening. Instead, I find I am staring at her breasts; I cannot take my eyes off them as, bra-less, they heave and bob with every shift and sigh. I try to imagine what they look like beneath the sundress. It is clear they are very large. If the elasticized smocking at the top of her dress were removed, would they fall wearily onto her lap or remain high and firm, attached proudly to her chest by muscles and ligaments not yet grown tired of carrying their bountiful burden? Are her nipples widespread and brown, or discrete, tight, and pink like mine? What is she talking about, I wonder, as I raise my eyes guiltily from their moving targets and focus knowingly on her lips and then her eyes.

I cross my legs, tuck my chin down, and place my right hand over my mouth, leaning my head slightly into it. This is one of my looks of relaxed concentration. I hope she registers it and does not notice how my mind has been straying.

But wait a minute, Leah. Why cut off this unconscious stuff? Maybe it will tell you something. Possibly, possibly, but it seems I should be at least vaguely aware of what the patient is talking about. Damn, maybe I should have gone all the way with my analytic training. Maybe if I had I would know what I was doing all the time, instead of only in periodic bursts.

Uh-oh. My eyes are off the kid's boobs now, but I'm still not listening. What is going on here? One of her sundress straps has slipped off her shoulder. I wonder if the dress will fall down. If it did, I could reach out and take one of those tits in my hand. I could heft the weight of it, squeeze it, bounce it around a little. Or I could tear that silly little sundress right off that snotty little bitch, grab her by the nipple, and pinch hard.

The primitive quality of my anger, the graphic image of reaching out maliciously to pinch Fromer's tit, remind me all at once of Ruthie and the terrible fights we used to have. She was younger than I and maybe prettier and had always been Daddy's favorite. I begrudged every moment my mother spent with her, calculating that every minute with Ruthie was one fewer for me. My jealousy was irrational, but that made it no less painful. And now Fromer is arousing those same feelings. I'm jealous of her all right, her with her big gorgeous boobs, a matched pair no less! She's young and she's free and she even has the audacity to take classes with Daniel. I'm angry with her, no doubt about it. And I'd like to hurt her, any way I know how. Like maybe by tuning her out, not paying attention to her feelings, just as I tune myself out so as not to have to deal with my anger.

I am uneasy. I shift restlessly in my chair. Why can I not get

127

comfortable this hour? Anger. I was thinking about anger. But there's more than anger, much more. There's the wistful side of it, too. And the erotic. I want to touch her breasts because she is young and beautiful. I want to make that youth and beauty mine. Miss Fromer has become a talisman, a goddess: if I embrace her, then all of her powers will flow into me.

Damn! I simply must focus on what is going on with her. Or is it possible that what is going on in me is a reflection of what is going on with her? I have been so busy with my countertransference problems that I have lost sight of the fact that my thoughts and feelings can give clues to hers: I embrace her to absorb her youthful sexuality just as she locks her legs around one man after another to absorb, through her own lust and some magic conjugation with them, their power. She uses men in much the same way that I once used them, to ward off her growing awareness of her own terrible emptiness, to reassure herself of her essential feminity, and to borrow from them the potency that she cannot find within herself.

How is it possible that it has taken me so long to understand her? She is about to lose me for a month to my vacation. And so she taunts me with her provocative behavior, her endless seductions, filling herself up with the men she knows she can always attract, bolstering herself to withstand the four weeks without me, flinging in my face the fact of my abandonment by showing me that she can bloody well do without me. Oh, Ilana, yours is a familiar plaint, a song that I have sung myself, and perhaps that is why the melody was so elusive. You may assume your defensive postures, masquerade as something you are not, but still I will discover you, as I once discovered myself. Only give us time and we will work it out. I know it. I feel it in my bones.

I settle back in my chair, able to relax at last, to listen to the continued flow of words that issues from Miss Fromer's mouth. There are only minutes left, but I will try to make them count. Despite my good intentions, I soon find that it is impossible for me to do much with what is left. And so I wing it through the rest of the hour on sheer *chutzpah* and experience, knowing that the material we haven't worked with this session will surely surface again. As I walk her to the door, I remember that Daniel never liked bleached blondes anyway.

Eric Johanson sits across from me in the big leather chair looking exactly as he has looked every Tuesday and Friday of the months I have worked with him. I cannot remember why he is here, but I sense that some primitive awareness of his own emptiness, his essential lack of center, has sent him to me and keeps him in that chair. He is a man who has followed all the forms, dotted every *i*, crossed every *t*. He pays his bills on time, never neglects his lawn, eats moderately, and goes to bed early. He has never taken an unnecessary risk. He does not drink excessively, even at parties, and has always been faithful to his wife. He works diligently at his research, which is pedestrian but respectable, and his publication record is good. His tenure at the university was assured early, and he is a regular teacher at the Sunday school of his church.

It is an utter mystery to him that his wife is dissatisfied. What she wants eludes him. He has dutifully kissed her upon returning from work every Monday through Friday of their married life, yet she has steadfastly accused him of being cold and distant. He knows that their lovemaking leaves something to be desired, but only because his wife has told him of her frustrations. For himself, he is satisfied, if she is willing. Sometimes he admits to a secret embarrassment or shame, for he suspects that as a lover he is less ardent and accomplished than he should be. He reads sex manuals diligently, but they do not enlighten him.

Although he takes his son to music lessons and occasionally attends his soccer games (if they do not interfere with his laboratory commitments), his wife says he shows no interest in the child.

All of this confuses him. He has tried his best and it hasn't been enough. Where was it written that warmth and spontaneity were requirements? He is a tolerant man, despite his many rigidities, and has never expected his wife to be a carbon copy of himself. He allows for her imperfections, her disorganized approach to the kitchen and the other household chores, her flamboyant taste in clothing and in art (a red wool winter coat! a Matisse poster in their bath!), her outbursts of temper or amusement. Indeed, he

129

has confided in me recently, he was perhaps attracted to her for those very qualities. "She seemed so lively," he remarked wistfully one day when he described their placid courtship. And now she is gone, bent on divorce, and she still has the red coat and the Matisse poster and the boy. And he is alone and does not understand.

Mr. Johanson uncrosses his bony legs and allows his knees to fall apart. He pushes his glasses up with the middle finger of his right hand, explaining as he does so. "It is hot today."

I wonder how he knows that, for I have never seen any evidence that he perspires. The office is air-conditioned and I do not feel hot, so I look at him more closely. Although his hands rest loosely on his knees and he is leaning back in the chair, his expression seems somehow strained. He is in the midst of one of his usual prolonged silences and I am at a loss as to how to cope with his resistance.,

I assume it is resistance, for so I have been trained to think, but of late I have begun to wonder if it is possible that there simply isn't any more to this man than that which he has so laboriously assembled. My own discomfort increases as his silence continues.

"I wonder what you're thinking," I say at last.

"Nothing," he assures me.

Nothing will come of nothing, speak again, I think, but I do not say it.

He catches his upper lip with his lower teeth repeatedly, and I watch him in fascination as the pale pink arcs disappear behind a white enameled barrier only to reappear and disappear again.

I look away embarrassed and wonder why I feel that way. The clock tells me that more than half the hour is left. I am uneasy without knowing why. Consciously I take a deep breath, then exhale slowly, as I search my memory of the previous hour for a clue to today. I find nothing.

He is still silent and apparently content to remain so. His eyes have their usual blank look and now his mouth is still. Will nothing ever move this man? I sit still, waiting for some insight to enlighten me, waiting for my unconscious to give me a clue. I feel definite tension in my right leg and know that very soon my back will start to ache. I shift in my chair, aware now of my growing impatience, and redirect my gaze to Johanson. How long has he been silent, I wonder? A minute? A week? A lifetime?

My eyes traverse his body like a ski slope, starting with his head, then moving in diagonals—first left, then right, then left again, across the frozen mini-mountain of his body. At last they come to rest at his crotch. His fly is open. He has begun to speak: some monotone irrelevancy about the lab. I know I should pay attention, but cannot seem to focus on his words. He falters in his story, so I murmur reassuringly "go on" and watch a shadow of myself rise out of the chair and cross to him.

I kneel before him on the carpet, my eyes now level with his fly. Oblivious, he continues, while back in my chair I set my face in a look of troubled concentration and proffer an occasional nod of interest. My hands dart out to his open zipper and swiftly release his soft, pink penis from its hiding place. I stroke it tentatively for a moment or two as it lies nestled against his perfectly pressed pant leg, then suck it surreptitiously into my waiting, open mouth. He does not notice. I lick, loll, and love it, but nothing happens. It stays limp and lifeless against my teeth and tongue.

I exert more effort, employing all the tricks I thought I had forgotten, caressing and cajoling, touching and teasing, nibbling and nudging, but nothing. He continues in his monologue, oblivious to my presence. I begin to suck vigorously, first slowly, then faster, working myself into a frenzy. I feel my hair come loose from its careful French twist, but in my mouth his penis is impassive. Tasteless, odorless, distinctly cool, it mocks me in its larval state. Hastily I tuck my hair back up, but it is no use. There is no hope for my hairdo so long as I continue to worry his penis, shaking it back and forth like a puppy with a rawhide toy.

I feel my anger rising in me, choking out my disappointment, and for a moment I am ready to bite and bite hard. But no, I think better of it and feel myself return to my chair. What an exasperating man, I think, as I wipe my mouth with the back of my hand. Along with my anger I sense my frustration and the magnitude of the rejection I have suffered. My hunger has gone unappeased, my womanness unrecognized. I am utterly negated: with his total passivity, he has controlled me completely, reduced me to nothingness, robbed me of myself as well as of whatever I thought I could have of him. He is as empty and dry as a gourd and I am ridiculous in my frenzy to fill myself, to quench my thirst at his reluctant fountain.

I work with him until the end of the hour, uneventfully, and have to stop myself from saying as I walk him to the door, "By the way, Dr. Johanson, your fly is open."

Ten minutes. I sit at my desk, eyes closed, and ponder the fantasy material that I produced. Some of what it means is clear, more is hazy. Come on, Leah. Do your stuff.

One: his personality, passive aggressive in the extreme. But I already knew that. Negativism. Anger. I sense anger. His? Mine? Where does it come from? His need to control, both himself and others. OK, that much is clear.

Two: his impotence. If you can't get it up, you can't get it off. Get it off? Cut it off? If you aren't a man, you don't have to act like one? If you don't act like a man, you aren't one? If you don't have a penis, you can't lose a penis? Castration anxiety? Sexual role confusion? Fear of women?

Three: goes back to one—unwillingness to give, anal retentiveness, confusion of genital and pregenital material. Is this best understood at a structural or a genetic level? Help. I'm losing it.

Four: this is your part of it, Leah. Countertransference. No, I'd rather do transference first. OK. Four: transference. There was a definite sexual signal there. A come-on. I saw it, felt it. He was hot, playing with his lip, sitting uncharacteristically with his knees spread rather than legs crossed. Trouble making eye contact. Open fly. And what was that story he was reporting while I was busy fantasizing—it was about a female colleague, a lady doctor who suggested a minor change in some aspect of his research, and he wouldn't go along with it, although it was, he admitted, an eminently reasonable suggestion.

Let's hit number five: countertransference; I am sucking at his penis. Why? My frustration with his therapy progress? Yes. My wish to take from him what he is unwilling to give? Probably. Does he remind me of Daniel? Perhaps. His precision, his rigidity, his lack of spontaneous warmth are excessive, caricatures of

Daniel's traits. But they are similar. And I do resent it. Not just with my patients, not just with Daniel. But with all the people I thought should nurture me more or better than they did.

You're faking it, Leah. You can do better than that. What about the penis-breast equation? Yeah, well what about it? I feel it, but it's confusing. Am I looking for a replacement breast? Am I trying to nurture myself by sucking at his breast/penis? Am I the castrated one? Involuntarily, my hands reach up. I cup my own soft womanness on one side, the slower-to-yield imitation on the other. I too am dry and empty. And afraid. So terribly afraid.

Harrington arrives early to his appointment wearing an elegant, ivory colored suit and a sheepish grin. He looks like a young English aristocrat, perhaps the owner of vast, Southeast Asian rubber holdings. He is dashing, colonial, romantic. The only things missing are a hat with an overwide brim and a cigar.

My heart pounds as I usher him into my office. He really is handsome. And he is the first man in more than a decade to have sent me flowers. Leah, I chide myself, abandon these foolish schoolgirl fantasies! This man is your patient, not your lover. I am appalled at the persistence of the countertransference. I thought I had rid myself of all this nonsense at last Friday's session. But that was before the roses arrived. I seat myself, carefully arranging my skirt over my knees, and I wait for Harrington to begin.

He is sitting across from me, staring down into his lap, nervously twisting his wedding band and breathing audibly. At last he sighs and looks up at me. "Hello," he starts softly, almost shyly.

I tilt my head at him in noncommital reply, raise my eyebrows perhaps a fraction of a millimeter, and wait for him to go on. I have already squelched the temptation to gush my embarrassed thank you's for the beautiful roses. We must deal with his gift in the context of the therapy, not as a social phenomenon, and certainly not in the spirit in which it was sent. After all, the fantasies and distortions we must explore and lay bare are his, not mine, I remind myself.

"Hello, again," he smiles up at me, raising his head and showing me his dark eyes and rugged profile.

He waits for a reply, but I say nothing. He shakes his head and looks down, then up again.

"Ah, Dr. Buchanan, you're a cruel taskmaster to make me work so hard. But maybe it's good for me. No one else has ever expected anything at all from me. No one has ever taken me seriously before. It's the curse of being rich and good looking, you know. I'm not being vain, you understand, just telling you how it is for us poor, wealthy, handsome devils."

He is striking a sarcastic tone, but every word rings true. Should I point this out to him, help him focus on the pain he feels when no one takes him seriously, or should I let it go this time, knowing it is a theme which will recur, and wait for him to explore with me the tangled transference issues that brought both him and his roses to my door these last days? I decide to wait—wait and do nothing. This much he can tolerate, he must.

He compresses his lips and stares at me, "You're not even going to bring it up are you? You're not even going to tell me whether or not you got the flowers I sent you? In the circles I travel in, that would be considered very ill-bred."

His anger is just below the surface.

"Well, did you? Did you get the flowers I sent you?"

"Yes, I did."

"That's all? 'Yes, I did,' " he mimics me and shakes his head. "Not even a bloody thank you?"

"I thought it might be more pertinent if we explored your feelings about sending the flowers, rather than mine about receiving them," I explain, more calmly than I feel.

He exhales noisily, then leans back in the chair. "My feelings about sending them," he muses, "well yes, why not? Though that's not what I really want to talk about."

'What do you really want to talk about?"

"You, Dr. Buchanan, you, I want to talk about you. I haven't stopped thinking about you since the other night. In fact, since before the other night. That's what brought me to your house to begin with. Only now, now it's even worse. You're in my mind twenty-four hours a day. All I want is to see you, be with you, near you. I can't wait for my appointments. They are the only two hours of my week that mean anything to me. Between times I feel so empty, so lonely. And now you're going away. I can't believe how much that affects me. I can't believe how I feel devastated just thinking about what it will be to be without you for a whole month. I mean this is really different. I don't understand it. I never feel this way when Monica goes off, or even Kelly Ann."

But, ah, I think to myself, you have felt this way before Mr. Harrington, that I know for a certainty; it is just too soon for me to point it out to you. I sit with my chin resting in my hands and I listen, waiting for him to go on. He picks up where he left off, delineating for me the emptiness and pain he anticipates when I go away, the warm sense of contentment that fills him when he is near me.

"And the funniest thing," he is telling me, "or maybe the most frightening, is that between times, when I'm not with you, sometimes I can't even remember what you look like too clearly, I can't even conjure up your face."

I listen to him and even as I do, I try to remember Dr. Isaacson. I close my eyes to see him, but he is not there. His face has faded in my memory, the features blurred like those on an early Polaroid snapshot that has not stood the test of time. I do remember his hair, how it began to thin as we both grew older together, and how he combed it over, Prufrock-like in his vanity. Also, I remember his height, and how surprised I was, when I finally stopped backing out of his office, to discover, as he walked me to the door, that he was not very tall. On those rare occasions when I wore high heels (did he know I wore them for him?), we stood shoulder to shoulder as I stared at is lips, trying to aid my ears in understanding the reassuring words he mouthed: "See you Monday (or Wednesday or Friday)."

Oh yes, his eyes are green, that I remember. And his voice, deeper than one would imagine in a man of such modest physical proportions, deep and resonant, like a trained singer's, with only a hint in it of the Germany of his birth, and then not so much in the words, the diction, the pronunciation, but really only in the

135

rhythm, the melodic quality he gave it. (Is it his voice I hear now, as I think I remember it, or is it that fellow on the radio who does those classical music education shows out of Detroit? Karl Haas. He always reminded me of Dr. Isaacson, the way he talked.) How little I have left of him!

One would think that he would be engraved in my mind, etched in acid on my brain, after all those hours we spent together with no external distractions, just he and I, hour in hour out, three times a week, summer and winter, rain and shine, except for his usual summer vacation, for five long years. And I am left only with the elusive image one reaches for in the morning upon waking from a vivid but fading dream. He, like Dr. Edwards, and like my father before them, is reduced to a dim but haunting engram, the flash I cannot focus on somewhere between closing and opening my eyes.

Especially odd, that, in light of the fact that I used to feel him inside me, an homunculus housed in my own body, telling me in stage whispers what was right and what was wrong, reassuring me that I would be OK, or admonishing me to slow down and take a long look before making an impulsive decision. He was so real to me and at times it was a comfort to know I carried him within my skin everywhere. Other times I wished to exorcise him and rid myself forever of his persistent, rational voice, so I could blindly unleash my own more-impetuous demons. He grew, filling me, bursting his own skin as he did so, flowing out to the ends of my fingers, tingling behind my eyelids, throbbing at my pulse points, warming my very scalp.

And then the sense of him was gone, and I no longer heard his voice, nor the voices of the ghosts who used to haunt me, but only my own. It was as if I had swallowed him and carried him around inside myself, a solid, friendly, but ultimately undigestible lump, until finally I transformed him, absorbing what I needed, discarding what was never really mine, and he was gone.

But the world wasn't empty anymore, as it once was. Because at long last, for better or for worse, I was in it.

Harrington is still talking, leaning toward me now, face somewhat flushed and very earnest, dark hair falling over his forehead.

"And when I went to your house the other night, I knew your husband wouldn't be there, I knew he was in Spain. Monica and I had dinner with the Fogels a couple of weeks ago; he rides with me, you know, and he mentioned that your husband was off on another research trip."

Damn Martin, I think to myself. How dare he muddy my patient's transference that way! He sure knows more about neurology than he does about psychoanalytic theory.

"Martin's my main source of information about you. Helluva nice guy, too. Good rider. A real natural athlete. Anyway, after that night at your house, after I found out . . . " He glances up at me and wipes his mouth with the back of his hand, "I mean . . ." I nod to encourage him, helping him over the unpronounceable fact of my surgery.

"Well, dammit, I just couldn't believe he left you like that . . ."

A thought begins to take shape in my fuzzy mind . . . like your father left your mother! I suddenly remember Harrington's father's death when Harrington had been only five years old. How is it possible that I haven't thought of it before? Does poor Harrington remind me too much of vulnerable little Sammy, denying his immeasurable loss with an infant's bravado?

Harrington is still talking. "I mean, if I were your husband, I would never leave you. I wouldn't leave you alone for a minute, let alone a month. I'd be with you all the time. I'd be there to take care of you . . ."

I listen fascinated as the dynamics emerge, explaining his behavior of the other night: My ardent lover, this little boy who wants to be near his mommy, to be sure that she is safe, that he is safe. He will care for her forever, take care of her, never let her out of his sight, so that, in turn, he can guarantee that she will forever be there to take care of him. He dare not run the risk of losing her, as he lost his father. Poor bewildered boy, in gaining his Oedipal victory he has lost his paternal protection. He must now be father and son, husband and child, all at once and forever.

I listen as his love song continues. I see no opening where I might insert the wedge of an interpretation. He has tugged loose his necktie now and unbuttoned the top button of his shirt. Such is

137

his ardor that he is sweating here in the frigidity of my air-conditioned office.

"You'd have no worries if you were mine."

He is slowing down now, his voice is quieter, less urgent.

"And I would care for you so tenderly. No, no worries at all. You wouldn't have to work. I'd bring you flowers every day. We would be so happy together. Anything you wanted I could give you. And I would give you. But most of all, we'd just be together, loving each other, just the two of us, always."

I listen dispassionately as Harrington paints for me the picture I have always wanted to see. There across the room from me, not three yards away, there sits everything I think I have always wanted: He is young, handsome, rich as Midas, and he adores me. He has asked me to be his queen. And all I have to do to have it for a day, or a week, or a lifetime, is to reach out my hand. Very gently, very slowly, very softly—oh yes I know just how I would do it—and, it, all of it could be mine. Here, now, in the glow of the positive transference, just as in the folly of first love, right now I can make my dream, his dream, come true.

I continue to listen, tracking my emotions as well as his, and I find that the fantasy-made-reality holds little charm for me. His adoration would cloy all too quickly, like too many roses in my living room. The very prospect of it is slightly sickening somehow. Or sick, anyway. This is not what my destiny holds in store for me, not even what I want it to hold in store. No. I will be for him what Dr. Isaacson and Dr. Edwards were for me. I will give him back to himself.

I sit across from Harrington watching as he winds down, waiting for the right moment to reach out to him, not with a crippling embrace, but with an idea that will help him see his world more clearly.

It is on my way home from the office that I first realize that, at last, my headache is gone.

8

I ANSWER the telephone automatically before the second ring. As I bring it to my ear I wonder if it is Miss Drake. She had seemed to be in adequate control after our telephone conversation Sunday.

"Leah?" a familiar voice questions, "Leah, this is Carolyn. I hope I didn't wake you, but I was afraid you'd be gone if I waited any longer."

"No, no, that's fine," I tell her. "How are you Carolyn?"

It is Martin Fogel's vivacious wife, a woman I have known for years. Did Harrington and I conjure up this call with his mention of the Fogels during his hour yesterday? This type of magical thinking still plagues me, even after eight years of therapy.

"I'm fine, Leah, fine. Isn't it terrible that we never talk anymore? And that's what I'm calling about. Our group is meeting at Sharon McIntyre's tonight. You still have the schedule, don't you? Why don't you let me pick you up around seven-thirty? It's right on my way."

"Oh, I don't think I'll make it to Sharon's, Carolyn, you go on without me."

"Are your sure you can't spare even a couple of hours? You haven't been for the last two or three months. We all miss you, Leah, really we do."

There is a long pause while I try to think of what to say. Carolyn is right, as usual. I haven't been to one of these monthly social gatherings since March, when I was the hostess.

"Come on, Leah, let me pick you up. It'll do you good to get out. We'll laugh a little. Or have you lost interest in our little group?"

Now she's got me, and she knows it.

"Of course not, don't be silly, you know how much that group has meant to me."

"Past tense, Leah?" Carolyn questions. She was never dumb.

"Touché, Carolyn," I laugh into the telephone, "pick me up at seven thirty. I'll be ready."

"Great. I look forward to seeing you."

Our goodbyes are simultaneous, and we hang up.

Fully awake now, I get up, wash, dress, and think about the day that lies ahead. Wednesdays are usually my day at the university, where I supervise and teach psychiatric residents. But, this is the end of July. The new residents for the year have just come in and are not ready for individual supervision. Classes don't begin until September. So my Wednesdays for this month have been free. I had intended to let myself sleep in and then take care of some of the errands and details that need to be attended to before any type of trip. Only a matter of days, really, until I pick up the children at summer camp, then fly to Spain to join Daniel. But I have slept so little and so badly these last weeks that many of the jobs I left for my day off are already done. There are still some bills to be taken care of and I have to figure out my route to North Carolina (which Daniel explained to me at least twice, with the aid of maps, but I didn't pay attention).

Minutes later I am seated at Daniel's oversized oak desk in the study preparing myself to do battle with the monthly bills. Usually it is Daniel who performs this odious task, for somehow it has come to be in the marriage that he does the bills and balances the checking account, while I wage the annual war with the income tax. I sigh as I sift through our obligations: telephone, gas, water, electricity, mortgage, credit cards. I dutifully make out checks for all that we owe, adding a precautionary $50 to the telephone company for long distance charges that have not yet caught up with us.

The pile is reduced to one unfamiliar looking envelope: my life insurance, the policy I took out when the twins were babies and increased greatly some years later. I pay it semi-annually so the statement is not one I recognize offhand. I write the check tight-lipped and unsmiling, thinking about my worth to the family, both alive and dead.

When I carved out a career for myself by going to graduate school and becoming a professional, I did so thinking I was very special. I had always done well in school, risen to the top of the class with very little effort. Only during those troubled early college years had I had difficulty with my school work, and even then, once my therapy was well under way, I had climbed from fifteen hours of F in my freshman year to Dean's List in my junior year. It just seemed natural for me to excel. People generally applauded me for it, and I blushed becomingly and went on.

I had planned to have a career, knowing I could not rely on anyone to take care of me, but then somehow got sidetracked when Frank entered my life. The publishing world seemed pale in comparison to the lights of Broadway. World Publishing was just a place I worked; I lived for my weekends on East 37th Street in Frank's comforting arms.

But, after I went back into therapy, the compartmentalized life I had structured for myself began to crumble and soon I was on my way to becoming a clinical psychologist. Then Daniel came along and, after we were married, urged me to take a year off from my job at the state hospital to write my dissertation. Before long the Ph.D. was mine, but my career seemed secondary somehow, only an aspect of what I was and who I wanted to become. After our move to Kentucky and the arrival of the twins, I was content to be a part-time psychologist and a full-time wife and mother.

It still pleased me at parties to be able to tell people, when they asked what I did, that I was a psychotherapist. Their predictable reaction always tickled me ("Are you analyzing me right now?") and gave me a sense of power. And when my friends began to think of trading daily duty at the diaper pail for volunteer work or a part-time job at some store or office, I had my own office to go to and a secretary who called me Dr. Buchanan.

Ten hours of therapy a week was a tonic for me, and the money came in handy for vacations or other little extras. But the balance slowly shifted and soon it was twenty hours a week, not ten, and sometimes I was tired. Daniel's salary never kept pace with inflation, he being as notoriously underpaid as most of his colleagues, and the money I brought home became an essential part of our income, not just a pleasant little pad to the checking account.

I began to realize that I *had* to work, that it was no longer strictly my choice, that if Daniel and I wanted the kids to have piano lessons and summer camp, if we wanted an occasional vacation, or a dinner out, then my working was indispensable. Daniel's salary could keep a roof over our heads and feed us, but that was about all. Anything beyond subsistence living required a double income.

It was then that it dawned on us that, if something happened to me, Daniel would be sore pressed to educate the children. I absorbed the shocking realization that I would *have* to work for the next thirty years, and that, if I couldn't for some reason, I had better find some other way to protect my family's interests. This was the other side of women's liberation, the through-the-looking-glass side that was never discussed at our monthly women's group. Buying professional liability insurance, disability income protection, and quadrupling my life insurance policy was a far cry from trading off with Daniel on dishwashing or bedmaking. Fun and games were over. This was the big time.

As I write the check to Security Connecticut I know for a certainty that I am nobody's little girl anymore. I stare at the signature I write so often, but which still seems strange to me, Leah B. Buchanan, Ph.D. (for this check is written on my professional account), and I wonder about the choices I have made. I feel that I know more somehow than that indomitable sisterhood, who thinks that being liberated means not shaving your legs or that husbands have to pitch in with child care and housework, so that wives can be relieved to pursue their own interests or not, as they choose. Not for them the pampered little-darling status of the dollar romances on sale at the supermarket checkout counter! They want more meaning in their lives.

I salute them silently as I seal the envelope that will carry my check to Connecticut, and I wonder if they are happy, or if I am, or if it matters. Sometimes I think it wouldn't be bad at all to be a pampered little-darling, a kept woman, anything but the busy professional with responsibilities more numerous than she can remember and a six figure price on her life.

With a barely audible sigh, I rearrange Daniel's desk the way he had left it, put the two checkbooks away, turn off the light, and carry the neatly stacked pile of envelopes downstairs with me. I will remember to mail them only if I lay them on top of my purse, and mail them I must, for there is no one else to take care of it for me.

I decide to take a walk to mail the checks, and I set off with the long-legged, determined stride that Daniel remarked on when he first met me. "You are a young lady with the gait of one who knows exactly where she is going," he told me one day as he watched me stride into the restaurant where I was meeting him for lunch.

I laughed, commenting that my long legs carried me forward through sheer muscular competence, but that my mind and heart were often left far behind.

"Ah," he had replied, ushering me toward the table he had chosen, "that is the mark of a true thoroughbred. A dangerous but endearing quality."

"Dangerous?" I echoed, "Why dangerous?"

"Because the thoroughbred strikes out for speed and distance and runs the risk of breaking its slim, well-shaped ankle in a chuck hole that any scruffy old ranch horse would instinctively avoid. That," he had continued, pulling out my chair for me, "is why a thoroughbred needs to keep company with a cow pony, that is if for some strange reason it chooses to run over the rough terrain of the ranch."

"There's rough terrain everywhere," I reminded him, nibbling idly at a breadstick, "except, of course, at the track. But what sensible horse would want to spend its life running around in circles?" I added, continuing the flirtation.

He raised the glass of wine he had ordered for us before my arrival and looked at me. "To the race," he proposed, "wherever it is run."

"To the runners," I amended, touching his glass with mine.

"No," he persisted, "we must keep things in perspective, the race is always more important than the runners. You wouldn't realize that," he explained, lowering his glass, "you're a psychologist, a social scientist. But, I am an historian, a humanist."

I had already fallen in love with him long before that lunch date and would have toasted anything or anyone he proposed, short of Adolph Hitler. I smiled and drank and wondered how I could be so lucky to be sitting in this dark, intimate Italian restaurant with this dark, sophisticated, handsome man. I knew I was attractive and bright, but after all, I was only twenty-five and he was forty-five and the most sought-after bachelor at the university. Yet he had chosen me, or so it seemed, for we had been keeping company almost constantly for two months.

The corner mailbox looms up before me. I deposit my payments, then turn down a side street and gaze into the summer gardens of my neighbors. Midsummer holds little in the way of charm. Even the hydrangeas are spent, and it is too early for morning glories or mums. The dew is still on the grass though, lending a lush, cool quality to its greenness, and, rambling over an occasional fence, the surprising orange of a trumpet vine blares out at me. I move on, more slowly now, eyes scanning the backyards and sideyards that I pass.

The creak of a screen door attracts my attention. Across the street, in front of a small Tudor style house, stands a pretty girl of about twenty, lighting a cigarette. She flicks the match into the fading hydrangea bushes before her, smooths the skirt of a clingy, side-slit dress of the style my friend Anna calls Contemporary

Streetwalker, and picks her way perilously through the gravel driveway in her high-heeled, backless shoes. I stare at her, trying to bring another picture into focus, a picture hazy in my memory, as if somehow smudged by the steamy summer day.

The girl looks at her wrist as she opens her car door, but the watch she seeks is not there. A quick glance to an open upstairs window of the trim little house, a muttered "damn," then she grinds out the cigarette under her fashionably shod foot, slides into the driver's seat showing a lot of bare thigh, and, seconds after the key is in the ignition, she is gone.

I watch the cigarette smolder on the pavement, for in her haste she has not snuffed it out completely. The spark at the tip hypnotizes me as it flirts seductively with the paper around it, trying to sustain itself. I walk toward it, to finish the job the girl has left undone, and feel the heat rising from the pavement. I am no longer on the quiet little southern street.

It is another early steamy Sunday, twenty years ago, and the street is East 37th near First Avenue. Clad in what we then called a black sheath, I have descended the steps of Michael Francis McKenna's apartment, my pointed three-inch heels tapping and my charm bracelet jangling. With my right hand I still the insulting noise of the bracelet, but I can do nothing about the shoes. My beaded black bag holds a lipstick, comb, and one stocking that doesn't have a run in it, a key to the Manhattan apartment of one of my college friends, two subway tokens, one of McKenna's paisley silk squares, which he usually wears tucked in a blazer breast pocket ("If you fancy it, darlin', take it, the color goes well with your Jewish Irish eyes."), and the white pearlized plastic case of the diaphragm I pack like a pistol in my purse. The diaphragm itself is elsewhere, I am reminded as I feel the wet stickiness begin to leak out into my panties.

McKenna is an actor, a "first-rate, second-class" actor, as he calls himself, who finds it amusing and lucrative to do the college circuit. Thus, I had met him at Brandeis University, where, as actor in residence for one brief week, he had titillated the theater arts department and indeed the whole campus with his Irish good looks and his urbane presence.

I played a scene from *Miss Julie* opposite him during one of my classes. He had been director and critic as well as Jean the valet. Flustered by the fact of standing so close to one who actually lived, if not within the inner circle, at least on the periphery of fame, one whose looks and demeanor graced him with such brilliance it seemed that he should have stood at the very center of that glorious circle, I flubbed my lines in hopeless confusion, lines I had known by heart for weeks.

He had been exceedingly kind to me, almost tender, as he drew me back into the scene, offering me his hand and gracefully leading me physically and emotionally to center stage. Playing opposite him had been like dancing with an accomplished dancer. He was so smooth, such a strong leader, that I finished the scene with a flourish, forgetting not only who I was, but who he was as well.

I was in a daze for the rest of the class, as the other lucky students played snatches of Ibsen or O'Neill with our talented temporary teacher. But the bubble burst when he read his mental notes to us later. For some reason, he had saved the Strindberg for last, though it had been the second scene the class had worked on that morning.

"Ah yes, Miss Julie, we come to you." He rose and paced away from us, hands clasped behind his back. With his broad shouldered, elongated frame, it seemed astonishing that he should be almost short.

(" 'Tis my cross to bear, darlin'," he told me later, as we lay side by side in his bed, "the good Lord gave me this magnificent torso," he indicated himself from chin to crotch, "and then stuck it atop these stubby, inglorious, little legs." I loved the self-mockery of the brogue he affected, and tried to comfort him by stroking those strong, stocky peasant's thighs.)

"Your interpretation of the role is, I think, impeccable," he said, spinning on his dancer's feet and startling me with the directness of dark blue eyes that he fixed, almost fastened, to my own, "but, my dear Miss Bronstein, you must learn to moderate your transports."

With this he rose almost on tiptoe, then rocked back on his

heels, crossed his arms over his chest, and with a negligent gesture, waved one hand at us, muttering "dismissed" just as—talk about timing—the bell rang.

Stunned, I sat in my chair, clutching my notebook to me. The word "impeccable" buoyed me up, but the phrase "moderate your transports" dragged me right back down again. McKenna had disappeared from the stage, and the room emptied. I had no class the next hour, so I sat there thinking about his words.

Theater was something new to me, something I had tried only after my release from the hospital. It had been an accident actually, my getting so involved in it. My major of English literature had drawn me into so many classes that were cross-listed with theater arts, that it was quite natural to become interested in other courses that some of my friends were taking.

The students involved in theater arts lay at the very fringe of student society, or formed a society of their own. They seemed looser, freer, more frenetic and intent. Their garb was different, as were their in-jokes, and even their language. They seemed to take my differences for granted and made nothing of the curious fact that I had been absent from school for a month, disappeared off campus three afternoons a week only to return late in the evening, barely spoke, and weighed in at an amazingly gaunt 103 pounds.

Soon I was one of them and even found the courage, with their support, to speak a small role in one of our Shakespeare classes. Everyone said I was good. Before the end of that semester I had taken the plunge. I lived, breathed, ate, and slept theater. It was a whole new world. I found that when I spoke the lines given me, I did not have to worry about what I wanted to say, and when the writer and director defined a character for me, I did not have to worry about who I was. I slipped in and out of any role, every role that was given me, tragic or comic, old or young, wicked or saintly. And, with the theater crowd, I could continue my roles off stage as well, for we did our bits constantly, to each other's great amusement and, I am sure, to the annoyance of many of the other students.

It was only in my therapist's office in downtown Boston, only there that I sat like an empty snail shell, waiting for some sign of a living creature that might inhabit it. My doctor sat patiently across from me as I huddled in his seemingly oversized chair. We waited together for the words to come and tell us what it could possibly be I was feeling. Once, just shortly after I left the hospital, three weeks went by without my uttering a word. The sheer act of my punctual arrival every other day, after an hour and a half on the train, was, I suppose now with the perspective of the other side of the desk, the beginning of a strong therapeutic alliance. After the three-week silence, I heard a voice say at last, as I watched the cigarette smoke spiral out of my mouth to be swept into the room air purifier, " 'My heart aches and a drowsy numbness pains my sense . . .'."

The voice was very tired, very far away. I looked over at him, wondering why he was reciting poetry to me, but his mouth was closed.

"Yes," he finally said, "I know. He describes it very well, how you feel. John Keats is one of my favorites, too."

And then he was walking me to the door, for the hour was up.

After more than a year and a half of therapy I had begun to discover myself a little, and the theater work, which had started out as yet another form of therapy, had become an obsession and a goal. Now, an expert was telling me that I wasn't very good at it. At least that was what I thought he was telling me. I mulled it over trying to determine which was more important, the fact that my interpretation was impeccable or that my transports were immoderate. It seemed as though the comment applied to more than just my acting ability.

A voice came out of nowhere. " 'Do ye like the dark because your deeds are evil?' "

I looked up. "Sean O'Casey?" I guessed. "I didn't hear you walk up," I added, "I didn't even know you were still here."

"Well, in a manner of speaking I wasn't. I was in the back mopping up. These acting classes are a drain, don't you think?"

He was offering me his hand.

"We'll walk a bit now," he told me, propelling me toward the door.

It was a brisk, early spring day. He wore a blue cashmere turtleneck sweater, dark trousers, and a camel-colored jacket with a silk square tucked jauntily into the pocket. It all worked wonderfully well for him, giving him an air of casual elegance that reinforced his native good looks. In the sunlight his straight, longish hair, combed back from his high forehead, looked more silver than gray. His chin, with that marvelous cleft in it, which looked so perfect with his face it might have been the work of a plastic surgeon, jutted forward, and he walked with his hands clasped behind his back, his stride determined as my own.

I felt ridiculous in my uniform of black leotard and tights, a dungaree skirt whipped about my knees by the March wind, and God help me, a pair of worn, dingy, gray sneakers. From my recently pierced ears hung a pair of heavy, silver earrings made from several links of chain and two outlandishly large Turkish coins, and my red hair was done in long Indian braids. The only makeup I wore in those days was black eyeliner, which bordered my upper lids, ending in a gratuitous upsweep nearly half an inch long at the corner of each eye.

McKenna talked as we walked, telling me things I didn't dare to believe. "You have a natural talent you know, Miss Bronstein, but you aren't always in control of your characterization. Acting is an art, my darlin', not an outlet. If you treat it as one, that's all it will ever be. If that's enough for you, so be it, but if you want to act seriously, you must work seriously. Your emotions and intuitions are tools of the trade, to be used in your portrayals. They are not furies to be unleashed in the service of your own inner madness."

I was having difficulty keeping pace with him for his legs, though short, seemed to carry him forward at a relentless pace, and his words, as well as the wind, stung me furiously. I wore no jacket at all, and the damp from the soggy, spring earth seeped through the holes in my sneakers. I was at the same time ecstatic to be walking with the great man and dejected by what he was telling me. I tried to keep up with his feet and his words, but it was a losing battle. My eyes burned, from the wind against my contact lenses I guessed, and I blinked furiously. He looked over at me.

"I've gone and hurt your feelings, have I?" he muttered, as if astonished that this could be so. "You're not about to cry, are you?" he added, spinning me around by my bony shoulders.

I didn't think that likely, as I hadn't learned how yet, or relearned how, as my doctor often reminded me. I shook my head solemnly at him, biting my lower lip, and stood there shaking in the wind.

"You're freezing, child," he fairly shouted at me, as my shoulders involuntarily shook beneath the grip of his hands. Rapidly he unbuttoned his jacket and wrapped me in it, muttering all the while about "beatniks" and "damn nonsense" and "kids who didn't have enough sense to come in out of the rain."

We were walking in a definite direction now. Clearly the promenade was over; McKenna had determined exactly where we were going. His jacket, nearly as long as my skirt, flopped against the backs of my legs, warming me through the combined miracle of expensive Scottish wool and the fact that it had been on his body only moments before. I felt grateful, and not at all concerned, until Faculty House loomed up just ahead of me. I stopped short.

"Feelin' a bit squeamish, Miss Bronstein?" McKenna murmured solicitously, tugging at his jacket, where it had fallen off one of my shoulders, and rearranging it for my comfort.

I looked first at Faculty House, then at him, then back to the glass, concrete, and steel structure that would spell expulsion from the university for me if I so much as set foot within its semisacred walls.

"It's against the rules for me, in there," I muttered, pointing vaguely with my chin, for my arms lay limp at my sides, as if paralyzed by the soft wool caressing them.

"Ah," he mocked me in his put-on brogue, "it's against the rules is it, and here I thought you had tired of my company."

He took me by the hand and led me to the left, heading for the back of the building. "Sure 'n' I wouldn't want to compromise your reputation, darlin'. All I'm after doin' is to feed you a cup of tea and take you to bed with me."

His forthrightness shocked and then thrilled me. All of it was oddly exciting and confusing. I dared a look at his face in profile and found it to be every bit as handsome from this close range as it was on stage or screen. It was a strong face, an open face, with a hint of humor about the eyes. I was inclined to trust him as well as like him. As I walked along with him around the hill on which Faculty House sprawled, its modern angles accentuating its resemblance to some strange, automated insect, I thought for a moment of three people: Steven, my college boyfriend, who had graduated and was now studying film out in California; Dr. Edwards, my psychiatrist, analyzing someone's dream in his office overlooking the Charles River; and my mother, running the asphalt-paving business in Cleveland.

Would I be walking like this with McKenna, I wondered, if Steven had given me the ring and the promises I had longed for before he went away? Would Dr. Edwards insist, come tomorrow's session, that I consider my actions just another bit of acting-out behavior, a confirmation of my burgeoning transference? And what would my mother think if she could see me now?

I giggled softly, then stole another glimpse at McKenna. He pulled me into the shadow of a nearby tree, leaned toward me, and in full Hollywood close-up kissed me tenderly, persistently, passionately on the mouth, until I was literally dizzy and breathless.

Images of Steven, Dr. Edwards, Mother, flew through my brain, as if shot by a movie camera, then rolled backward at far too fast a speed. They receded from me, blurring, turning into nothing more than a stream of colors that were somehow tied up with soft lips pressing, skilled fingers seeking, and the haunting aroma of a gentleman's cologne so sophisticated and expensive that it made English Leather smell like soda pop by comparison.

I followed my soon-to-be lover blindly up the hillside, stumbling a little against him, not caring anymore if I was expelled from Brandeis, for only the moment mattered. I was nineteen years old and being seduced by a movie star. Shaker Heights seemed very far away.

Just how we ever entered Faculty House is hazy in my mind. I was in a daze, not just as I waited, but after he appeared. Clutching my green book bag to me, I stood in the center of his room as he took his jacket off my shoulders. The neatly made twin beds seemed to stare at me reproachfully. Was this where eight years of Hebrew School had finally led me? I took a deep breath, closed my eyes, and waited for my seduction to continue.

McKenna gently pried my book bag from my arms.

"Here now, let's have a look at you," he crooned at me, deftly loosening my skirt. "Step out of it darlin', there's a good girl, and kick off your shoes, why don't you?"

I did as I was told, grateful, as always, that someone seemed to know what to do, eager, as always, to please. I stood before him clad only in my leotard and tights, while he appraised me.

"A bit bony, Miss Bronstein, but not bad nonetheless. Your legs are really quite good, you know."

I felt like a Negro slave being put up for auction. But it didn't matter as long as he liked what he saw.

"Ease out of this now," he went on, helping me shed the black dancer's uniform. "It's embarrassed, you are, is it?" he muttered, "or frightened maybe?" he crooned on. "No need, no need. You're very lovely really, you know, and I'm a gentle old man."

His talk distracted me from my nakedness, and it was only after he embraced me, caressing my back and my flanks with long lazy stroking gestures, that I realized he was still fully clothed.

"You're not old," I reassured him, looking up at his intense blue eyes. "You're beautiful. I mean, I've never seen a man like you, not up close."

"How old do you think I am," he asked, still stroking my backside with his cool hands.

"You must be about thirty-seven," I lied, knowing he must be forty, maybe even forty-two.

His laugh was wonderful. It shook his whole chest, projecting across the room, as if meant for an audience.

"I'm past fifty, my dear, yes, and old enough to be your father. Indeed, I have a married son, older now than you. I'm a grandfather for Christsake."

"Is your grandchild a girl or boy?" I asked, not knowing why.

"Now that's what I like about you Miss Bronstein. You listen to a person. You respond to what they say. I've noticed it in class all week. She's a girl, only sixteen months old. But enough of this. I'll show you her picture later."

He stepped away from me and I was left naked in the center of the room. I crossed my left arm over my breasts and hid my crotch with my right.

"No, no, don't cover your breasts," he told me, pulling my left arm away. "They're quite marvelous, you know."

He described first the left one, then the right with a practiced fingertip. The nipples jumped up shamelessly as I looked down at myself appraisingly. Steven said they were like bananas, but now this famous actor had told me otherwise. Marvelous, he had said, and high and round and firm. I was giddy with delight, quite convinced that McKenna knew more about tits than Steven.

McKenna leaned over and kissed me again full on the mouth, a long lingering kiss that lasted several moments before the tongue came into play. I thought I would swoon. My arms went up around his neck and my legs threatened to give way. My ecstasy was interrupted by a smack on the bottom. Startled, I broke from his embrace and eyed him suspiciously.

"No, it's nothing kinky I'm after, little one, only a wee small fetish of mine. So, into the shower with you. I like my girls fresh and clean and sweet smellin'. Use plenty of soap, and don't forget to wash your teeth. There's a powerful smell of cigarette about you, and I cannot abide it."

Dutifully I padded into the bathroom to do his bidding, thinking how odd men were. This one liked my breasts all right but couldn't stand my smell.

I finish grinding out the cigarette and walk on, lost in my memories of Frank and of the love affair I clung to for five long years. The excitement and the magic flood me, and I am breathless with remembrances. Why and how did it all end?

A dove rises in reluctant flight before me, wings whistling as it flies. I look around me. I am only a few short blocks from home. The dove coos mournfully at me from a nearby dogwood tree.

I continue my walk, wondering about the choices I have made: my profession, Daniel, the children, this quiet little street in this quiet little town, rather than the noise and light and glamour of Broadway. Have I chosen wisely, well? For a moment I am wistful for Frank and our brunches at P. J. Clark's and our dinners at Sardi's and our nights in his oversized bed. But then I force myself to remember that the dream was not as perfect as my memory of it. I walk on, think on. It is 1960, and I am twenty-three years old.

I sit tailor fashion on Frank's bed, sewing the second button onto one of his favorite sport jackets. His muttered "damn" had sent me scurrying only moments before for needle and thread in my offer to help him in some way. It didn't matter, he reassured me, he had others he could wear. But no, I would tighten the loose button, remove the irritating evidence of his thickening middle, smooth out the roughness of the day.

Pleased with my domesticity, I sit sewing blissfully, the in-and-out movement of the needle through the fine fabric giving a pleasure to my fingers, my whole being, that I never knew could come from so simple a chore. The cashmere blazer caresses my bare knees like some luxurious lap robe, for Frank's silk kimono has fallen open over my cross-legged body, as I sit hunched over my tender task. I hear him singing in the shower, now loud and comic, then soft and tender, as he flits from opera aria to Broadway tune, to suit his whim.

I pick up the sleeve of the jacket to check the buttons there and, finding them all sewed tight, I rub it across my face remembering the day Frank took me with him to his tailor. How astonished I had been to discover that by tailor he did not mean merely a man who handled alterations: his tailor actually made his clothes.

I wandered moonstruck among the bolts of fabric—Chinese silks, Egyptian cottons, French linens, British woolens—amazed that a human being could have such an embarrassment of choices. Frank was there for a final fitting. I watched him from a safe distance as the skilled hands of the tailor hovered now over Frank's proud shoulders, then shifted to his waist where, with magical nip and tuck, they produced an illusion of slimness that visibly pleased Frank, until they finally came to rest, after flicking an imaginary piece of lint from an unfinished pocket.

"That suits you, I think, Michael," the tailor said, as he stepped back and squinted his cool appraisal.

To me the tailor himself was as elegant a man as I would ever hope to meet. Had he been introduced to me as a baron or a duke, I wouldn't have been surprised.

"It takes real panache to wear that tweed the way you do. And, too, the colors, well, the colors . . ."

This statement he left unfinished, making just a hint of a gesture toward the perfection reflected.

Frank nodded his acquiescence, appreciating his own image in the mirror, where for a moment our eyes met.

"Are we boring you terribly, darlin'?" he asked solicitously. "Here, come along now and tell us what you think of the fit. We want a woman's eye, don't we Bill?"

I looked down, embarrassed, and shook my head.

But Frank persisted, "Come along, now don't be shy, Lay-uh," he went on, "Bill's a master at his trade, but he's only a man, after all. Tell us what you think."

Looking up again, I told him more abruptly than I intended, "I haven't much experience with imported British tweeds and custom-cut clothes, Frank," consciously using the name he has told me only I may call him. "You look marvelous in it, that's all I know," and, turning toward Bill, in a whisper, I added shyly, "You've done a fine job, sir."

Then I walked away pretending great interest in a stack of silk squares lying carelessly spread on a neighboring table. As I went I heard Bill comment to Frank, "Where did you find this one? She's not an actress, is she?"

"No, a student at Brandeis University—a real brain."

"Legs aren't bad either."

I walked on, removing myself, I hoped, from earshot of their exchange. My feelings were mixed: angry, humiliated, pleased. I might have been a bolt of fabric they were discussing so dispassionately and appreciatively, pointing out my merits to each other, a new import, a rare find. I brushed the irritating image from my mind and waited for Frank to finish with his fitting. I was with him. That was all that really mattered.

I am still rubbing the sleeve back and forth across my cheek and lips when I hear the shower water cut off. Frank is stepping out getting ready to shave. Looking down at my lap, I find that the button is sewed properly and I start to bite off the needle and thread with my teeth, then think better of it.

"Frank," I call out, "have you a scissors or something?"

"There's a little pocket knife on the tray of my valet chair. Among my change and keys."

I find it easily, surprised I haven't noticed it before. It is small and silver, light and cool, when I hold it in my hands. Clearly it is sterling, another bit of the finery with which Frank likes to surround himself. His initials are inscribed in bold block letters on the side: MFM. So symmetrical, I wonder for an instant if his mother had been prescient, choosing such a perfect name for her actor son. Or was it really his given name at all, I wonder for the first time.

"It's a lovely little thing," I call back to him as I open the blade and cut the needle and thread away, then carefully trim the loose threads left from the previous sewing.

"Where did you get it, anyway?" I ask, too casually, feeling certain it is a gift chosen by one of his women.

"Oh, it's just a little *tsotsky* I picked up somewhere" he demurs, and I know the subject is closed.

Tsotsky, one of the Broadway Yiddishisms that peppers Frank's carefully cultivated speech, *tsotsky*, a plaything, a toy, something cute but of little real value. I fondle the silver *tsotsky* and am off in another reverie, this one taking me much farther away in place and time than Bill's elegantly appointed tailoring and men's furnishings establishment.

Ed's New York Steak and Seafood House is neither in New York, nor, according to my father, is it any longer Ed's. Ed sold out two years ago to open a restaurant in Akron, some fifty miles south of his previous Cleveland establishment. His Steak House had become sufficiently popular, though, that the new owner retained its lengthy title. Anyway, everyone always referred to it as just "Ed's." It is one of those wonderful eateries that strikes a happy balance between comfort and the easy elegance of dining out: soft white cloths on large square tables, oversized linen napkins, perpetually refilled water glasses and butter plates, crusty rolls brought to the table still warm from the oven, moderate prices, and friendly service. Dining at Ed's is a rare treat for our family, which does not usually frequent restaurants except for an occasional foray to Howard Johnson's.

So an early Saturday evening at Ed's is something very special indeed. I can hardly sit still in the chair, which I refuse to admit is a little large for me. Sammy bounces in his high chair, banging his spoon upon the tray, until the waiter comes with the basket of rolls and Momma distracts him with a breadstick. Ruthie, perched on the booster seat that allows her to sit more comfortably in her chair than I do in mine, spreads butter on her roll with six-year-old seriousness. Al, at sixteen already estranged from such family doings, has chosen to go to a movie with friends.

I look across the table to Momma and Daddy. She is sipping her drink through a straw. It must be some special occasion, for I almost never see them order a cocktail. Daddy has asked for an imported beer to go with the red snapper he has ordered, in keeping with his strictly kosher views. Mother's Moscow Mule, a delicious-looking potion composed of vodka and ginger beer, has preceded her rare steak, which Daddy encouraged her to order. Apparently it is enough for him that she keeps his home strictly kosher, for he always watches her dietary infractions with amused pleasure when they dine out.

I think my mother looks very smart, sipping her drink through the tiny, double-barreled straw. And I wonder how it is that this lady who, attired in flour-dusted chintz aprons bakes *challah* and strudel, knows about such things as Moscow Mules. I am nearly ten years old and am beginning to be aware that parents lead a double life.

Daddy is pleased about something. A case he has settled for a client will bring in a great deal of money. Is that the reason for the celebration? He is talking about the paving business, too. He may be able to devote more of his time to his law practice it seems, but he is reluctant to give up the business.

"It's such dirty work, Joe," my mother sighs, "so hot, and sticky, and tiring."

My father acquiesces but reminds her that law is dirty, too. This apparently, is a joke, for my mother smiles and touches his muscular arm where it rests near her on the table.

"Besides, hon," he reminds her, "asphalt paving can be quite lucrative."

I listen, fascinated, and watch the looks that they exchange. The world of adults has taken on new interest for me lately. I also wonder whether lucrative is spelled with a *c* or a *k*. I remind myself to ask them, so I can look it up when I get home. I need to know the meanings of words and have made a friend of the dictionary. I never forget a word that I look up myself. Lucrative, I repeat in my mind. It has a cool sound that reminds me of a shaded brook. But when I repeat Daddy's sentence to myself, I cannot find a meaning. I close my eyes and visualize the letters of the word, now with a "c", then with a "k." I cannot decide which looks better. Opening them again, I find myself looking between my mother and father toward the table beyond.

A short man with a mustache is pulling out a chair for the most beautiful lady I have ever seen. She is a tall, slender blonde wearing a fur coat that looks like a leopard skin. As the heavyset man helps her off with her coat, a pair of white shoulders is revealed, for underneath the fur the lady is wearing a scoop-necked black dress. The man drapes the coat over the back of one of the extra chairs at the table and sits down, not opposite, but beside the lovely lady. Her perfume floats our way as she fluffs her long platinum tresses over her perfect shoulders. Looking at her I decide that she is lucrative.

"Leah," my mother whispers, "it's rude to stare."

I avert my gaze, then catch my mother sneaking a glance that way. She nudges my father's arm and leaning toward him says, "Joe, do you think that she's his wife?"

"Nah," my father replies after a short appraising glance, "she's just a *tsotsky*."

I look over at the woman again and wonder what he could possibly mean. *Tsotsky.* I know the word. But what I know of it does not fit his sentence. When Daddy comes home from work he sometimes is annoyed by the clutter of toys in the den.

"Leah, Ruthie," he calls, "get in here this minute and clean up all these *tsotskys.*"

And when he returns from a business trip, he sometimes greets us holding out a brown paper bag.

"Look in there," he says, giving us a broad wink, "I brought you each something from Chicago, nothing big, just a little *tsotsky.*"

I look down at the Salisbury steak the waiter has just slipped over my left shoulder. I have ordered it to appear more grown-up than Ruthie with her perpetual hamburger platter. My mushrooms and gravy look good to me, but the grayish green string beans beside them run a poor second to her crisp fries. Sammy is happily picking up tiny bits of Mother's steak from where she has placed them on his tray. I generously pass him four of my string beans and one chunk of my meat, without a mushroom.

The leopard lady is drinking a cocktail now from a beautiful long-stemmed glass. Her drink has a big red cherry in it, which she picks up by the stem and pops into her equally red mouth. "Lucrative" I know I can look up in my dictionary when I get home. But who will tell me about *tsotsky*?

"Is something the matter with your meat, dear?" Mother inquires. "You haven't touched it."

"No, Momma, I was just thinking."

"Well, stop thinking and start eating," my father admonishes, "before it gets cold."

"Yes, Daddy," I tell him as I bite into the gravy-smothered meat. It tastes delicious to me, especially the mushrooms, and I forget about the lady as I consider my meal including the possibility of Ed's Famous New York Cheesecake, if I make a clean plate.

At twenty-three I know what my father meant by *tsotsky*. It makes me feel vaguely uncomfortable to think about it as I close the Sheffield blade and return the little silver knife to Frank's valet

159

chair. With a toss of my head I try to rid myself of the memory, knowing full well that it will come up as an association in the course of one of my hours with Dr. Isaacson. He will look at me unblinkingly as I retell the incident and wait for me to draw the conclusion he knows I know must be drawn.

But that is Monday in Cleveland and this is Saturday in New York. I shelve the unwanted ideas in the back of my mind and walk into the bathroom to find Frank. He is standing with his back toward me, a large velour towel wrapped around his waist, shaving with a straight razor in front of a still partly steamy mirror. The whole room seems bathed in light, and his silver hair is so bright that he looks like an angel or a god.

I walk up to him, the kimono still open, and wrap my arms around him from behind, pressing my bared breasts onto his naked back. I stand there nuzzling him a moment, inhaling the scent of his freshly scrubbed skin. I feel the muscles in his back move as he continues shaving, reaching behind him once to give my derriere a pat. He seems to take my affectionate presence for granted and never deters me from my frequent need to touch him. After a bit I open my eyes and look into the mirror to find his face. It is then that I notice the sunlamp clamped like a mechanic's trouble light to the frame around the mirror. I step back.

"Jesus Christ, Frank, no wonder your eyes always hurt so much. You can't do that, I mean, stare into a sunlamp like that."

"Ay on't are if I'm ind as ong as I'm an," he mutters incoherently, lips curled over his perfectly capped teeth, as he tries to shave the incredible cleft in his chin.

"What?" I ask stupidly, staring at him.

He shakes off his razor into the sink, rinses it, wipes it carefully on his towel-wrapped torso, and repeats, "They don't care if I'm blind as long as I'm tan, my darlin'," and with that he reaches up and flicks off the light.

"Frank, really, you'll hurt your eyes, you musn't do that. Use the sunlamp while you're resting. Wear those little shades on your eyes. You know."

I am zealous and solicitous, genuinely concerned for his welfare. He pulls me to him and strokes my hair, trying to hush me, but I go on. "Frank, it isn't worth it, really it isn't."

160

"You're wrong, little one. It is. It's my way of life. I haven't time for long naps with sun shades. I have this face, this body, a modest talent, and nothing more. I exercise, take dance lessons, tan myself, have my hair coiffed, and buy the best clothing I can find. I am on, all the time, selling myself even when I smile at the waiter who serves us Bloody Marys at P. J. Clark's—where we are going in about twenty minutes. So shower yourself, love. We haven't much time. I'll leave the lamp off in deference to your contact lenses. Besides, in your role of the endearing young ingenue you don't have to be tan. Peaches and cream will do fine."

While he is making this little speech, he strips me of his kimono, turns on the water in the shower and, before I can protest, he is gone.

I stand under the stinging jets and wait for something to sink in. *Tsotsky:* a plaything, a toy, something not to be taken seriously. *Tstosky,* the little silver knife, Frank, myself . . .

I look up in time to cross a street and still I think about Frank. Another year passes in my memory.

"Frank," I begin tentatively.

He raises one silvery eyebrow and waits for me to go on as he licks the last luscious drop of sour cream from his spoon. We have been sitting on his oversized bed eating blueberries lavished with sour cream and brown sugar, one of his favorite treats. It is a Sunday morning in June, not city-hot yet; the open window brings in breezes and the slower-paced Sunday sounds of voices and sporadic traffic.

"Frank, I 'm thinking of leaving the publishing house," I tell him, waiting for some sign that what I will say next matters to him.

"Go on," he murmurs, as enigmatic as Dr. Isaacson.

"I just don't think I want to spend the rest of my life editing other people's copy," I continue.

"That's understandable," he encourages.

"Well, I'm not sure what to do next," I hedge, hoping he will tell me.

"Come to New York, Leah-bschoen," he teases, licking the empty spoon seductively.

161

"Do you mean that?" I whisper.

"Why not?" he replies.

"I could sublet my apartment, I suppose," musing aloud, as if it were a new idea, "or get out of the lease entirely, maybe, and quit my job and just move here and look for something."

"Move here?" he echoes, again like Dr. Isaacson, but he sounds apprehensive.

"Here to New York," he clarifies, smiling at me.

"Yes, to New York and to here."

I indicate his bed, his apartment with my blueberry spoon. He looks incredulous.

"Here?" he questions.

"Well, yes, here, if you'll have me. Of course I'd contribute to the rent, as soon as I get a job."

"But that's impossible," he exclaims.

"Impossible for me to find a job? Well, I know it won't be easy, but I'll have good references from World and even though the market's tight I'm sure I could . . . " ·

He cuts me off. "Impossible for you to live here, with me," he explains.

"Why impossible?"

I can feel my lower lip begin to tremble, my eyes well up with tears.

"Don't you love me? You always say you love me."

"Of course I love you, Leah, to the extent that I love, I love you. I love my children, too, and my grandchild, even my wife sometimes. I love New York and Paris, I love Chekhov, I love blueberries and sour cream, for Christsake. Loving is one thing, Leah, living together is something else."

"But we do live together sometimes, Frank, and we never fight. We live together on weekends and all of my vacations. And, and, and you miss me when I'm not here, you say you do, you even send me airline tickets."

"Yes, yes, that's all true," he reaches over and ruffles my long hair as if I were an appealing but wayward collie dog.

"I do love to be with you, Leah. You're young and pretty and terribly clever and you're dynamite in bed. You demand nothing

162

from me, you're not a sychophant, and you make me feel like a king. But I certainly don't want to live with you. That really would be tiresome. Besides, I'm a married man."

I am crying in earnest now.

"Get unmarried," I tell him, "get unmarried to her and married to me," I sob on, conscious of the stupidity of my request and of the fact that my nose is running.

"Marry me and we'll live together and make love, dynamite love, and babies, too."

It is all out in the open now. Frank strokes my hair fondly, then holds a tissue under my nose.

"Blow," he orders.

I do.

"Again."

I do again.

He wipes my nose tenderly, thrusts the blueberry bowls onto the nightstand, and pulls me to him. I am safe in his arms, but only for the moment. The bottom falls out of my heart as I realize that my secret is out and our affair too is blown.

"So," he croons to me, "my lovely little Leah, my beatnik, my Bohemian, my Miss Julie, my rebellious little Jewish iconoclast . . . so, underneath your convoluted sophisticatd exterior beats the heart of a pure-blooded, middle-class American girl."

"Is that terrible?" I ask him, for even if he will not be my husband he is still my lover and my teacher.

"No, not so terrible, if it's what you want, my darlin'," he says, slipping into his mocking Irish brogue.

"But I don't want it with just anyone, Frank, I want it with you."

"Well, it's a sad lesson you'll be learnin', lass, but we mortals don't always get what we want," he chides me.

"I know that," I murmur into his shoulder, "and I accept it and I'm willing to settle for less."

"Well, you shouldn't be," he tells me, all the while stroking my hair.

I ignore him and continue with my new tactic. "Tell you what," I wheedle, as winningly as I can, "I'll just move to New

York and find a little place somewhere and a job and we'll go on just as we have, is that all right with you?"

"You don't need my permission to move to New York, Leah. New York is a very big city, and I don't own it. Move here if you choose. Spend weekends with me when we both feel like it. But don't move to New York for me, because I may not always be here for you."

"Are you going somewhere else?" I ask naively.

"No, yes, well yes, in a way I am. I travel a lot in my work, you know. I go wherever I can to make a buck. I'm not always lucky enough to have a live theatre job or a part in a TV series. But even if I were to remain in New York permanently, I wouldn't always be here for you."

I have extricated myself from his embrace, for it no longer comforts me. I sit on his bed hugging my knees and staring at him. I know he is telling me the truth, that he has always told me the truth, but I wonder why this is the first time I have heard him.

"Don't be so downcast, little one," he continues, his eyes full of tenderness and concern. "This is part of life, part of growing up. We're having an affair. A lovely affair. And we're both enjoying it, I think. But that's all it is, all it was ever meant to be. I never promised you anything else. I never promised you anything more."

He waits for this to sink in, for me to answer. Why am I so stunned when everything he says is true?

"Then you won't always love me?" I question, "You don't always want to be with me?"

He watches me, waits for me to understand. But I am stupid and incredulous.

"You can't really love me, Frank," I shake my head at him, "not the way I love you."

"Ah, Leah, I do love you, I do. But, as you say, perhaps not the way you love me. I'm thirty years older than you, don't forget. It makes a difference in the way we see things."

"Maybe," I concede, "but it doesn't have to make a difference in what we want."

"Yes, Leah, it does have to make a difference, at least for me it does. Even if you were only five years younger than me, it would change nothing. No, that's not true. It would change one thing: I wouldn't even be here with you. You'd be middle-aged like my wife, and I wouldn't even want you. I want, I *need* youth, the firm, healthy feel of a young body, the pliability of a young mind. I'm a veritable vampire who lives off of youth."

He leans toward me and playfully bites my neck, then begins to nuzzle my ear.

"Let's not talk anymore about it," he has shifted gears completely and is beginning to stroke my breasts, "let's not talk at all," and he pushes me down on the bed, covering my protesting mouth with his. My body arches up to him, eager as ever, as if the preceding conversation had meant nothing. I let him love me in the way he knows how, and I revel in it, all the time knowing that something profound has happened, but not certain yet what I will do about it, or when.

Afterward, we lie satisfied in each other's arms.

"God, you're good," he tells me as he rubs his chin against the nape of my neck.

He is holding me spoon fashion, and I stare off into the hazy spaces beyond the bed, for without my glasses anything beyond my nose is shrouded in mystery. I am wondering if I am good. Good in bed? Is that what he means? If so, then no one else has ever appreciated me the way Frank does. But then, all my other lovers have been boys, selfish boys, and Frank, Frank is a man. Do the men I pick up in bars think I'm good? Do they wish they knew my name and phone number so they could hump me again, maybe in their own beds rather than in dingy motel rooms or the backseats of their cars? How can I be good when I behave like that, for doesn't good entail more than just drawing up your knees, rotating your hips, gasping, moaning, and feeling or feigning ecstasy?

"Am I?" I mutter, surprised to hear that it has come out aloud.

"Mmmnh?" Frank murmurs.

"Am I good, Frank? I think I want to be good."

"Sleep is good. Sleep, now shh . . ." and he nuzzles me some more.

It feels good. I close my eyes and try to give myself up to the feeling of strong arms encircling me, warm breath on my neck, the rhythmic pulsations of another living body near mine, but my eyes spring open.

Frank sleeps, but I do not. I find myself thinking of Grampa Bronstein. He is sitting in his favorite chair, looking down at me benevolently. He leans forward, tugging at his neatly clipped Vandyke beard and says, "*nu, na'arla, vas machst du?*" Well, little fool, what are you doing?

"Nothing, Grampa," I reply, "nothing," and I am suddenly ashamed.

When Frank wakes I am already up, showered, and dressed. He yawns and stretches luxuriously, then pats the bed beside him, indicating that I should come to him. I have never known anyone who is as sensual as he is. I seat myself obediently near his tousled head. He sniffs appreciatively.

"You smell good, clean. I love it when you smell like that."

He pulls me to him for a quick morning kiss. How can I give this up, I am thinking, this is the only thing that makes me feel alive. His warmth fills me even through the gentle brushing of our lips alone. I will die without it, I think. Then I remember Dr. Isaacson and amend the thought: I will be so sad without him.

"What shall we do today, Leah-bschoen?" he asks me.

"Whatever you want to do Frank," I reply, as I always do.

I have no wishes other than his. I am all too aware that my plane will leave at seven and that I will be back in the lonely confines of my Cleveland apartment by nine-thirty. I will shower again, go to bed, and in the morning rise like an automaton and drive to my dull job at the publishing house.

The only bright spots in my week will be the hours I spend with Dr. Isaacson and the class I take in abnormal psychology at the university. Funny, I haven't told Frank about the class, or even about Dr. Isaacson. For the first time it strikes me as odd that I should have left those facets of my life out of my reports to Frank.

Of course, I don't tell him about the night terrors and the strange men I pick up, whose increasing frequency and numbers have driven me back into therapy. It seems natural to leave those things out. But why haven't I chosen to tell Frank about my class or about my therapy?

Frank has begun stroking the bare underside of my forearm. It sends involuntary shudders through me. He kisses the inside crook of my arm, then my wrist, and laughs at me.

"Leah, you're wearing me out. I'll have to get my son to come over and spell me for awhile. Take pity on an old man."

I am not amused. I pull away with such force that I surprise myself.

"You're the one who started fooling around," I reply resentfully, "and don't taunt me with your son."

"Well, well, don't get your Irish up, Leah. This isn't an O'Casey play."

"It isn't an O'Neill play, either, I hope," I snap back at him.

Then, for some reason, I giggle. The hatchet is buried. Frank decides we will have a Bloody Mary at P. J.'s, then I will watch Frank go through his exercises at the dance studio. After that we will while away the remaining hours here before I depart. Maybe then I will tell him about my opportunity to work at the special school for psychotic children. I wonder if he will be interested. I wonder if I am.

Clearly I have to do something. My job at World Publishing is not taking me where I want to go, and where would I be going, even if I moved to New York? I have always known, ever since I was a little girl, that I had to be able to support myself. That was one of the main reasons I rejected the idea of going into theater. Too risky. My modest talent could never have carried me to the top, where I wanted to be. It might not even have paid my rent.

I could climb to the top or near it in publishing, I suppose, but that holds no appeal for me.

I sigh to myself, thinking of the sometimes-appealing, sometimes-appalling little waifs whom I observed at Dr. Hess's school only last week. She invited me there after I had turned in what she dubbed a "superior" paper to her Abnormal Psych seminar. Something about the terror and confusion in some of the children's eyes haunts me. Maybe I should accept her offer.

"The job is yours if you want it, Miss Bronstein," she had told me. "Our regular assistant teacher is moving to California with her husband. This school can't function with one teacher. I'm impressed with you as a student, and you seem to have some maturity and experience, which one doesn't see in many young people anymore. I can't offer you much in the way of salary. But you'll learn a lot, and if you're interested in continuing your study of psychology you'll get one tuition-free course per term. I'll need your answer before the end of the month. The fall term begins in September, but you'd be on the payroll as of the first of July. And, oh, yes, I'd want you to go to school this summer to pick up some special education courses. The center will pay for that, of course, and for your time while you're in school. Three hundred fifty a month plus tuition and books. Think about it."

I muse over the possibilities as I watch Frank tie a silk square casually at his throat. He doesn't wear open collars, even in summer, for fear that someone will see that his neck is getting crepey. With his broad shoulders and narrow hips, he could pass for a man of thirty from the back. And, from the front, he could be forty, even with his silver hair.

But he is neither. He is fifty-four. And he doesn't want me to live with him. He wants things just as they are. But for how long? I am nearly twenty-four, and my goals are still unset. I must begin to carve out a career for myself. Three hundred fifty dollars a month won't keep me warm when I am in my fifties, like Frank. But, by then I might be something more than an editorial assistant or an assistant teacher. I could be a full-fledged editor, or I could be a psychologist like Dr. Hess, if I took an advanced degree. Or even a therapist like Dr. Edwards or Dr. Isaacson. . . . Yes, I could support myself easily enough if I earned my doctorate in psychology. Teaching, psychotherapy—any number of doors would open.

I watch Frank comb his beautiful hair and think how far my reverie has taken me from him. Managing the anxieties of a dozen wildly disordered preschoolers is a far cry from brunching at P. J. Clark's. As I ponder the choices, thinking of such new ideas as "my future" and what will make me "feel better about myself," I am astonished by my creeping puritanism. Has Dr. Isaacson crept so completely into my soul?

I arrive at my front door, still thinking about Frank. Although I can see the affair quite clearly now, with the perspective of twenty years, my nostalgia is overwhelming. For one instant I think maybe, just maybe, I'll telephone him, just to say hello. I close my eyes and picture him, me, us, as we were in that faraway time. But then I remember that he is past seventy years old by now, an aging actor struggling to find good character parts. And I am past forty, a married woman, a mother of two, with only one breast. I enter my house and let the screen door slam behind me.

9

WEDNESDAY EVENING——

I SIT in Sharon McIntyre's carefully appointed living room sipping a glass of white sangria and wondering what I am doing here. There are eight of us tonight, eight women who have known each other casually for as many years. We started meeting monthly like this when our children were quite small and in a play group together. At that time, the incessant chatter and endless movement of our busy toddlers kept us from completing even the briefest conversation. One of the women, maybe it was Sharon herself, suggested that we get together periodically at each other's homes for an evening, without the children. None of us really expected the idea to catch on the way it did. We knew that our friendship was based in large part on mutual need, on that starvation for adult companionship that many young mothers feel, whether housebound or working. We thought the monthly meetings would fizzle out, as the play group had when the children outgrew their need for it and moved on to school.

But, despite the fact that each of us went off in a different direction, this one to attend to a disrupted career, that one back to school, another to community work, we continued to meet and enjoy each other. Occasionally, someone moved away, leaving a void that might be filled by a new face in town, and so the group grew and changed in composition but there was always a core of us who rememberd its beginnings, those faraway mornings when sticky-fingered two-year-olds invaded our laps and conversations.

At first I had been reluctant to join, never having been much of a joiner. I had always preferred my relationships close, intimate, and one to one. But, when the children were preschoolers, I really came to rely on this bunch of sensible ladies, whose cheerful conversations seemed to help me keep my sanity. Seeing them was more than a pleasant social excursion: it served to remind me that there were others who shared my parental concerns.

As the children grew older and I grew more comfortable with being a mother, I began to feel somewhat estranged from the women in the group. I saw no real point of contact at all, except for the accident that we were all the same sex and had children nearly the same age. Tonight I am feeling that acutely.

Perhaps my long reveries about Frank this morning are at the root of my disaffection this evening. After all, I have never told any of these women about Frank. But then why should I? Romance and excitement were never the topics that glued us together. These are the ladies who saw me through toilet training and the twins' first day at school, not through broken hearts and hopeless love affairs. Our friendships are based on good humor and warmth, not on the shared intimacies and easy confidences I exchange with Anna or with Jeanne. And, although I am glad for the joking camaraderie and friendly support I receive from the women who surround me here tonight, I can't help feeling that something important is lacking.

Years ago I complained to Dr. Isaacson about loneliness, lamenting the fact that all my really good friends lived out of town. He raised an analytic eyebrow at me and said, "How convenient."

Soon after, I began the arduous task of developing new friendships with people who lived where I lived. Now I find myself feeling cut off again, longing for Anna or Jeanne while all around me at this very meeting are women who call me "friend." Is this just a repetition of the way I behaved so many years ago? Have I isolated myself anew by not attending meetings regularly, by not sharing my innermost feelings with the women at those meetings, by not probing theirs? It doesn't seem the same. For one thing, I am more dignified now, more reserved. I do not bare my soul to every woman who is willing to have a cup of coffee with me, anymore than I bare my body to every man who is willing to buy me a drink. Besides, I am older now, busier. I have family obligations, a career. I haven't the time to cultivate new relationships with endless telephone conversations and three-hour lunches. I can't just snap my fingers and take off to the movies, or New York, with people I enjoy. Everything is different now.

I look over at Carolyn, who is sitting across from me nodding attentively at something Betty Zuckerman is saying. Carolyn is the one I had hoped for the most from, the one I thought would become a real friend. Her quick wit and energy attracted me; her easy way of relating to her children set an example for me. She helped her kids bake gingerbread men on ordinary weekday afternoons and seemed unconcerned about Play-doh in her shag rugs. I wanted to be around her more, to see how it was done. And I was curious about her life before she met Martin, when she had worked as a special assistant to Bobby Kennedy in Washington.

But although I spent a lot of time with her, long happy mornings over coffee while the twins and her two children wrought cheerful havoc in her family room, I never got to know her any better. She adroitly parried all the questions I asked her about herself, answering my inquiries about her years in D.C. by deftly turning us to a discussion of politics or social issues. It soon became clear that her life before Martin and the children was a closed book, which I for one would never read.

Superficially open, she was really profoundly private. I respected that but thought we could still be close friends. Then one day she asked me how I happened to become a psychotherapist. I told her about my job working with disturbed children and went on to say that my own experience in psychotherapy had had a lasting impact on me. She looked stunned.

"You were in therapy?"

I nodded.

"Why, how fascinating," she said, recovering herself. "Whatever made you decide to do a thing like that?"

I looked at her, incredulous. She seemed to think that going into therapy was something like deciding to dye your hair. It just never occurred to her that anyone she knew could need it.

After that conversation I should have known better than to confide in her about Daniel. But, she had brought her children over to play with Jacob and Hannah one morning, after he and I had had a terrible scene the day before. It was the time I had planted the beet seeds where the lettuce was supposed to go. I was feeling intensely sorry for myself, had a backache from all the gardening, and, as if all that weren't enough, I had just gotten my period. In a fit of candor I told Carolyn all about it.

She listened for awhile, then interrupted, "If things are that bad, Leah, why don't you divorce him?"

I was shocked. Did she know me so little that she thought I would divorce my husband over a packet of beet seeds? Would I abandon the man who fathered my children because he brandished a hoe at me? I had been looking for comfort of the "oh you poor dear" variety, and she had hit me over the head with the baseball bat of divorce.

In Carolyn's world, every problem has a solution: a hungry child gets peanut butter on whole wheat bread, a tired husband gets a warm kiss and a cool glass of wine, an unhappy wife gets a divorce. After that day, I expected very little from Carolyn. How can you tell a friend that she has failed you when she doesn't even realize that you have asked anything from her?

I continued to see Carolyn from time to time, but, as our children grew older, it was they who exchanged visits, not we. We waved to each other cheerfully from our cars as we dropped off the kids; we shared quick cups of coffee when we picked them up.

And so it went with all the women in the group, women whose idea of friendship seems to consist of "touching base" with each other, as they call it. Am I really the only one who requires more?

Perhaps it's immature or just plain crazy to cherish the idea of having "girl friends," the way I do, to want more than whatever is exchanged when two or three married couples spend an evening together or when eight women gather for a monthly ritual of gossip and coffee cake. Girl friends. Even the phrase is outdated, I guess, since women's liberation. But it perfectly characterizes the warmth and camaraderie of an essentially preadolescent relationship, where everything is shared and competition and rivalry have not yet reared their ugly heads.

Girl friends, real girl friends like Anna and Jeanne, nod sympathetically when you are having trouble with your spouse and never-ever advise separation or divorce. They remind you by recalling anecdotes that even you have forgotten, that your children, who have acted willful, stubborn, rude, stupid, or neurotic, are really warm, charming, stable, brilliant and loving. They reassure you that you are a good mother. They compliment you on how you look when you have a new hairdo that your husband thinks is silly, and they are willing to go with you to Bergman films that he despises.

In turn, they invite you to dine with them at tearooms their spouses won't set foot in. They tell you that you are definitely not too old to have an affair, if you want one, but agree with you that extramarital relationships can't be what they are cracked up to be. In short, they give you something a man never can: they act as a mirror to your own narcissism, reflecting to you other aspects of yourself, allowing you to be utterly selfish, at the same time that they hold out to you the idea of what you are and can become.

I gaze around the room at all these smiling women who chat sociably and who seem so relaxed with one another. Is there really no one here who feels the way I do, who could understand me, whom I could understand? How can I be so isolated, I who have always relied on other women for support?

I think of Anna and how it wrenched my heart when Daniel and I moved to Kentucky and I had to leave her warm, caring presence behind. And of Jeanne and the shy acquaintanceship I struck up with her, amazed to discover as our friendship grew that I had found a kindred spirit in the South. Our camaraderie grew, based not on common background but on some inner empathy that perhaps only chemistry can explain. And then, two years ago, after her husband died, Jeanne moved to Cincinnati, and I was devastated anew.

Was it really worthwhile, I wondered, to open oneself to someone like that, to urge that someone to open herself to you, only to find, some months or years down the road, that cruel circumstance would force the two of you apart, and that there were gaps that not even long distance phone calls could bridge?

Anna and Jeanne still mean as much to me now as they did five or ten years ago, but I miss our frequent meetings and nearly daily chats. They are gone from me, and I have been unwilling or unable to replace them.

These friendly women who surround me here tonight, who joke and laugh with me, who keep my children for an afternoon, who brought cakes and casseroles when I recuperated from my surgery, these are women whose company I can enjoy, but there is not one of them who seems to want the kind of friendship I need. They seem content to stay on the safe surface of relationships, at least with me, and it is neither polite nor feasible to press them toward anything more. And maybe they are right. For if I disappeared tomorrow, I could be easily replaced in this group, where not even one woman has ever seen me weep. Nor have I seen their tears nor heard their heartaches. Is it possible they have none, or do they just prefer not to share them with me?

Charlotte Anderson's distinctive voice interrupts my reverie. She is talking about her fourteen-year-old daughter's new-found interest in boys. Several of the women have children older than my twins. They all seem worried about adolescence, as well they might be. I listen sympathetically for awhile, wondering how I will feel when Jacob and Hannah are set adrift by the times in a sea of sex and drugs. Will they stay afloat or at least be able to keep their heads above water? Have Daniel and I given them the ballast they need to keep them from capsizing in those very muddy waters? My babies, they are so young. . . .

Betty Zuckerman, a positive woman with positive opinions, proffers the information that her niece had several affairs that the family knew about, indeed lived with a young man quite openly for a time, before she finally settled down and got married last

176

year, and entered law school, too. The general consensus is that that is different because Betty's niece lives in New York, and besides, she is older than fourteen.

Betty raises an eyebrow and points out that she doubts that her niece was much older than fourteen when she had her first sexual experience, and that the sexual mores in our town are probably not as far different from those in New York as we might like to think. There is an uncomfortable silence in the room.

Janet Robertson, a slow-speaking woman whom the group tends to think of as a model mother, leans forward in her chair. She has been a schoolteacher for nearly twenty years and has the schoolteacher's definiteness of diction. What worries *her*, she says pointedly, is not so much the *fact* of premarital sex, it is the *impact* that such sexual experience has on the whole social fabric.

"After all," she continues, "a girl who has indulged in *that* kind of thing is going to have *difficulty* remaining *faithful* in her marriage." Point made, she leans back again.

Betty jumps in immediately, "Surely," she stammers, "you're not arguing in favor of virginity?"

"And why not argue in favor of premarital virginity?" replies Janet. "I happen to see it as a positive value."

Carolyn Fogel, the arbiter of the group, suggests that it's really a very individual thing, isn't it?

I swish the melting ice around the bottom of my glass, watching as an orange slice alternately rises and sinks in the tiny pool of water. What am I doing here? Should I explain to them what I know to be true, that they are talking about two separate things, that the ability to develop warm and lasting relationships, faithful relationships, if you will, develops in the first three years of life and has little or nothing to do with the other thing they are talking about, namely adolescent acting-out behavior, specifically sexual acting out? Should I offer myself as an example? I smile at the sheer audacity of it! These women are my friends. I have known them for years. But do I really know them? Do they know me? I haven't even told them about Frank: five long years, more than twelve percent of my life! And my time with Frank was a love affair, something even Janet Robertson could understand.

But what about the nameless, faceless men who peppered my

177

past? What do my friends know of such things? What do they know of the terror and loneliness that sent me stalking the night in the streets of Cleveland, or of Hungarian bars where no one ever heard of white sangria, but where a stinging shot of Kessler's was followed by a draught of cold beer? What do they know of strong-sinewed, beer-bellied men from Republic Steel, whose bearlike, sweaty embraces could chase away the night terrors for awhile? What do they know of anything outside the safety of their own carefully appointed worlds? And faithfulness? What do they even know of that? They think of faithfulness as a function of the body, while I know it to be a function of the mind.

I look around me at these seven women who are my friends. Seven women sipping sangria and discussing the perils of pre-marital sex. Why did I ever consent to let Carolyn bring me here tonight? I feel as alien as if I had just stepped off an unidentified flying object.

Yet they smile at me, include me, are convinced that I am one of them. I inspect their faces, their clothing, their hair. I listen to their conversations. All of it is so utterly predictable, so right. They are so complacent, so smug, so self-satisfied. They are just plain insufferable.

I long to say or do something that will shock them. What if I leapt up and said, "Hey girls, wanna see my prosthesis? It even has a nipple." Or suppose I loudly stated during a lull in the conversation, "I am having an affair with one of your husbands." But it wouldn't work. If I pulled out my prosthesis and passed it around the group they would all look at it and say, "How interesting." And as for their husbands, why would any one of them even consider sleeping with a mutilated woman like me?

As I formulate these thoughts I feel ashamed, for I know that I am being unfair to my friends, none of whom has ever done me any harm. I feel edgy and irritable and seem bound and determined to blame them for my mood.

Carolyn asks me to pass her an ashtray. Even this maddens me. She is one of those people who smokes only socially. She doesn't even have enough character to be an addict. As I pass the ashtray to her she smiles me a thank you. I return her smile guiltily. Looking

178

at her honest, intelligent face, I am sick with my own hypocrisy. What am I doing here, accepting the hospitality and friendship of these women and then sitting in judgment on them? What makes me think I am better than they are, just because my experiences have been different? Don't I share their world now? Am I not every bit as carefully appointed as they? Isn't that exactly what I worked so hard to achieve with Dr. Edwards and Dr. Isaacson?

Suddenly I am very lonely for Daniel. Of all my friends, he is the only one who can really understand. Funny, I am thinking of him as a friend. And it is his friendship that I am longing for now. In some ways we are alike, he and I, in some few ways we are. We share some experiences that my other friends know nothing about, and a view of the world that they will probably never know. Daniel the cowboy, Daniel the merchant seaman.

How can I say I am like him? Am I not more like Betty Zuckerman, a nice Jewish girl who grew up in the city? I glance at Betty and she smiles at me. No doubt she sees in me an ally, another woman in the room who cannot in good conscience cast a vote for virginity. Is she trying to encourage me to speak up? I listen for a minute.

The conversation has taken another turn while I've been musing. They're on public versus private schools now. Sharon is passing out more sangria. I hold out my glass. She fills it, then moves on with her icy pitcher. I think of Daniel again. I know I have been faithful to him for more than fifteen years, and I feel reasonably certain that he has been faithful to me. Yet, when he was a merchant seaman he screwed whores in every port, sometimes even when he didn't feel like it, but only because it was the thing to do in port. He does not remember their faces or their names, and maybe the thought is repulsive to him now (I remember his saying, once, how lucky he felt that he never got the clap), or maybe he doesn't think about it, or maybe it doesn't matter.

And that's how I feel about my steelworkers. And even about the teachers, doctors, stockbrokers, and lawyers, whose arms and legs and backs and bellies sweated over and under and beside me in the night. Hairy or hairless, muscular or fat, fleshy or bony, they were

179

there with me, together for a moment, a breath, a gasp, a sigh; and in that moment I was real, at least to them, and I was not alone. The nauseating fear that rose from my stomach was momentarily dispelled, and when they were gone I was left only with emptiness or sadness or shame, all infinitely more bearable than fear.

Closeted with Dr. Isaacson over the years, I learned to sit still with the night shadows, to let evening fall, and to stay in the dreaded confines of my own body, my own four walls. And the nightmares receded, more manageable at a distance, until, wrapped in the blanket of my growing attachment to Dr. Isaacson and his way, I felt I could contain them, package them, and carry them into his office. There we inspected them together, opening them gingerly and slowly, and I cried and laughed and shouted over their paltry contents and watched them disintegrate in the morning light of our analysis. Then, when night came, my own arms and legs and back and belly sufficed to keep me safe, and, when I felt alone, I longed for somebody—and not for any body anymore.

Who but Daniel understands and shares this with me? When I told him all about it, he was unimpressed. Holding my hands in his he said, "So, we both spent many years at sea. Something else we have in common."

And that was the end of it. If he worried about faithfulness, it was not in terms of my previous promiscuity, but only in the context of the difference in our age; for he feared he would grow old too soon to keep me happy. That worry faded over the years as we settled into marital familiarity and found that our sexual appetites were more closely linked to our moods than our ages and that we had many things to occupy us, and sex was only one of them—and not the most important.

Daniel. I think I knew that I chose him for the children even before we had the children. But I knew it for a certainty that crisp fall day that Hannah and Jacob were six and had been going to first grade for a week or two. At first either Daniel or I had walked them to school, but they said they were ready now to walk by themselves. The distance was not great and there was a crossing guard. Only our own mad, parental fears stood between them and their independence.

We acquiesced. Daniel stood at the front door, adjusting his Harris tweed cap.

"Daddy," Jacob scolded. "You promised . . ."

"Well, I'm not walking *with* you," Daniel muttered, "at any rate not beyond the corner. I'm just going out to get a newspaper." And so he followed them down the street as far as the corner.

I could see the twins, lunch boxes swinging, mouths chattering, as they turned right, and Daniel as he followed them, first with his body, then with his eyes, straining after them with ferocious protectiveness, keeping his promise to the children not to walk with them all the way to school, at the same time keeping his promise to himself to care for and guard them forever.

Daniel at the corner on the pretext of needing to buy *The New York Times* strained after them, his seaman's eyes and ears following their every move until at long last he sighed and reluctantly abandoned them to the custody of old Mr. Jamison, the crossing guard. I knew at that moment, as I had known before and would remember after, that in choosing Daniel I had at last done right.

Sharon is up again and heading for the kitchen. I realize it must be late, as she's undoubtedly going after the coffee and cake, which ritually close these meetings. Feeling guilty about my lackluster performance as a guest, I blink back my tears, then join her to help with the serving. Sharon is a perceptive woman. Besides, one would have had to be as insensitive as a stone to have missed the fact of my disaffection from the group all night. She asks me what's the matter and I tell her "nothing."

She shakes her head, then walks over to me and says, "Leah, I'm worried about you. You haven't been yourself for a long time. Are you all right?"

I want to tell her that I am myself, that this is just another self from the one she usually sees. I want to tell her that I feel frightened and alone and do not know where to turn. I want to sit down on one of her carefully refinished kitchen chairs, lay my head down on her heavily waxed cherry table, and weep hot, salty tears. I want to reveal myself to her as I have never done before, so grateful am I

181

that she has said that she is worried about me, and I want her, in turn, to reveal herself to me.

But it all seems too complicated somehow, complicated and wrong. For if she is really so worried about me, why haven't I heard from her in over two months, and if she cares about me so much, why does she reserve her concern for a chance encounter at a monthly meeting that I might not even have attended? I reassure her that I am fine, just fine. Perhaps a little more tired than usual, but fine all the same.

"Well, of course you're tired! You've been working like a dog forever, and you haven't had a vacation for two years."

Puzzled, I look at her. "I had a vacation just a year ago," I remind her. "I take a vacation every summer."

She shakes her head in disbelief, "Some vacation, my dear. Not exactly my idea of a good time. . . . Last year you spent your vacation in the hospital, or don't you remember? Honestly, Leah, you're just not fair to yourself. It was bad enough when you had to have your surgery. And you and Daniel and the kids were all so unbelievably brave about it. But then as soon as you recuperated, you just went right back to work."

I review the events in my mind, realizing she is right. Daniel and I had planned to take the kids to Vermont to visit my sister Ruthie and her family last summer. All of us had really been looking forward to it. But at the end of June I discovered the lump in my right breast, and by the tenth of July I didn't have a right breast anymore. I tried to convince Daniel that we could have part of our trip anyway, part of our vacation. We'd fly instead of drive, curtail our activities. Daniel thought I was crazy. My surgeon agreed.

By the time I was really back on my feet, more than a month had passed, and the children were getting ready to start school. My patients needed me, I told myself. And it was important to reestablish a normal routine for Jacob's and Hannah's sakes. My mother had been with us for awhile to help out. I felt it was important for the whole family just to be by ourselves after she left. The vacation had been no vacation at all. I had absented myself from my patients' problems, worries, and fears, only to run headlong into my own.

182

"Perhaps you're right, Sharon," I tell her as I pour eight cups of coffee, "maybe I really do need to get away."

"Well, of course you do, and the trip to Spain will be just the thing. You say Daniel's always at his best when he's busy with research, and that he likes to play Indian guide. There probably isn't a corner of Seville that he hasn't poked into by now. He'll keep you and the twins busy from morning until night with those cathedrals and museums and markets that he goes so crazy over. Just don't let him wear you out, Leah. You really need a rest."

"I'm not that bad off now, am I?" I smile.

Sharon goes serious on me for a minute, "Aren't you?"

I laugh and pick up the tray with the coffee. "Don't worry about me. I'll be fine. And don't worry about Daniel wearing us all down in Spain. He's very much the Spaniard, don't you know. A big believer in the siesta. There will be plenty of time to relax. As near as I can tell, the whole country is closed from two to five everyday."

"Very civilized," says Sharon, preceding me into the living room with her famous walnut torte.

She is greeted by the appreciative "oohs" and "aahs" of the other six, who are now all sitting cross-legged on the floor in a tight, cozy circle. They scoot back a foot or two, clearing a space for Sharon and me, or for the coffee and torte.

"Oh, yum," exclaims Carolyn, "this will set me back two weeks on my diet."

Everyone eats appreciatively for awhile and Charlotte asks Sharon for the recipe.

"I'll type it up for the next meeting," Sharon says agreeably.

"Just type one and drop it off at the bookstore," says Betty, "I'll be happy to make enough copies for everyone. It'll give me something to do. Besides, they owe me at least the option to make a few copies on the machine. God knows they don't pay me anything."

The group murmurs sympathetically in its usual supportive way.

"That's what we were talking about while you two were in the kitchen," Janet informs us, ever the schoolteacher, "how some of us have to slave away for peanuts, even if we've spent years on training, or, worse still, have to work for minimum wage in some office or store 'cause we don't have a marketable skill or maybe don't want to work full time because of family commitments. I mean, it's really the hours and vacations that keep me in teaching. What other job would give me the freedom to spend time with my family like I want to?"

Sharon puts down her coffee and says, "You're right, Janet, and that's one of the reasons I haven't gone back to work—at least for money. My children are younger than yours. They need me. Where would they go after school if I had a full time job?"

"Join us at the bookstore, lady," Betty interjects. "Four hours a day for four dollars an hour. No fringe benefits, no retirement. For this I went to college, wow!"

"You're the lucky one, Leah," says Carolyn, "you've got a career, a profession. You can name your own hours, your own price. You don't have to answer to anyone. You're really lucky to have that Ph.D."

All eyes are upon me as I swallow a piece of walnut torte and chase it with a gulp of coffee. This is a chant I've heard before, and it never fails to raise my hackles, but I smile pleasantly, washing the anger right down with the torte. I verbally agree with Carolyn's assessment of my blessed good luck while I seethe inwardly, and not from the heat of the Sanka. They always make it sound as if the doctorate I sweated over for five long years had been handed me by the Blue Fairy. "Here Leah, this is something you should have, it will always come in handy." And she flies off in a puff of smoke, carrying her goodies to the other fortunate few who have been graced by her favor.

Deftly, I turn the conversation back to the group, neatly channeling them into a discussion of meaningful volunteer work versus meaningless paid labor. Sharon is particularly hot on this point, and I know it will take the pressure away from me. After all, ever since the Blue Fairy gave me my magical doctorate in psychology, I've been a whiz at handling people.

I look around my group of friends and try to imagine what they were doing while I was living alone in a fourth-floor walk-up, grappling with advanced statistics and neurology and fighting my night terrors.

Betty and her husband had spent a year backpacking in Europe before they were married. Sharon and hers were saving up money for the expensive stereo equipment and tasteful antiques that now surround them. And while they were making love or money or babies, I was carving out the career I am so "lucky" to have. Do they imagine that the Blue Fairy's graciousness extends even beyond that good-luck diploma that hangs on my office wall? Do they believe that the fifty fat bucks an hour flies conveniently into my pocket, like baby-sitting money that I can finger greedily on my way home? Do they have any concept of what it takes to keep that office operational: money for rent, telephone, furnishings, office equipment; money for secretarial and telephone answering services; money for stationery and postage; money for both sides of my social security, for malpractice insurance and disability income protection; money for my retirement plan and for quarterly tax estimates; and money socked away in the bank for a vacation once a year, because every hour I am away from the office is fifty dollars I don't earn while the office operating expenses relentlessly pile up.

And beyond the money comes the worry: where will the referrals come from, will they keep coming? What if it's a lean month, or worse still, a lean year? Or what if I'm overbooked, overtired, overworked? Do I dare turn down a referral and alienate those precious referral sources who could well start sending their patients elsewhere? Better to work a little later, a little longer, getting home at seven instead of six or spending Saturday mornings in the office.

And so it goes until I'm uncertain whether to pray for fat times, so I can make more money, or lean times, so I can spend more time with my family.

These are issues that have never concerned any of the women friends I am with this evening, I realize, as I look around at them. And all at once my anger is spent. They are different from me, that is all. Different because they never saw themselves as the sole source of support for their families. Different because they always

185

believed they could ultimately count on some man to take care of them and their offspring. But I never did. I had my mother's example. Who, after all, was stronger, more hardworking, more reliable than my father?

Forty hours a week in his law office, the courts, the law library. Then who knows how many more out on the paving job, measuring lots and drawing up estimates evenings and weekends, getting the work crew out at 6:30 A.M., stopping by at the end of his day to supervise them—more often than not, ripping off his suit jacket, tugging off his tie, rolling up the sleeves of his white-on-white shirt, and donning an old pair of coveralls so he could pitch in and show the "mens," as he called them, how it was done. He did it all: pleaded cases in court at 10 A.M., raked hot mix at 6:00 P.M. Then he was home for supper, just late enough to make my mother angry, pouring powdered Boraxo into his asphalt-speckled hands and scrubbing them as Sammy, Ruthie, and I looked on.

"Eins, zwei, drei," he counted, teaching us the words, as the fingernail brush flashed back and forth across his hairy knuckles, and *"vier, funf, sechs,"* Ruthie would say. *"Sieben, acht, neun,"* I chimed in, and then, as he rinsed those massive hands under the flowing tap water, inspecting them carefully like a surgeon, Sammy would look up and shout in glee, *"zehn!"*

Daddy always dried his hands so slowly and thoroughly. We waited impatiently, hopping from one foot to another. Al, more often than not, was upstairs in his room, already separated from us by his adolescent moods. But when Mother said that dinner was on the table, we all appeared, washed, combed, and quiet, and sat down together to our meal. That was one of Mother's laws: a family eats together. And it was always just so. The food might be simple, but it was attractively served: a hot main course, two steaming vegetables in contrasting colors, or one vegetable and a salad, a potato dish or some noodles. There were dishes for everything. I never saw a catsup bottle or mustard jar at our table. Even the condiments appeared in sparkling, cut-glass dishes or pretty little bowls. My mother wiped her busy hands on a tea towel in the kitchen and then joined us at the table.

"It smells delicious, honey," Daddy would always say. Or, "It looks good enough to eat," he would tease.

For the next half-hour, life was good, whole, valuable, even if marred by a spilled glass of milk, a harsh word, a quarrel. It didn't matter. We were together. The dinner table was our oasis at the end of a long day. It was a gift package that my mother prepared lovingly each evening for my father, and we children were privileged to sit around the table and watch him unwrap it before he shared it with us all.

My father. So large and so alive. I remember him vividly or not at all. Dead a long, long time. I guess it doesn't matter how long you're dead. But who could ever imagine him dead? It just never occurred to any of us that he would stop like that, stop and not return—die, go away, give up, and leave us all alone. For a while, my mother set his place absentmindedly each evening, as she moved trance-like around the dining room, preparing her nightly offering. Ruthie or I would unset it, as Mother stood distracted in the kitchen, head cocked to one side, listening for his footfall on the stairs. It never came. She continued to cook her meals; they were always tasty, nutritionally balanced, attractively served. But, after a while, we stopped eating in the dining room.

"It seems cozier in the kitchen, don't you think?" Mother lied.

And we all nodded our agreement. Besides, Al was often too busy to sit down with us anymore. He'd grab a sandwich and then run out again, busy with his girlfriends or his clubs.

"*Eins, zwei, drei,*" Sammy would chant, banging his spoon against his glass, as he waited for Mother to pour his milk. "*Eins, zwei, drei,*" he would repeat, smiling broadly. But neither Ruthie nor I would ever answer.

I take a last bite of my walnut torte and savor the mocha-flavored whipped cream that tops it for a long moment before swallowing it. I look around me at the pleasant, cheerful faces of my friends and hear the comforting sounds of their conversation and laughter. Why am I not at ease? I was thinking about my father.

Mentally I survey the group and realize that each and every one of them still has her father. I have even met some of them, old men who talk about football and stocks. My father never looked old. These fathers sometimes give their daughters advice, especially about money. They guide their investments, if they have

187

any, and make recommendations about how to handle income tax or life insurance. Sometimes, my friends report, their husbands and their fathers hold different views about money and how it should be managed. Such information awes me.

My conversations with my father were about Hebrew School, or astronomy, or caterpillars. Never about money. What interest has a ten-year-old in money? My father took care of all of that for us. He didn't want my mother to worry about anything. He would always take care of her. He did not even allow her to go to the corner of an evening for a pack of cigarettes, back in the days when she still smoked.

"I'll get them for you," he'd say, donning his jacket, "a woman shouldn't be out alone after dark."

In nearly twenty years of marriage my mother never wrote a check. She ran my father's house, cared for his children, lit his Sabbath candles, warmed his bed. He said, he promised, that he would take care of all the rest. And he did. Competently, efficiently, reliably, cheerfully—until he clutched at his chest and dropped dead, leaving my mother to pick up the pieces.

My mother was, still is, a clever woman. When the numbness left her limbs, maybe even before, she took over. We never heard her complain. Al soon left the house to go to college, and only Ruthie and Sammy and I were left. I watched Mother through my thick glasses, watched her as she ran the house with one hand, the asphalt-paving business with the other. She listened to me conjugate French verbs while she made out the payroll.

"You're a smart girl, Leah," she would tell me. "Someday you'll be something. A doctor maybe, or a lawyer like Daddy was. You'll be important and successful, and you'll be able to take care of yourself."

"*Etre,*" I answered. "The verb to be: *je suis, tu es, il ou elle est, nous sommes, vous êtes, ils ou elles sont.*"

"Very good, Leah, very good. Keep studying. Maybe you'll win a scholarship to college."

Then shifting to another favorite scenario, "You'll meet someone wonderful," she would tease me, "wonderful and rich. Remember, it's just as easy to fall in love with a rich man as a poor man . . . "

I knew the refrain, "and twice as comfortable, Momma, I know."

One time I added thoughtfully, "But you didn't."

"No," she sighed, "I didn't." And she ran the checks through the checkwriting machine, letting me help her finish the job.

By the time I was in high school, no, even before that, I knew I had to be something. I could never settle for just a job after college. I had to have a career. Women who count on husbands to care for them can work in department stores or boutiques or be school teachers until their husbands finish medical school. They can fiddle with volunteer work, doing good for others, attending luncheons, giving teas. Women who know they may be left widowed at forty with young children on their hands, such women make other, different plans.

I walk out with Carolyn, each of us lauding the torte and the general success of the evening as we go. Carolyn and I chat briefly at the foot of Sharon's driveway, exchanging pleasantries about the children and our various summer plans. She fishes in her oversized straw bag for her keys and we both get into the car. The drive to my house is a quick one and, before I know it, Carolyn pulls into my driveway, turns off the engine, and reaches into her purse for a last, social cigarette. Apparently, she plans to sit and talk awhile. Should I invite her in, I wonder? No, it is late, too late for that.

I watch her as she lights up, thinking how sophisticated she looks as she leans against the door frame and exhales grandly through slightly flared nostrils.

I remember when I was a sophomore in college and one of the senior boys, an obnoxious rake named Charlie, told a table full of girls at the Student Union, including me, that only women who could flare their nostrils could have orgasms. We all sat there like idiots, snorting in and out, and exercising muscles in our faces we didn't even know we had. He looked on in amusement for a while, then turned and shuffled off, admonishing us over his left shoulder to keep on practicing and let him know when we had got it down. I never did learn how to flare my nostrils, I realize, as I stare fascinated at Carolyn's retroussé nose. I wonder even as I gaze at her whether old Charlie was on to something. Is Carolyn better in bed than I am?

Carolyn interrupts my thoughts by repeating, "Well, what about it, does Saturday night suit you?"

I realize she has extended some sort of invitation, to what I do not know.

"Saturday night," I echo, trying to figure how to get out of it, "well, really, it's lovely of you to think of me, but Daniel will be calling that evening and I'd like to be here to receive his call."

"Come after his call then," Carolyn encourages me.

"No, no, that will be quite impossible. He's bound to phone late, eleven or so, because really it will be morning for him when he calls, because of the time difference you know," I stammer on, realizing that my excuse is lame and transparent and even illogical, but for some reason Carolyn accepts it.

"Let's see," she thinks out loud, "Friday night we play bridge, so that's out; OK, what about Thursday night? That's tomorrow. Now, Leah, you can't say no. You don't even have to get a baby-sitter. Just come around six-thirty. We'll be very relaxed, very informal. We'll grill out on the patio. I positively won't take no for an answer," she insists, "you have to start getting out some. We're all getting worried about you. You've turned into a regular recluse."

The smoke from her cigarette drifts my way. I wave it aside. If she's worried about me, I think, she should snuff the damn thing out. It no longer looks sophisticated to me, but dangerous. I sit in her car inhaling her secondhand smoke, endangering my lungs. Cancer lurks everywhere, I am convinced of that. And it is only a short hop from a breast to a lung. I roll down my window the rest of the way, hoping the night air will rush in and cleanse me. I dare not take any risks. I do not want to have dinner with her and Martin on Thursday or any day. They will blow smoke in my face and serve me carcinogenic steak. The danger is too great. I glance over at Carolyn. She has finished her cigarette and is smiling at me. The threat is gone. She is my friend.

"Well, yes, that would be nice," I answer, "but do let me bring something—potato salad, or cole slaw, or dessert, maybe."

"If that's what it takes to get you over, all right. Bring your cole slaw, the one with the caraway seeds in it. Martin loves that. Then it's settled, we'll see you tomorrow, right?"

"Right," I answer staring at her frank and open face.

She is my friend, isn't she? Aren't all of them?

If only one of them would reach out to me, talk to me, ask me how I feel, in the way that Anna and Jeanne always do, then perhaps I could respond. Or am I so tired and disillusioned that I prefer to remain isolated, hidden behind the glib facade I constructed carefully so many years ago. But perhaps it is better this way. For I haven't the energy to give any of them anything in return, and I would feel obligated to do so if they held out a hand to me. I have no time now to cultivate new intimacies, no inclination to reveal myself to someone who does not already know me, no energy to respond to yet another person's human needs. Between my family's needs and my patients' needs, I am pretty much used up. I have nothing left to give. And while that is an all-right state of affairs with old friends like Jeanne and Anna, it would never do with new. At last I know the reason why I feel so alienated from Carolyn and Sharon and all the rest. Time was when I thought sex was what separated us as I thought earlier this evening at Sharon's. But now I realize that it is death. My brush with cancer, like my escapades with strange men, has made me different somehow, or so I believe. I am privy to secrets that they have not discovered. I cannot share my fears with them because I may not share my knowledge with them. I am alone.

Lying in bed that night, despite the three glasses of sangria, I cannot fall asleep. I think about the children in their camp in North Carolina. Hannah, I have heard from just the other day. I know she is happy—happy and safe. But Jacob, I haven't heard from him in nearly a week. He must be all right, and happy, too. Didn't Hannah say he was swimming all the time? And isn't that one of his main joys? Besides, the camp is reputed to be a beautiful spot. The children say so in their cards and letters. All the other children and parents we know who have been there say so. Daniel said so after he drove them there nearly three weeks ago.

He had insisted that he be the one to take them there, even though it meant renting a car. He wanted to spend the time with them before he took off for Spain. His plan was to drive them there, then continue on to Washington, D.C. Once there, he would spend a week at the Library of Congress, then fly to New York and Madrid.

It was a thoroughly good plan, as all of Daniel's plans are, clearly thought out, then clearly executed. I felt a little left out somehow, but there was really no reason for both of us to make the long trip. I would, as he pointed out, be making it all alone a month later.

How many more days until I see Hannah and Jacob, I wonder? This is Wednesday night. I pick them up a week from Sunday. Ten more days. I sigh and turn, but sleep does not come to me. I try to envision the route I will take to camp. Daniel showed it to me on the maps he left for me, but it still remains unclear. All I can see are the mountains, the mountains I must go through to reach my children. Daniel is a good mountain driver. Mountains are his habitat: Wyoming, Mexico, Argentina. But I am an Ohioan, a flatlander. I am made uneasy by mountains. I like to look at them, but I am cautious of driving in them.

I sigh and turn again, musing about maps and mountains. Perhaps I can circumvent them. Nowhere is it written that I have to follow the same route as Daniel. I close my eyes and mentally travel through familiar territory: the Ohio River Valley, Cincinnati, Western Pennsylvania, Pittsburgh. There are those damn mountains again! I have driven the Pennsylvania Turnpike many times and am no fonder of tunneling through mountains than of creeping along their switchback ridges, as we do when we go out West. I shake my head. Going north is no solution. If there is a solution, it escapes me.

As I fall asleep the mountains loom up before me like a wall, my children waiting on the other side.

10

THURSDAY——

THE cole slaw sits in a covered dish by the back door, alongside my purse. I am ironing in the kitchen, getting ready to go to the Fogels. It will be an informal evening, I know, just as Carolyn promised. Perhaps another couple will be there. We will sit ouside on the patio Martin finished last fall, while Martin grills steaks and Carolyn passes out glasses of perfectly chilled Chablis. I admire their seemingly easy life style. How did they get so comfortable with themselves, each other, their niche in the world?

Daniel and I are never so easy, so comfortable. When we take our meals outside, we are bothered by the flies. I dutifully carry out the iced tea and paper plates. The children are delighted. But we are unsettled and ill at ease. Daniel grills the hamburgers impatiently, thinking of the air-conditioned splendor of his shade-darkened study.

It will be different tonight at the Fogels, relaxing and calm.

Martin's oversized hand will sweep away any audacious fly that dares to land on the perfectly grilled steak, and Carolyn will be ready with a joke, a smile, another glass of wine. Surely it is impossible that the waters of their lives are as unruffled as I imagine. No doubt I invent this perfection to contrast my perception of my own less-perfect world.

Suddenly, I am sick of my interminable habit of analysis and angry with the doctors and teachers who schooled me in it. Why can't I just think a thought without dissecting it? Why can't I not think at all?

I shift the skirt of the dress a quarter turn on the ironing board, smooth the fabric, and continue with my ironing. I like the mindless motion of my hand, back and forth, back and forth, among the gentle folds of the light blue skirt. The steamy heat rises up to me, envelops me, and I begin to sweat. I think of the air conditioner upstairs in my bedroom, but am too lazy to unplug the iron and carry it, the dress, and the board upstairs. I remain in the kitchen. Back and forth, back and forth again, the texture of the cloth, the smell of the steam, transport me.

The same motion, the same feel beneath my fingers, but the skirt is yellow now, lemon yellow, and the air around me damp but cool. I am in the basement of my mother's house and it is summer, July, the summer before my senior year in college, the summer after I met Frank. I am getting ready to fly to New York that afternoon, to be with him. I know he likes the way I look in yellow, my sunburned skin, my reddish hair made even warmer by the sunny tone. So I am pressing this favorite dress of his to wear that evening, although I know it won't be on me long. I am thinking of him and of our evening together and of how it will feel when he holds me close. I grow weak in the knees and literally have to grip the ironing board for support. The mere thought of our embrace has made me feel faint. Right there in the basement of my mother's house, ironing a yellow cotton shirtwaist, dreaming of my lover. I am nineteen. I can swoon just by closing my eyes.

The dress before me now is blue, not yellow. Two long decades have passed. I smile over the foolish girl, so in love she does not even need her lover's presence to fill her with ecstasy.

I smile, but I feel oddly wistful. Those feelings are gone. They will never come again. Not with Daniel, not with Frank, not with Harrington, not with anyone new. Even if I had both breasts and a week in Bermuda and several glasses of champagne. Those feelings belong to youth and to the unanalyzed. Who was it who said that analysis is the giving up, the relinquishing of infantile wishes? I do not think I have given up the wishing, only the hope of having those wishes fulfilled.

The stove clock tells me I am running late. My reverie has cost me several minutes. I step out of my bathrobe and slip on the freshly pressed dress. It is still warm.

11

FRIDAY——

FRIDAY. How did it get here so fast? Despite the turmoil of the past week, it seems only yesterday that Harrington was at my door. When did the pace of my life change? If the children were here they would be chanting "T-G-I-F, thank God it's Friday." For them the weeks are still long, as they once were for me. But now, one day blends into the next; I turn around, and it is Friday once again.

I can remember a time when my weeks, too, were endless, when the stretch from Monday to Friday was an eternity that I measured out in the number of times I would wash my hair. I stood in the shower on Monday night rubbing the suds into my scalp and thinking, only four more times, four more shampoos, and then I'll be in Frank's arms. Giddy at the thought of it, I pictured myself flying to him, his silver hair and movie-star good looks singling him out for me in the crowd waiting at the airport gate. Friday night, four whole days away, ninety-six hours. Would I live that long, could I survive it?

And now, now I snap my fingers and April is gone, then May, and suddenly tomorrow is September, or even the New Year. The pace of my life moves quickly, relentlessly, as if someone had pressed the fast-forward button on my dictating machine. TGIF, I smile to myself as I say it out loud. But where did Tuesday and Wednesday and Thursday go?

I am very, very tired. Not only is it the end of a long work week, whose only therapeutic high point has been the resolution of my own countertransference problems with Harrington on Tuesday, but I stayed too late at the Fogels last night, drank too much wine, and barely functioned at the office today. During my afternoon appointments, I spent much of each hour surreptitiously biting the back of my right hand to keep from nodding off. It was foolish of me to have gone out two nights in a row. I discovered long ago that I must be asleep before eleven, or I cannot focus properly during my therapy hours. Being a psychotherapist is like being an athlete: you have to be physically and mentally prepared for each game. Perhaps I will go to bed early tonight, tomorrow night, Sunday night; then maybe I'll do better next week.

Friday night. The house seems especially empty. It is past eight o'clock, but it is still light. I have finished an egg salad sandwich and a glass of skim milk. I feel unsatisfied. I pace the house, looking for something. I wish the children were here. And Daniel. If they were, I would light and bless the three Sabbath candles in their gleaming brass holders. And Daniel would recite his carefully learned Hebrew phrasing over the wine, for we agreed when the children were still babies that we would rear them as Jews and would maintain a Jewish household for them, our atheism, and Daniel's lukewarm Presbyterian upbringing notwithstanding. Either Hannah or Jacob would then make the *motzi* over the *challah*, and then we would proceed to a hearty meal of chicken or roast meat, the table set with our best dishes and our good silver flatware. For, as the great sage has said, just as the Jews have kept the Sabbath, so has the Sabbath kept the Jews.

I love the Sabbath. I have always loved it. Even at the height of my hatred of religion, when I swore no child of mine—if one were

198

ever born—would be tainted by the lies, guilt, narrow-minded-ness, and confusion that religion inevitably carries with it, even then I treasured my memories of the Sabbath.

My mother always gave the house a thorough cleaning on that day so that by the time we heard my father's footsteps in the back hall, every mirror, window, glass, and spoon sparkled. The smells were warm and wonderful: rich, golden chicken soup; brisket surrounded by roast potatoes and carrots; *farfel* with onions, green pepper, and mushrooms. All of these delicious odors were punctuated by the underlying pungency of lemony furniture polish and the startling sharpness of ammonia. For no dirt, no germ was ever welcome in our household, but on the Sabbath their banishment was complete.

And my usually tense, angry, or worried father, put down his briefcase at the door, donned a white satin *yarmelkuh,* and stood at the head of the dining room table, a king in his household.

"Va'yahee erev, va'yahee voker yom hasheeshee," he chanted. And it was evening and it was morning, the sixth day.

"Va'yachal elohim bayom ha'sh'veyee, micol malachto asher asaw . . . Vayishbot bayom hashveyee," he chants on, in my memory, passing the edge of the serrated bread knife ritualistically over the *challah,* whose white satin cover he lifts. And on the seventh day, all of God's work was completed; and he rested on the seventh day.

My father's eyes are shining, all the strain is gone. When he lifts the cut crystal goblet that holds the glass of sacramental wine, the bluish red liquid casts a glow over all of us around the table: my mother, smiling but distracted, no doubt already thinking about serving up the soup; my older brother, silent and still, compress-ing himself and the adolescent energy and anger that threaten to overwhelm him; my younger sister, wide-eyed and serious, staring at my father with the adoration of a repentant sinner for a forgiving god; my little brother, still too young to understand, excitedly shifting from one foot to the other, waiting for the salted chunk of bread that he knows will soon be placed in his freshly washed fist.

I am consumed with love for each and every one of them and for our shining house and for the candles whose warmth I pray will never go out. Later that night I will climb contentedly into bed, the Sabbath made perfect by the benediction of cool, clear, crisp linens, fresh from the laundry and the line.

Shaking off my reverie, I decide to light the candles. The brass *menorah* is dull and tarnished, for I have not used it since the children left for camp; but it will have to do. I carefully insert the plain white candles, find a match, strike it, and begin to chant as I light them. I do not cover my eyes as my grandmother did, nor do I throw a handkerchief or shawl over my head, nor do I circle the candles with my hands three times. These gestures have always seemed too superstitious and pagan to me. They embarrass me in a way that the lighting and chanting do not. I hold my hands out to the flame in a gesture like my own mother used. Is it a blessing of the light really, or more a reaching out toward the warmth and beauty of the Sabbath? Or is it just another primitive ritual, the worship of the sacred fire?

"*L'hadlik nayr,*" I sing, unembarrassed now, "*l'hadlik nayr*" I am almost crooning, "*shel sha-a-a-a-bat.*"

No answering voices pipe in with their "amen." I watch the play of light and shadow on the white dining room walls. I hear my father's voice in my memory, the booming baritone voice that he used only in the shower or at the *schul.* But he doesn't say "*shabat,*" as I and my children do. He says, "*shabos*" in the *Ashkenazi,* or eastern European style, that we all used before the State of Israel was created and it was decided to follow the *Sephardic,* or Spanish pronunciation of the words.

It is September, in my memory, a September Sabbath morning. My mother is busy with my baby brother. My sister is playing with her dolls. My older brother is still asleep. My father is putting on a tie. Is he going to his office? I am bored with my stack of library books, most of which I have already finished. I want to draw or write, but Daddy won't let us do that on the Sabbath, for writing is defined as work and work is forbidden. When he has to go to work, that is different, he has explained, for where he works is not a Jewish place where the Sabbath is kept; but at our home, we must keep the Sabbath. And besides, he only works when he absolutely has to. I recognize all of this explanation as an equivocation, but I forgive him because he is my father.

200

"Honey," I hear him call to my mother, (until I was seven I thought her name was "Honey") "I'm going to *schul* this morning."

That's right. I remember. Since Grampa Bronstein died he goes whenever he can, most Saturday mornings and at least several evenings a week, to say *Kaddish* for him.

"Daddy," I murmur, and then louder, "Daddy, can I go with you?"

The expression on his face shifts from surprise to annoyance and then, I think maybe to pleasure and pride.

"All right," he answers, "if it's all right with your mother. But, don't you delay me, Leah," he admonishes.

I jump up from the dining room chair and run to change my clothes, from long pants and a tee shirt to one of my better school dresses. I pay special attention to brushing my hair and arranging it into the neatest ponytail I can manage, for my father is very partial to my long, auburn tresses and has often told me when we watch television together that my hair is prettier than that of any of the June Taylor dancers, whom I see as the epitome of beauty. I run back to the dining room, the center of almost all family activity, to show my father I am ready. My mother looks up from the block tower she is helping Sammy build.

"It's cool this morning, Leah, don't forget to take a sweater. Your blue one would be nice with that dress."

I run back for my sweater, eager to do whatever I am told, for I know I am being given a special privilege and I don't want them to change their minds. My mother helps me with my sweater, then pulls out my long ponytail from where it is caught between my sweater and dress, and, as she smooths it over my shoulder, she whispers to me, "This will be longer than the children's service that you are used to, Leah, but don't you fidget."

"I won't, Momma," I promise and kiss her quickly on the cheek.

I bend to kiss Sammy, too. "Do I have to kiss Ruthie?" I ask, making a face, for Ruthie and I are only three years apart, share a room, and are generally at each other's throats.

"No, dear, you just go ahead. Ruthie is happy with her dolls. And she's much too little to sit through such a long service."

Amazed at the extent to which my good fortune has grown, I fairly skip out of the room into the front hall, where my father is waiting.

We walk together, my father and I. For, unless he absolutely has to go downtown to his office, he does not drive on the Sabbath. It is about two miles to the synagogue, a perfect walk for a cool autumn morning. Although I am long-legged for a girl of ten, I must take three or four steps for every two of my father's strides. Six foot two, over two hundred pounds, he is a giant not only in my memory, but in his generation. He carries his blue-velvet *tallis* case in his right hand. His left hand swings free. Impulsively, I catch it in my own, then look up at him. The sun glints off his glasses, and underneath the shaggy brush of his mustache his lips part in a smile. We walk together, my father and I.

Beside him at the synagogue, I stand and sit, sit and stand, following the prayers as attentively as I can. My Hebrew is good, for I am a diligent student at religious school, as well as public school. But despite my diligence, my mind wanders and I frequently lose my place in the prayer book. For the service, which began well before we arrived at ten, will continue until twelve and will include a long reading from the Torah as well as all the other prayers and songs, not to mention the sermon.

My father looks peaceful and contented. The worry lines in his forehead and around his eyes are, for once, relaxed. Perhaps God was right to give man a day of rest, to forbid him from any work at all for at least one twenty-four hour period each week. My father certainly needs it. Relaxation is not a word in his vocabulary. For him it is just another name for idleness.

Yet, here in the synagogue, he seems relaxed. I like to sit beside him. I am proud of his knowledge of the prayers, his rich voice, his ability to sing all the melodies. Every once in awhile, during a lull in the service, he looks around him and then acknowledges, with a quick nod and whispered "good *shabos*," a friend in a different row. The friends sitting closer to us reach over for a handshake, their fringed *tallises* swinging as they lean over the seats.

"My big daughter, Leah," my father indicates with a fond arm around my shoulder.

The friends chuck me under the chin, or pat me on the head. "She *davins* so well, Joe," one mentions, "just like you."

My father beams with pride, and I am glad that I have paid such good attention to Mr. Goldberg and Mrs. Levenson in my Hebrew classes.

The morning wears on. The Torah is reverently removed from the ark, resplendent in its silver ornamental crown and heavy embroidered cover. It is marched around the room to a rousing Hebrew hymn. The faithful, including my father, reach out to touch it, not with their bare hands, but with the fringes of a *tallis* or a prayer book. They then plant fervent kisses on those fringes, those books. I am too shy to stretch out my hand. My father places his fringe, which has just touched the passing Torah, to my lips, to share with me this special blessing, this intimacy with God's word.

I watch the pulpit now as those who attend theTorah gently disrobe it and lay it on the special table, where it is then unrolled. They bless it and begin the long reading. My Hebrew is not good enough to reveal to me what the passage is about. But I know that the rabbi will later quote from it in his sermon.

I lose interest in the ritual and daydream for a while. My hands reach down to the seat, where I see the fringes from my father's *tallis* have draped themselves. His eyes are closed, whether in concentration on the words of God or in sleep I cannot tell. I lift the corner fringes and begin to twist them idly in my hands, finally braiding and unbraiding them to the rhythms of the chanting Torah readers. Intent on what I am doing, I lean too far forward and drop my prayer book with a loud crash. Frozen, I look at my father, certain that his eyes will open in rage. To my astonishment he winks at me, retrieves the fallen book, and holds it up for me to kiss, the dictated custom, as if a Jew must always beg forgiveness if he treats a book unkindly. Relieved, I lean back in my chair, and wait for the service to move on.

More prayers. The sermon. More songs. Up and down. Up and down. My father is singing *"Yismachu b'malchusacha."* May they who keep the Sabbath rejoice in thy kingdom, *"Shoimray, shoimray,"* he sings, not like an American Jew, but in the eastern

European accents of his father and his father before that. *"Shom-ray,"* I have been taught, with a long *"o," but "shoimray"* I sing, too, like the little old grandfathers and grandmothers around me, who, like my father, sway back and forth as they sing, eyes closed or half-closed, secret smiles playing about their lips, rejoicing in the keeping of the Sabbath.

It is 1947 in a Conservative synagogue in Cleveland, Ohio. The surviving remnant sings on in scattered handfuls, not about their bitterness or the depth of their sorrow, but about the joy of the keeping of the Sabbath. And with his "oy" instead of "o," my father memorializes them, the Jews of Poland and of Czechoslovakia and of Germany and of Hungary and of Russia and of Austria.

Of course, I do not think about any of this in 1947, as I stand beside my father in the *schul*, first singing softly, then loudly, in the ancient language that will become the official language of a new nation in less than a year. I think only that I love the melody and my father and the joy that the Sabbath has brought me.

12

SATURDAY——

I WĀKE suddenly to loud noises below my window. My eyes open, and I see that it is morning, and light. I squint at the alarm clock on the night stand before me. Seven thirty? Eight thirty? I cannot tell. The noises translate themselves: a truck's engine, a door slamming. Voices in the driveway, male voices. The garbage men, I decide, and begin to allow myself to drift back to sleep.

I sit up with a start. No. It is Saturday. It can't be the garbage men. I reach for my glasses and concentrate on the clock: 8:35. Footsteps on the back porch. A knock at the door. At last my brain takes charge, as I pull on a bathrobe and head down the stairs: Martin Fogel and Dick Robertson! I can't believe it. They were serious Thursday night at the barbecue. They have come to knock down my kitchen wall.

I open the door to them and blink into the sunlight. There stands handsome Martin in a blue workshirt and painter's overalls. Dick, looking shy and awkward, stands beside him, carrying a large toolbox that seems to be very heavy.

"Whatsamatter, Leah, did we wake you? Why we thought you'd have breakfast cooking by now, and I don't even smell any bacon," Martin teases, as he slides past me into the back hall.

Dick is right behind him.

"Good morning," is all I can manage to muster.

"You were always quick with the repartee, Leah," says Dick by way of greeting.

He sets down the toolbox, and both walk toward my kitchen.

"Listen, you guys, you aren't really serious are you? I mean we were just kind of talking the other night, hypothesizing . . ."

"Like hell we were, Leah! That's your line of work, not mine. I'm heavy into action, lady."

It's a running joke between Martin and me. Neurosurgery is his speciality, and he is forever reminding me that my efforts at delving into people's minds are far too indirect and crude.

"Be serious, you two. You can't do this. I can't let you. It's too much work. There's no way I can let you spend so much time and energy on my house. You have houses of your own. Besides, Daniel doesn't even know about it, and, and . . ."

"Leah, you and Daniel have been talking about this kitchen ever since you bought the house. It's an impossible kitchen. You said so yourself Thursday night."

Martin is doing the talking again, per usual. But Dick is enjoying it all immensely, as he smokes a cigarette and studies my kitchen wall.

"Now all we're gonna do," Martin taps the wall with a crowbar he has pulled from the toolbox, "is knock down this one wall here," he gesticulates, "and open up this space for you so you can expand into here, just like we were saying the other night. Then you can put in that nice breakfast bar and some new cabinets. Leah, believe me, it's a piece of cake. Easy. Right, Dick?"

Dick nods his agreement and stubs out his cigarette absent-mindedly in the Christmas cactus on my kitchen table.

I size up the situation and decide they are in earnest. Can I really let them do this thing that I want done so much? Do I dare do it without consulting Daniel?

"Are you two sure you want to waste a perfectly beautiful weekend on my kitchen wall? I mean there's no way I could ever repay you and besides, it's going to be hot today . . . Martin, what are you doing?"

While I've been talking, he has stuck his crowbar into the door jamb and begun to pop off a piece of woodwork.

"Piece of cake, right Dick?"

"Piece of cake," agrees the mustachioed French professor.

"Leah, are you just going to stand there in your bathrobe or are you going to pitch in?"

"What do we need, I mean, do you need anything?" I ask.

"I think about two two-by-tens—Dick will get those from the lumber yard—and, oh yeah, about a case of beer. Oh, and Leah, you better mask off the dining room and living room with plastic drop cloths or old sheets. There's going to be lots of plaster dust. Everywhere."

Their enthusiasm ignites my own. I feel my excitement rise, overthrowing the caution that has pervaded me of late.

"OK, we'll do it. Are you guys blocking me in? I need to go to the store."

"Better dress first, Leah, they frown on that kind of thing here in the South."

I look down at myself, barefoot, in my sloppy bathrobe. They have seen me without my prosthesis. I wonder if they noticed my lopsided frame. But they have been more interested in the wall's structure than in mine. And so have I.

When I return twenty minutes later from the liquor store with a case of beer and a sack of ice, I am astonished at the amount of progress Martin has made in Dick's and my absence. He has stripped off almost all of the woodwork and trim from one door-way and the baseboard is rapidly yielding to the onslaught of his crowbar.

"What should I do with all this stuff, Martin?" I ask him, sizing up the growing pile of molding and trim pieces.

"Stack it in the garage or the basement or somewhere. Careful of the nails. Knock 'em in with a hammer if you can. Don't throw any of it away though. You may need it when you finish off. It's hard to match the trim from these old houses, and besides that's quality stuff. Whatever you don't use in the remodeling, you can burn as kindling. Daniel'll love it. It's as dry as tinder, over fifty years old."

All the while he is talking to me, his skilled surgeon's hands are prying loose more and more woodwork. He has already begun to sweat.

"Jesus, Leah, I love to do this stuff. It's fun. Wanna try it? You can move as fast as you want, and it doesn't matter if you make a mistake. Here," he hands me the crowbar. "You work on it awhile, and I'll get the beer from the car."

I take the crowbar from him and stand staring at it, dumbfounded.

"Go ahead, Leah, try it. It's a crowbar, not a phallic symbol, it won't bite you."

Very gingerly, I poke at a piece of molding.

"A little more pressure, Leah, a little leverage. Good, you're getting the feel of it."

I push, wriggle, push some more, and feel the wood begin to yield. It pops loose, intact, and clatters to the floor at my feet. There is immense satisfaction in seeing it there. I am destroying the work that someone else's hands did before I was born. It doesn't matter. It feels good. I move on to another piece as Martin brings in the beer.

"Where do you want this ice, Leah?"

"There's a Coleman down in the basement, Mart. Just bring that up, please, and dump it and the beer in there, OK?"

Another piece of woodwork yields to my touch. Martin opens two cans of beer and hands me one.

"I haven't had breakfast yet," I demur.

"Go ahead, Leah, it's good for you. Consider this a continuation of Thursday's party. You can eat something later."

The beer tastes cold and slightly sour, and it goes down very easily, just as easily as my usual morning orange juice. The giddiness I feel already must be from what we are doing to my kitchen, for the alcohol couldn't possibly be in my bloodstream yet. I sit down on the Coleman cooler sipping my beer and watching Martin, who has already finished his. He wipes his mouth with the back of his forearm, tosses the empty can into the wastebasket, flashes me one of his usual engaging smiles, and picks up the crowbar.

"Well, back to work," he says as he turns to a particularly stubborn piece of wood trim over the closet door.

"This has to go," he explains, grunting a little, "because it'll be in the way when we finish pushing through here."

I nod at him appreciatively, although I do not understand how he has determined that. I watch with interest as he attacks my kitchen systematically. He is an altogether attractive man with chiseled features and blond, blue-eyed, Aryan good looks. The muscles of his forearms tighten as he wields the crowbar expertly.

"I'm on vacation now, ya'know, Leah, and," the stubborn piece of wood yields to his persistence, "this is really a good way for me to begin it."

"Some vacation! You're working your butt off in somebody else's house."

"Yeah, and by the way, when are you gonna get off yours and help? Grab a hammer and start knocking some of those nails in, so you and Daniel don't rip your hands to shreds when you go after one of those hunks of wood this winter."

Martin always speaks with authority. I do what I'm told without questioning.

"Anyhow, not even Carolyn can think of anything for me to do in our house, now that the patio and back addition are done."

Mentally, I catalogue the work Martin has done on his own house, work he could well have afforded to hire out, but he prefers to use his own two hands, which are apparently as skilled at carpentry as they are at neurosurgery. His kitchen is a showplace, the kids' bedrooms are replete with built-in furniture and cabinetry; the new bathroom he worked on last summer is as well equipped as a small spa, and the recently completed back addition gives them the equivalent of a vacation home in their own backyard.

"You're the psychoanalyst, Leah."

"Psychologist," I correct him, still sensitive about not having finished my analytic training.

"Whatever. Anyhow, you must realize that the work I do at the hospital and even my teaching and research, well, it's all detail, pressure, and perfection. Intense. Anyhow, my dad's a carpenter, or was until he opened his own business, you know, the store that has been so successful for him. He sells all the stuff that people need for home remodeling. It's made him a rich man, at least compared to what he made as a carpenter. So maybe when I do this kind of work, it solves my Oedipal conflicts or some other myth. You believe in all that junk, don't you?"

He puts down his crowbar and wipes his hands on his pants.

"I mean, if you think about it, it's cheaper for me to come over here and tear up your kitchen than to go out to your office and lie on your couch and pay you fifty bucks an hour. So you're really doing me a favor, not the other way around, see?"

"Whatever you say, Martin, you're the doctor."

"Right, and don't you ever forget it," he adds, launching into one of his favorite routines: the M.D. versus Ph.D argument.

"Yeah, I know," I reply, "I'm not a real doctor to begin with, and besides, I'm only a girl."

Dick's pickup screeches into the driveway, interrupting Martin's and my mock battle. I rush out the back door, curious to see what he has brought. Martin follows a moment later, carrying an armload of wood trim, which he proceeds to stack carefully in the garage.

"I hope you got all those nails, Leah."

"I hope you've had a tetanus shot within the past five years."

"Very funny."

Dick lets down the rear of the pickup grandly, arm outstretched toward its contents.

"*Voilà*, Madame, *votre* two-by-tens."

Two enormous beams of wood confront me.

"What are they for?" I question.

Dick and Martin exchange a knowing look.

"Well, you know how we were talking Thursday and drawing sketches of your kitchen, and I asked you which way the joists ran in your basement, and then we all agreed that this wall we're tearing down isn't a support wall?"

210

Martin is talking, but Dick interrupts, "The two-by-tens will keep the ceiling from falling, Leah, when we knock down the wall."

"I thought it wasn't a support wall . . . "

"Well, we don't think it is but, after all, it is weight bearing, and you don't want a sagging ceiling."

"Are you guys sure you know what you're doing? I mean, is it dangerous?"

"Life is filled with dangers, Leah, you should know that, you've read lots of Victorian novels," quips Dick.

"Will someone give me a straight answer? I mean, is the ceiling going to fall on us?"

"Not once these two-by-tens are in place, my dear," Martin reassures me. "Go ahead, touch them, they're for real. Why, we could support anything with two two-by-tens. Ask any carpenter, isn't that so, Dick?"

"Dick isn't a carpenter. He's a French professor."

"I'm insulted. I only do that for a living, and a meager one it is. Leah, trust me, we could hold up the cathedral at Notre Dame with those two-by-tens. Now, step aside, while we unload. And get me a beer, or have you two drunk them all already?"

"How do you guys do it," I ask, handing Dick the requested beer. "I'm tipsy on the one I just had, and I didn't even finish it."

"We had breakfast. And besides, we're men."

The two-by-tens are unloaded and waiting in the backyard. I wonder why they've taken them off the truck, since they obviously don't plan to use them yet. All the woodwork is down, but the wall is still up. Dick explains that he and Martin will undoubtedly have to trim the two-by-tens and they can do that more easily in the yard than on the truck.

I am sent to hunt up an extension cord heavy enough to handle Dick's power saw. Like Martin, he is a do-it-yourselfer. He and his wife, Janet, live in an old farmhouse in a quasi-rural setting, just at the edge of town. They have transformed it from semisqualor to rustic charm through relentless good-humored effort.

Daniel and I feel hopelessly citified and unskilled alongside most of our friends, all of whom seem to feel as at home in the world of the hands as they do in the world of the mind. On weekends the men carpenter, plumb, and electrify their homes. The women run up curtains, quilt quilts, and put up pickles, jams, and jellies. Daniel and I seem unfit for any kind of craft. He is not lazy; indeed, he spends long arduous hours gardening every summer. And I am content to cook recipes whose lists of ingredients spill onto a second page in the cookbook. But we have no skills in the area of craft or home repair, and we take no pleasure in it. Sometimes I envy Carolyn and Janet their handy husbands. But I suspect Daniel envies Martin and Dick their handy wives, too, when he finds a torn lining in his favorite sport jacket, for example.

When I return with the extension cord, Dick and Martin tell me they want to get started on the wall. They will help me mask off the doorway to the living room and dining room. I tell them I don't mind cleaning up after the dust, but they both laugh, assuring me I'll have plenty of dust to clean up after, even with the masking off of the doorways. We go to work and soon have the kitchen and back hall area fairly well sealed off with some old plastic drop cloths Daniel used when he painted Jacob's bedroom.

When Martin puts on a surgical mask and Dick covers the lower half of his face with an oversized handkerchief, I realize they are serious about the plaster dust. I go to Jacob's room and borrow an old pair of his swimming goggles, to keep the dirty stuff off my contact lenses. Then I return to the kitchen to help the men attack my wall.

The morning moves on and the plaster dust, together with the July heat, envelops us. Conversation ceases, made impossible by Martin's mask, Dick's bandana, and my own reluctance to swallow more of the gritty dust than I have to. The silence is human only; we are surrounded by the thud of the crowbar as it butts the wall, the crunch of the lath as it is ripped away, the crash of the huge chunks of plaster as they hit the floor.

Once in a while I stop my attack on the stubborn wall and stoop over to scoop up another load of debris and deposit it in one of the empty cartons Dick told me to bring from the liquor store. The cartons fill rapidly, marking our progress. Dick helps me carry several out to the curb. Hot and sweaty, the chalky taste of plaster in our throats, we drink can after can of beer, tossing the metal tabs carelessly on the floor.

My giddiness spirals along with my exhaustion. I work along-side the two men, feeling myself to be one of them. The sinews on their arms stand out as they strain against the wall, which yields reluctantly to their onslaught. The dust settles upon us streaking our sweaty faces, fogging my swimmer's goggles, hiding among the dense, blond, curly hairs on Martin's arms and the sparse, silky, black ones on Dick's.

Martin moves to the other side of what remains of the wall and climbs the stepladder, hatchet in hand. He wants to chop loose the remaining lath where it is attached to the ceiling. Most of the plaster is down now, except for odd bits that cling to the old gray wood strips. I squint up at him where he stands above me, but cannot get him into focus. The beer, or the chalk dust on the goggles, lends him a hazy look. His nose and mouth are covered with the surgical mask, but his intensely blue eyes are naked as he looks down at me. gesticulating with the hatchet. I feel faint, frightened. Instinctively I reach for my breast, but it is gone.

My bra is empty on the right side. I move my hand upward until it meets what it is seeking. With all the sweat and physical effort, the silicone substitute has shifted up and to the left. I look down in horror and see my prosthesis perched on my sternum, peeping out of the V of my shirt like some Cyclopean eye. I step backward, confused and ashamed, and trip over a half-filled car-ton of debris. Dick reaches me before Martin can get down the ladder, and tries to help me up, but I am paralyzed, both arms crossed over my chest to hide my shame. I close my eyes, complet-ing my caricature of a dead saint in respose. I do not want to see the hand I know Dick is stretching out to me, I do not want to see Dick, I do not want to see Martin, and most of all, I do not want to see myself.

"Leah, let me help you up," Dick is saying softly, "just take my hand now and . . . "

But Martin interrupts him roughly, "Get up, Leah, open your eyes and get up."

I obey half of his command and open my eyes. I do not, cannot, get up. Dick, I see, is kneeling beside me, about to put a protective arm about my shoulder. Martin stops him, leans over, and repeats his command. I shake my head, still mute, unable to look him in the eye.

Martin changes tactics and tone, "C'mon Leah, we all know it's there, take it out or something, we've got work to do."

"Take it out?" I repeat, disbelievingly.

"Well, for Christ's sake, Leah, it's too hot and you're all sweaty. There's plaster dust everywhere. See for yourself. The stuff is gritty. It'll ruin that thing. And you probably paid a fortune for it."

I run a tentative finger over the rubber nipple poking out just above the button of my shirt. It comes away gritty. Martin is right, per usual. I look up at him and then over at Dick. They are both uneasy, uncertain of where to go from here. Suddenly I begin to laugh. They look at one another, perhaps they think I am hysterical.

"No, no," I laugh, shaking my head, and offering them each a hand so they can help me up. "I'm OK, really I am. It's just that it's funny. It is funny, isn't it?" I indicate my chest with my chin. "I mean, it's sad, but it's funny, too. After all, who ever saw a lady with a tit in the middle before. Please guys, tell me you think it's funny."

"Leah, stop being such a good sport," Martin admonishes. "Go upstairs and wash that thing off before the plaster ruins it, and then come back down here and help us finish this job."

Dick follows me shyly part way down the hall as I head for the stairway. He puts a hand on my shoulder, "Are you OK, really?"

"Yes, Dick," I answer him honestly, "I really am OK."

The three of us sit companionably together at the redwood picnic table, grateful for the shade of the pin oak tree. The sandwiches I have brought from Kroger's deli taste delicious, and I think of Daniel who always remarks that "hunger is good sauce." It is nearly two o'clock and there is no breeze, but we have washed off some of the gritty dust and the relaxation of our picnic

214

has made us feel cooler. I wear no bra now beneath my work shirt and feel quite comfortable. Not only am I cooler without the heat of the rubber and elastic against my skin, but I feel at ease sitting across the table from Martin and Dick. They do not stare at me. They pay no more nor less attention to me than they ever have.

I have no difficulty understanding their minimal reaction. They are both intelligent men, relatively sophisticated, reasonably empathic. What confuses me is my own reaction, which, after the initial shock, is as prosaic, as matter of fact, as theirs. No big deal. Not any more serious than dropping your pocketbook in front of a male friend and having a tampon fall out in his view. So what?

I munch on my potato chips and take a swallow of iced tea. I have had enough beer to last me all day. Martin has been talking about his vacation plans, which include a trip to Cape Cod. Dick is into his "poor French teacher routine," teasing Martin and me about our lucrative professions.

"Yes, Martin will be on the Cape with his family, enjoying the ocean breezes, and, Leah, you'll be traipsing off to Spain for the rest of the summer, while Janet and I and the children will be here in hot-old, humid-old Kentucky, chopping morning glories out of the vegetable garden."

The lunchtime banter continues at our backyard picnic. I sit comfortably between Dick and Martin, joking and teasing, my left breast perspiring damply where it rests against my chest wall. I smile to myself as I finish my sandwich and tea. I am one of the boys at last.

13

SUNDAY——

IT is nearly 9:00 A.M. when I walk down the stairs and am struck by the odd quality of light coming from the kitchen. Even before I turn down the hallway, I can see the morning filter onto the wooden floorboards. I am puzzled by the difference, until I raise my eyes to the space where only yesterday there was a wall: open, empty, clear. I am shocked by the difference. The room looks twice its former size. My shock shifts to pleasure and then pride as I realize with a definite thrill that I have done this thing. Martin's and Dick's part shrinks as I consider my own. It is not that I have forgotten their arduous attack on the cement hard plaster and staunch wooden laths, nor do I minimize the importance of their labors, their busy knowing and doing, for without them surely it couldn't or wouldn't have been done.

But I am struck by the magnitude of my own daring and audacity. I did it! I. Me. Leah Bronstein Buchanan.

I hug myself, giddy from the view. I have broken out of my

claustrophobic kitchen into the spacious light of this whole new room. Above me the new ceiling beams stick out stark, raw, and bare. Naked wood—vertical, dark with age—stands guard in the corner, bits of crumbling plaster clinging to it. And the greenish linoleum, with random splotches of red and black and white, like a poor imitation of some Jackson Pollack canvas, that linoleum which I have alway hated, is now uniformly chalk gray, except for the few footprints I have tracked in it. Apparently, my busy mopping yesterday was in vain.

I step into the dining room, ducking through the plastic drop cloth that droops above me, having lost one of its masking tape moorings, then stop myself short to keep from tracking more plaster in with me. Reaching out, I run my finger over the dining room table and find that it, too, despite the drop cloths, sports a coat of gritty gray.

I retreat to the kitchen. The persistence of the plaster is nearly unbelievable. Martin was right for laughing at my shrugging off the notion of sealing off the other rooms. I leave my slippers at the bottom of the staircase, hoping not to track the dust upstairs, then trot up barefoot, two steps at a time. My mood, despite the plaster dust, is more than cheerful. It is expansive.

I start to dress, but cannot find my prosthesis. It is not in its usual place in my lingerie drawer. I must have laid it down on the dresser when I got ready for bed. But no, not there either. Leah, you're getting forgetful in your old age, I tell myself, then retrace my steps of the night before into the bathroom. Not on the window ledge, not on top of the toilet. Damn. I took a bath before bed last night. Maybe, with the twins and Daniel gone, I've grown careless, blasé, and have left it on the edge of the bathtub. My eyes scan the white porcelain, but find nothing other than one of my own red hairs, which I fastidiously remove and throw in the wastebasket. I am about to leave the room when I spot it staring blindly down at me from its perch among the shampoo bottles and cream rinses that crowd the acrylic shelf hanging from the shower head: my nemesis, the Blob. I pick it up gingerly, with the same minor revulsion I felt when I picked up the hair.

A thing which by natural right is a part of our bodies becomes an object of disgust once it leaves them; a hair, a scab, a drop of blood, a dribble of mucus, nail parings, dead skin, urine, feces, debris from our noses. We look at them sometimes with detached curiosity, but other times with frank loathing, with shame, before we wrap them in tissue, or mop them up, or hurriedly flush them away.

I heft the surprising weight of my breast's false twin (8 ounces, at $12/ounce) in my left hand, then poke it with the forefinger of my right. The silicone gel does its job, receding slowly to my touch. The pinkish, fleshlike material that surrounds it dimples inward, almost but not quite, like skin. Without really thinking about it, I turn on the water in the sink, test it on my wrist to achieve the tepid temperature I associate with baths for the newborn, then wash it beneath the slowly flowing water. When it seems clean enough to suit me, I wrap it in a towel, then gently dab it dry. As I do so, I wonder just exactly what is going on in my head.

I wind through the labryinth of my own associations to discover that I have characterized the prosthesis first as a discarded part or product of my body and then as a baby. I have alternated betweeen love and loathing for this odd facsimile of the organ that makes me a mammal. All of the first things I thought of are dead, useless, to be discarded. But a baby, a baby is something different altogether: it is the one thing that comes out of, separates itself from a human body, and is then treasured and adored.

I lay the terry-wrapped package down on the toilet seat and begin to pace the hallway outside the bathroom door. There is something more here that needs to be thought out, but for the moment I am blocked.

On the wall of the hallway hang snapshots, certificates, diplomas, awards, school pictures. A cheerful collage of black and white and color. Hannah's face zooms out at me, strawberry-blonde tendrils escaping the braids she loves to wear, curling forward onto her freckled cheeks. Jacob's eyes stare at me solemnly from his second-grade picture, in striking contrast to his partly toothless smile. I pass a newspaper photo of Daniel, handsome and erudite, seated behind his massive desk, wearing the mustache he sported for a year or two after our sojourn in Argentina.

I make my turn at the end of the hallway and walk back toward the bathroom, slowing my pace as I try to recover the thought that almost popped into consciousnesss a moment ago. Sunlight glinting off the glass of one of the picture frames draws me to it, and there, side by side, I see the footprints of the twins on the pink and blue certificates that the hospital gave us, with all the birth information: Jacob Edward Buchanan, 6 lbs. 6 ozs., 20 inches long; Hannah Elisabeth Buchanan, 6 lbs. 3 ozs., 20.5 inches long. I remember the usually laconic obstetrician, smiling as the delivery room nurses wrapped each of the babies tenderly, then handed one neat package to Daniel and the other to me, the best presents ever. I remember the tune that floated through my mind as Daniel and I stared teary-eyed and speechless into each other's faces: *"...we will raise a family, a girl for you, a boy for me, oh can't you see how happy we will be . . ."*

I come to a dead stop, just short of the bathroom door, as the thought I have repressed finally surfaces, breaking water like a trout rising to a fly. I catch the silvery glimmer of my own memory and try patiently to reel it in. Steadily, slowly, with a fisherman's poise and skill, I draw it to me, knowing the joy and excitement of the sport. But as I land it, I feel the same sadness I sometimes feel when fishing with Daniel, for the trout lies flopping and gasping on the bank, no longer shimmery and graceful, until Daniel mercifully kills it and slips it, still at last, into the creel at his hip.

My recollection stares at me, glassy-eyed like a dead fish, but I have landed it; it is my own: the dead baby, the less than six-month child, less than two pounds (did they ever tell me how many inches?), the little girl who never breathed, ejected prematurely from my body, to be discarded like a scab or a fallen hair. She was never named, never buried. But we mourned her nonetheless.

We even mourned the bloody fetus that preceded her the year before, the product of my first pregnancy, which lasted only three months. That, too, must have gone into some hospital garbage can.

I close my eyes and shudder, then force myself to open them and think. Why do my miscarriages come to mind today? I check the date mentally: it is summer now, and both of those incidents took place in winter. No anniversary syndrome here. My period? Am I about to get my period? Am I mourning the loss of yet another child, one not yet conceived, is that what has made me think of the ones I lost? No, I finished my period a few days before I went to Cincinnati, I remember. What then, I wonder, moving forward, then stopping again, this time in the doorway to the bathroom. My eyes fall on the towel-wrapped package on the toilet seat, and then I know.

It is my breast, the one I lost, that I am mourning, for it too, like the nameless daughter and the embryo I aborted, had been part of my body until it was unceremoniously lopped off and ultimately tossed into the trash—once pathology was through with it.

I lift the prosthesis and unwrap it, then slip it carefully into the right cup of my brassiere. Adjusting its position, I tighten my strap and gaze critically at myself in the mirror. Because my surgery had been a simple mastectomy, because the tumor had been encapsulated, there is no damage to my upper arm. With my bra on and the prosthesis in place, I look quite intact. Now all that remains is to learn to feel that way.

I go into the bedroom to finish dressing. As I do so, I remember my misery after I lost each precious pregnancy. I remember especially the sadness of the second time, for that baby had been so real to us, with its lively kicking inside me. Daniel and I had turned to each other in the night, hating the new flatness of my formerly rounded belly. We clung to each other and even wept, lonely for the thumping of the third party who had kept us so happy and hopeful on previous nights. So we had mourned together, healed together, loved together, and out of that love we created together the twins, who all but erased the agony of those other times, miraculously transmuting our melancholy into pure unadulterated joy.

After the mastectomy, it was different. Daniel tried to comfort me in the night, but I held my body aloof from him. He was afraid to embrace me, and I was afraid of his embraces. My body ached at first, but then it healed, and still we slept on opposite sides of the bed. The subterfuge of my physical discomfort became a barrier between us. We held hands from time to time, exchanged occa-

221

sional good night kisses, chaste and passionless, but we did not share our sadness. The loss had been mine and mine alone, or so I reasoned, and I chose to bear it alone.

The tears I wept were wept silently, secretly, with my back turned to Daniel in the big bed, as I explained to him that I could not sleep on my right side. Sometimes he snuggled up to me from behind, but he never knew where to rest his protective right arm without hurting me. And I never told him. I grieved alone and resented him for not grieving with me. In the past, our tragedies had been shared and had brought us closer together. But this one I guarded jealously, and it drove us apart. In my selfishness, I paid no heed to his fears or his regrets. And Daniel, being the man he is, never voiced them.

Daniel. I have shut him out, ignored him, erected a wall between us, just as I so often accuse him of doing to me. And he has neither criticized, nor complained, nor cajoled, as I do when the situation is reversed. He tolerates spaces, distances, better than I do, maybe even requires them. He is not threatened by our separation, because he is certain of our love. He is older than I am, but even so, time is on his side. He knows the meaning of patience. He can wait.

I rush to the nightstand and the telephone, thinking for a moment I will call him and in that way close the gap between us. But I stop myself, realizing the futility of the gesture. He cannot respond to me with gushing words of reassurance. That is not his way. He can only be there for me in the sense that he always has been, always will be. His vow to me was spoken seriously. He waited forty-five years before he trusted himself to make it to any woman, and then he made it to me: *"for richer or for poorer, for better or for worse, in sickness and in health, till death us do part."* Amen. He meant it then. He still means it. All I have to do is remember that.

I walk down the stairs again and inspect the kitchen. I am restless and excited. Old habits die hard: I want to share my excitement with someone. I hear myself framing my breathless sentence of surprise, "Guess what? I knocked down our kitchen wall! Yes, really. And the room looks twice the size . . . " But there is no one to tell my tale to, for Daniel is gone and, despite the good will of all the women I met with the other night, I haven't the heart to talk to any of them. In the end, knowing even as I do it that it is sure to be a mistake, I choose to share my triumph with my mother.

She answers on the second ring, her voice clear and strong. Is it really possible she is past seventy years old!

"Leah! Well, this must be mental telepathy. I was just thinking about you."

(She always says this. Is it possible that she is always thinking about me, is she really psychic, or is this just her way of one-upping me?)

"How are you, Mother?" I ask her.

"I'm fine, darling, just fine. In fact, I'm getting ready to make another little trip. I was going to phone you later to tell you all about it. Fern and I are going to Chautauqua. Her son, Arnold, is *very* successful, you know, and he has a summer place there and he's letting us use it this coming week. Isn't that lovely?" she goes on.

"Yes, Mother, just lovely. But, tell me, how are you feeling? How is your leg?"

"Oh, I can't complain, Leah, I'm doing well. Dr. Wright says he can't get over how well I'm doing. He thinks I must have lied to him about my age. 'Frances,' he tells me, 'there's no way you could be as old as you say. Your bones are very, very young.' Of course, I don't have the mobility I once had, Leah, my dancing days are over, but, then, I have no one to dance with anyway since your father's gone these thirty years."

And she is off.

I wince as she dredges up my poor, dead father, as if his demise were news. She wears her widowhood like a precious jewel or like a badge of courage that adds distinction to her life. Sometimes it seems to me that my father's death is the central event of her personal history, the moment toward which everything that preceded it led and from which everything that followed took meaning. During my therapy I hated her for her constant reminders of it. All my shining moments of joy and triumph were tarnished by

223

her pointed editorials about how sad it was that Daddy couldn't have lived to see this day, or how hard it was for her to have such *nachas*, such pleasure, without him beside her. I watched her teary eyes at my *bat mitzvah*, confirmation, high school graduation, and college commencement and felt guilty and bewildered that my accomplishments could bring her so much pain. Daniel and I got married quietly, in a judge's chambers, and I received my doctoral diploma by mail. I could no longer bear to see my happinesses bring her so much grief, or, perhaps I felt angry and resentful and simply would not share them with her anymore.

How foolish of me to have phoned her about the wall! If I were to tell her about it, she might even find a way to drag Daddy into the remodeling of my kitchen: "If only Daddy could have lived to see you wield a crowbar, Leah," I hear her lament. But then I feel disloyal, as I always do when I think such thoughts, and I undo them by reminding myself that, although she is insufferable about my father, she is not a complainer, not about hard work, not about physical health. No. She is a good sport, a good soldier, who can be counted on to carry on, no matter what.

I remember when she had the accident. It wasn't too long before my surgery. My brother Al called me and told me about it. She had been crossing a parking lot, on her way to meet Fern for lunch, as a matter of fact.

I can picture her in one of her smart little afternoon dresses and the too-high heels she always wore to compensate for her short stature. She has—had—a bouncy gait and a habit of pursing her lips in a sort of silent whistle when she is on her way somewhere and is alone. She always does that, for example, when getting off airplanes. It makes her look so casual, so young, so self-assured. But I know she really does it because she feels just a little afraid. Isn't she, after all, my mother? In her heart of hearts, isn't this assertive, domineering woman just a little shy—like I am?

There she is, whistling her way across the parking lot, headed for the shopping mall and the restaurant where she will meet Fern, when out of nowhere comes this big blue Buick, doing fifty. It speeds past her and knocks her down. Her leg is broken in three places. I hear the crunch of bone, her subdued and startled cry of pain. I picture her lying there on that sunny, Saturday afternoon, trying to control herself, trying to figure out the ladylike way of handling this bewildering situation.

By the time Al reached me in Kentucky, she was already in surgery, for her leg was so torn up that it had to be completely rearranged. I got the first plane I could, but even so, didn't arrive until the next day. Al was at the hospital with Mom, pacing and smoking nervously. As I touched him by way of greeting, I noted that all the color was gone from his face. He looked worse than she did, there, where she lay, talking cheerfully and trying to keep Al's spirits up. The cast and the machinery that kept her in traction overwhelmed her, making her look terribly small and vulnerable.

"This is my elder daughter, Leah," my mother told the private-duty nurse. "Dr. Buchanan, actually," she went on to confide, "my daughter the doctor."

Her pride embarrassed me, as always. No one thinks of a Ph.D. as a doctor. Every time she goes on that way I can only think she is disappointed that I have taken the wrong degree, that I wasn't a real doctor after all, just as she is disappointed in my choice of husband (Daniel should have been a Jewish cardiologist), and in the modest life we lead (we should have a summer place in Chautauqua and a fifteen-room house, like Fern's Arnold).

I went to her where she lay, started to sit down on the edge of the bed, thought better of it, then just leaned over and kissed her. Her too-brave smile vanished, and I felt the tears on her cheeks and her strong arms wrapped around my neck like those of a frightened child.

"I'm glad you came, Leah," she admitted.

"I'm glad, too, Momma," I murmured, thinking of all the times that she had come for me.

Al escaped to the coffee shop. Hospitals have always made him uneasy. And then it was just Mother and me, for the nurse had made herself busy elsewhere.

I stood there wondering how it could possibly be that I was the strong one standing up and Mother was in the bed. Nearly two decades of fevers, upset stomachs, skinned knees passed before my eyes, and it was always she who was turning my pillow to the cooler side, carrying a tray of hot tea and dry rye toast, blowing on the skin as she applied the Merthiolate. The order of my universe had been upset. It is not right for the child to minister to the parent.

My mother is still talking on the other end of the telephone. "But then you're a lot like me, Leah," she goes on. "You heal so quickly, so beautifully. That's why you've made such a remarkable recovery from your surgery, dear. And thank God for that."

"Yes, Mother," I echo, "thank God for that."

"I thought you were an atheist, Leah," she chides me.

"Well, yes, it was just an expression."

"Anyway, dear, I have to run. Fern and I are going out for brunch today. She'll be by for me any minute. How are Daniel and the children? I had the most darling postcards from them from their camp. When are you coming to Cleveland, dear? Why don't you come up here and spend a few days with me while they are all away?"

"You won't be there, Mom," I point out to her.

"That's true, true. Well, I'll be coming to see you after you and Daniel and the children come back from Spain. I wouldn't want to miss the children, dear."

I close my eyes and hold on to the phone for a second wishing she would drop everything, her trip to Chautauqua, her brunch with Fern, and just come to visit me, just me.

"Or maybe I'll meet you in New York when you fly back. That way I could see Samuel, too. And we could take in that new show everyone's talking about."

Her energy is boundless, or so it seems to me. And even though she now wears support stockings and those sensible shoes she hates so much, and even though she walks with a limp, for one leg is now somewhat shorter than the other, and even though she is past seventy and sometimes repeats herself, she is still the plucky little lady who rescued me more cheerfully, more efficiently, and more often than I could ever do for her.

"Have fun, Momma," I remind her, "and give my love to Al and his family."

"Thank you dear, I will, and I'll call you when I get back. And you kiss those gorgeous children for me, when you see them, that is. But I'll talk to you before that. Leah, you're taking care of yourself, aren't you?"

"Yes, Mother, I'm taking care of myself."

We both know what that means.

"Goodbye, dear."

"Goodbye."

And she is gone.

I hang up the phone, then lay it carefully on the floor, for there is no wall for it to hang on, as it used to. I never even mentioned the kitchen to Mother, I realize, as I survey the wide-open mess around me. I wonder what she would have said. I wonder what Daniel and the children will say! I pull down the remaining plastic drop cloths and wad them up to stuff them in the trash. The sun is shining through the kitchen window and all the way into what used to be the hall. I picture the breakfast bar, the new cabinets, a dishwasher next to the kitchen sink. I pull the butcher-block table back to the kitchen from the corner of the dining room where Dick helped me move it yesterday, and I place it where the wall used to be, then center the Christmas cactus on it. Even the leaves of the plant are gray with plaster dust. I'll have to spray them clean later.

I slide each of the four chairs around the table, then step back and look at what I have done. It is my kitchen. Spacious, as I have always wanted it. I stand gazing at the unfinished edges of the wall, the crumbling plaster and broken lath, the dust everywhere. I decide I like it. I like it just as it is.

14

MONDAY——

I HAVEN'T been able to keep process notes all summer. I know I
need to, but for some reason I resist
the idea. After each patient leaves, I find some excuse not to: I have
to go to the bathroom, I have to make a phone call, I have to start
the next hour. I know what Saul would say, but even his heavy-
browed stare has no impact on my resistance. I am impatient with
my patients. My borderlines bore me, my narcissistic character
disorders put me to sleep; even Mrs. Matthews turns me off. I
yawn. I stare out the window. I fidget in my chair. I develop that
miserable sciatica that starts mid-morning as a gnawing discomfort at the base of my spine, works its way by noon down my leg
like a hot electric wire, and finally, by the end of the day, edges up
my back to my neck and shoulder, at last shooting down my arm
so that my entire right side is in agony.

Come on, come on, come on, I think, as they stumble through
their repetitious complaints, or sit sighing at me. Please, deliver

me at least a sexy dream, a little transference anger, a neat piece of acting-out behavior.

With each passing hour, the temptation to seize control grows. I will wrench whatever resistances they have from them. I will show them how to live. I will tell them what to do. And why not, really? Surely, I could do a better job of it than they do. And wouldn't they be grateful if I told them when to marry, when to divorce, when to take a job, when to quit, whom to love, whom to hate, what to say to their mothers, fathers, husbands, wives, children, lovers, lawyers, and creditors? Isn't that what they ask me to do every day of their lives? And, wouldn't it be easier, ultimately, for me to carry the weight of their worries on my back forever, than to try to teach them—ever so slowly, painfully, and patiently—to bear their own burdens, or harder still, to lay those burdens down?

Sometimes, at night, as I lie in bed, trying to fall asleep, I am one of them again. And I hear my voice crying, "Hold me, hold me, never let me go. Please, please, take care of me, just take care of me."

My mailbox is full of surprises. A postcard from Daniel! And, right behind it, a letter from Jacob. This is better than two dozen roses. I slide the postcard with its technicolor picture of the famous Seville cathedral behind the rest of the mail, not wanting to see its message yet, then I quickly tear open Jacob's envelope and read: "Dear Mom, Rick said I couldn't go swimming if I didn't write to you today. I was going to write you anyway. It just isn't fair to have to write two *different* letters to your parents! Hi. I'm having a terrific time. I've already passed my intermediate swimmers. When I get the patch, will you sew it on my suit? I want it for our trip to Spain. I'm learning some diving. Wait until you see me. Do you think there are any swimming pools in Seville? Or can we go to the ocean? Do they have diving boards at the beach? I'm also making something really neat in woodcraft, but I can't tell you because it's a surprise. Hannah will definitely turn into a horse before the end of camp. Don't be surprised if when you pick us up all she can do is whinny. (It could be a welcome change from all her usual yakking.) Mom, please bring my allowance money with you when you come. I want to buy some stamps and other stuff in Spain. Daddy sent me a terrific postcard with some great Spanish stamps on it. I also want my wristwatch. Don't forget. OK? Hope you are fine. How are the flowers we planted? Well, got to go. We are going on a hike this afternoon. I'm taking the compass you and Daddy got me so don't worry I won't get lost. See you soon. Love, Jacob. P.S. Don't forget to water the flowers."

He sounds fine. It will be an easy letter to answer. After Hannah's worries about breasts, I was afraid Jacob might write to say half the boys in his bunk were having wet dreams. But I guess he would address that type of concern to Daniel. I reread the letter, then reread it again. No doubt about it, he is, like his sister, cheerful and happy. They have gone off to overnight camp and have not fallen apart. They do not appear to be suffering from the horrible separation problems that plagued me both at camp and at college. The sins of the fathers have not been visited upon the children. Daniel and I must be doing something right.

Now, now I can turn to Daniel. I turn over the postcard and I read, *"Te espero. D."* At first I am disappointed. Only two short words, in a language not his own, and an abbreviated signature! I wanted more. I wanted a long letter filled with love and support and apology. But this is what I got. I translate carefully. *Te espero.* I wait for you. But *te espero* could mean something else, something more. I expect you. I wish for you. I hope for you. It means all of those things. I turn the phrase over in my mind, say it gently to myself, listen to the sibilant *s*, the rolling *r*. The intimate *te* reaches out to me like a caress. He waits for me in Spain. He misses me. He longs for me. I try another translation: I await you. D. Yes. This is Daniel. Brief, precise, and to the point. He neither minces nor wastes words. He is embarrassed by emotion. He reaches into a foreign language to tell me what he cannot admit in his own words, except under duress. In the intimacy of our first naked embrace, he whispered, *"Te amo y te quiero,"* and now, sixteen years later, he reminds me, *"te espero."*

I close my eyes and press the stiffened paper to my chest, as if the warmth of Daniel's message might thus be transfused directly into my heart. He awaits me in Spain. And the children await me in North Carolina. Suddenly, it seems perfectly clear to me that what I need is to be with them, with him and with the children. Only their presence, I am now convinced, will return to me the equanimity and peace of mind I need, just as I was convinced a month ago that only their absence would allow me to think clearly. Why, I wonder, am I seated here in my living room in Kentucky, rather than there in Seville with Daniel? Why didn't I go with him to Spain? Why didn't we all go together?

I love to travel with Daniel. He, who seldom seems at ease in his own environment, is completely at home on foreign ground. With a map in one hand and a guide book in the other, he leads me and the twins in and out of unfamiliar places, smiling over his discoveries. He is never too tired or in too much of a hurry to take an unmarked road. His sense of adventure is endless, embracing out-of-the-way restaurants, as well as famous museums and cathedrals. He urges on us octopus, mango, goat meat, cactus fruit—a taste of this, a sip of that—and all of it delicious. He shops in open-air markets buying things he cannot name by pointing to them and nodding. He, who cannot wait three minutes in line in an air-conditioned supermarket, has endless patience for the dickerings of toothless peasants, who speak to him in accents he can barely approximate.

I see him as he was in Mexico when we were last there together. His English cap pulled down over his face to shield his gray blue eyes from the afternoon sun, he takes each of the children by one hand and leads them toward the Museum of Anthropology. I am hanging back with the camera. He poses with them in front of the gigantic statue of Tlaloc the rain god. He lifts first Hannah, then Jacob onto the ledge before the monstrous idol, then turns to face my camera. I wave them into position, a little farther left, yes, that's good.

"Cheeeese," the twins are saying, and Daniel grimaces, "*Queso.*"

I snap the photo, and they are frozen in time, Hannah tugging at her sundress, Daniel standing tall with his slightly rounded scholar's shoulders, Jacob twisting his head to glimpse the statue of Tlaloc, who gazes obliviously out over the Paseo de la Reforma.

I am in Mexico again. The sun is shining. The smog is smothering. We are living in a too-expensive, furnished apartment: everything from candelabra to toilet bowl belongs to the *señora*. I often wonder what awful images are conjured up in Jacob's and Hannah's minds as I caution them daily, "Don't spill your milk on the *señora's* rug" or "The *señora* won't like it if you climb on the bookshelves."

They live with the *señora's* presence as do I (I do not like making love in the *señora's* bed).

Daniel is at his archive. The children are in school. I shop, go to museums, clean the house perfunctorily. Mexican women, above a certain class, are very chic. I feel drab and matronly. My faded denims are conspicuous when I pick the children up at school. They would be fashionable only if I wore them with a pure silk blouse, 18-karat gold jewelry, and Gucci boots.

I have come to feel naked without fingernail polish and take to wearing it, but it is almost always chipped. Mexican women do not spend their evenings attacking old aluminum pots with rusty Brillo pads. They have maids. Daniel thinks I should have a maid, but even in pesos we cannot really afford it. Besides, I do not like their dark, resentful shuffling around the small apartment. Even when they are cheerful I feel ill at ease. Grampa Bronstein marched for Eugene Debbs. How can I keep a *muchacha*, a *sirviente*?

I become increasingly depressed; my identity has been peeled away. I have no career here and cannot even play the gracious hostess-wife, for we know few people we can entertain.

I take the children to the park, searching for a friendly face to chat with. I am met by the curious stares of maids, pushing their charges on the swings. Mexican mothers above a certain class do not take their own children to the park.

We join a sports center with a swimming pool. I love to swim. The women are not there, only maids with the children. Where do the mothers go? One fine day at the pool I see a woman about

233

my age with her children and a maid. She is sunning herself in a string bikini that reveals long golden limbs, uplifted breasts, and a perfectly flat abdomen. No sign of a varicose vein or a stretch mark. How did she bear those children? I look suspiciously at her forehead, wondering if they sprang from her brain like Pallas Athene from Zeus. But there are no telltale marks there, not even the hint of a wrinkle. Her skin glistens in the sun as she anoints her body with oil.

The maid frolics in the water with the children, then asks whether the *señora* would like to take a dip.

"Ayyy, no," comes the reply, for the *señora* has just gotten her hair done. But, noblesse oblige, she reconsiders, and, tentatively touching her hair, she delicately lowers herself into the water. She reaches for the younger child, holds him out at arm's length, murmuring *"ayyy mi corazon,"* and makes kissing motions with her mouth. The toddler squeals in delight, but before an enthusiastic foot or hand can splash water on Mama's hairdo, she has returned the baby to the maid.

Mother gives the older child a parting pinch as she emerges from the pool, plucks at her bikini where it barely covers her perfectly rounded bottom, and allows the water to slide easily off her oiled limbs. She pats herself with an oversized Turkish towel, gazes into her compact mirror and reapplies her lipstick, then sinks exhausted into her morning nap.

I watch her for most of the morning and note that her children clearly adore her. They respond to her few words and occasional caresses with the ecstatic wriggling of small puppies. Jacob and Hannah, on the other hand, complain to me if I try to read for five minutes, and they clamor rudely for their water toys.

I tell Daniel the weather is growing too cold for gringos to swim outdoors, and we let the membership lapse the following month.

Weeks pass. I decide to have my hair done. I go to a fancy salon in Polanco near the *Puerto de Liverpool* department store. I dress for the occasion and apply an extra layer of lipstick, my darkest shade of nail polish.

The maestro looks at my thin hair and long face. He seems discouraged, then inspired. With five snips he rearranges the geometry of my head, moving the part, changing the planes where hairline meets face. He motions to his assistant, hisses out some instructions in his sibilant Mexican Spanish, and leaves. Waving the blow dryer above my head like a magic wand, the assistant transforms me from a wet bedraggled creature into a bleached-out carbon copy of her Mexican sisters. I look at myself and confess that I am pleased.

I hurry to the school to pick up the children and am met by Jacob's awed appraisal, "Mommy, you look so beautiful, you look like one of the mothers of the *chiquitas.*"

There is no higher praise. Even Daniel, who prefers my hair quite long, compliments me. But within days my glamour fades, as the flipped-up curls flop down, and the dark polish suffers defeat amid the pots and pans.

I remind myself that I have a Ph.D., that I am an intellectual, that I have more important things to do than cultivate my face and my body like a gourmet's vegetable garden. I tell myself that I should pity these women for their empty lives, their superficial relationships with their children. Daniel agrees with me emphatically, but I notice that when we are invited to a Mexican home for dinner he stares at the lovely hostess in appreciation as she rings for the servant to clear away the last traces of a luscious mango mousse. And he nods sympathetically as she explains in exasperation that when the cook first arrived it had taken hours to teach her how to chop an onion.

I sigh over my memories. Maybe this summer's arrangement is better after all.

Daniel belongs in Spain. His research has drawn him ever backward into the past, where every good historian longs to go, until he has exhausted the archival material of the New World, history there has blurred into archaeology, and he has been drawn inevitably to the Old.

The twins belong at summer camp, where they can swim and ride and joke with children their own age.

And I belong where I can work. At least for now. Money issues have intervened. There was no grant for Daniel this time. The fact is, we need the income I can generate at my office. So I am here and they are there and that is that. It is, after all, only for a short time. A month is not a year. It is a hiatus, not a separation.

Carefully, I fold Jacob's letter and put it back into its envelope. I slip Daniel's postcard in behind it. I must remember to save the stamp for Jacob. I carry both of my treasures with me out of the living room. As I go, I catch a glimpse of Harrington's roses out of the corner of my eye. They are overblown, half of the petals scattered on the table below them. I carry the vase full of fading flowers out to the kitchen and dump them unceremoniously into the trash.

15

MONDAY NIGHT, TUESDAY MORNING——

IAWAKE startled to a room flood-
ed with moonlight. The transition
from sleeping to waking is so
immediate that I am at once alert and disoriented. Where am I?
What time it it? I reach for my glasses on the bedside table, then
squint at the clock. 2:00 A.M. It seems it is always 2:00 A.M.

The night is beautiful, for the moon is nearly full, and my new
habit of sleeping with the curtains open allows me to watch it rise,
crest, and set, depending upon the extent of my insomnia.
Although my windows are wide open, I hear nothing. Even the
summer insects are silent. Do they sleep, dream, or stare into the
night, worrying about the winter months ahead? My glasses do
not help me to see clearly. I remove them and settle back, this time
on Daniel's side of the bed, my head resting on Daniel's cool
pillow. My right hand seeks each of my ear lobes in turn, questing
for and finding the tiny emerald earrings that Daniel bought for
me in Colombia so many years ago. It pleases me to find that they
are there, in my body, even while Daniel is not.

My right hand leaves my left ear lobe and travels slowly down my neck, fingers caressing my collarbone, until it finds my left breast. The nipple is erect and I smile at my body's willing wistfulness. I feel the smile fade as I begin the odd ritual that has become a focus in my life: Left arm crooked at the elbow beside my head, right hand on my one remaining breast, with practiced fingers I press and palpate in a parody of love, seeking, seeking—and praying not to find—the tiny lump that might foretell my doom. I feel the sweat beads forming on my upper lip as I retrace my circular path, looking for a second time, and then a third. My nipple is soft again, the excitement of sex replaced by the fear of death, but I have found nothing to alarm me.

A shudder passes through my body as I think of my narrow escape. Once again I have been spared. My examination has revealed just what the doctor's revealed a month ago: nothing. The only test I ever wanted a zero on.

I lie shivering in the summer moonlight, frightened beyond imagining. All my previous narcissistic worries seem like garbage. The lost breast is small potatoes. I have had cancer, damn it. I might die. I hug my damaged body and I weep. With perfect clarity, it comes to me: I don't want to die. I hear the words and realize I have said them aloud. So I repeat them into the night, the darkness, stating them, perhaps to the God I lost faith in, even before I was analyzed. I don't want to die, I state calmly, to no one in particular—to myself.

I look out at the moon again. Without my glasses it looks like a large fuzzy globe, suffusing the world with soft, milky light. I see Grampa Bronstein smiling down at me from the moon's muzzy face. He is offering me something. Ach, Leah, he seems to say, life is not so bad, have a lemon drop. Or did he say death is not so bad? I am not certain. I lie in bed and listen. Daniel's clock strikes five bells, 2:30. I am still awake. Still alive.

I sleep fitfully, sleep and wake, then sleep and wake again. The moon moves past my window slowly as I hover between waking and sleeping. I am afraid to abandon myself, to let myself lose consciousness. I watch the moon jealously as if keeping it in view may somehow save me, but I do not know from what.

In my dream I see Daniel and the children, but they are very far away. I must get to them. With all my energy I try to move one foot in front of the other, but my progress is infinitesimal. My limbs are leaden, and the air is like molasses.

I abandon my efforts to run or walk, and I am swimming. The air is not molasses, but water, cool and clear. The distances are vast, but I am powerful as I lift my head up to catch glimpses of my darlings waving me cheerfully forward. My usual breast stroke does not move me fast enough, so I trade it for a trudgen crawl, pulling the water toward me, first with one greedy cupped hand and then another. My legs thrust out in a rhythmic scissors kick, propelling me onward, and my shoulders ache with the effort.

I turn my face up quickly, gulping air, too much in a hurry now to allow myself the luxury of looking across the water. But I know that they are there, waiting for me, and that I will see them, touch them, hold them soon. All that matters is that I continue swimming, breathing, diminishing the distance that separates me from them.

When I awake I am still swimming, lying in an uncharacteristic prone position, head turned to the left, right arm stretched forward over Daniel's pillow, left arm flung out behind me, mouth wide open. The moon and Grampa Bronstein are gone. I cannot see the clock but I know the time by the birds' singing outside the window. Five-thirty, I make it, by bird time. I turn over and then, despite myself, I fall asleep again.

I am in my office, and it is crowded with patients. Some are crying. Others point at me accusingly. Hands reach out to clutch me. I step backward, only now I am in the sanctuary of some familiar synagogue. I am at the pulpit, cradling the Torah in my arms. My patients are the congregants, murmuring in prayer, or they are Nazis, or an unruly mob. I open my mouth to lead them in song. I sing. They continue their muttering and seem to be moving toward me. They press forward, unmoved by my chanting.

I cannot let them reach me, for they might, in their madness, defile the Holy Law. I continue singing, but they do not seem to hear me. I implore. I admonish. I hold my words and the Law forth to them like an amulet or a charm, or like a crucifix in the face of a vampire. But the Law means little to them, for they have hidden hungers that must be satisfied. I step back, clutching the Torah more tightly in my arms. The angry, frightened mob continues to advance upon me. I look around me wildly for some sign.

I see Daniel. He is holding out his arms, as if to take the twin scrolls from me. I hesitate for a moment, for he is making the sign of the cross before his face, ducking his head and kissing his thumb, like a devout Puerto Rican baseball player. I thrust the Torah into Daniel's arms, and Grampa Bronstein is beside me, very bent, very old.

"That's right, *na'arla,*" he whispers. "Daniel is a judge for God."

And he is gone, carrying with him the faint scent of lemon drops.

The mob, the sanctuary are gone. It is outside air I am breathing now—Western, mountain air. We are hiking somewhere in the Rockies. Daniel is carrying one child on each shoulder.

"For Christ's sake," he chides me, "take one of them. I can't carry both of them up this goddam hill alone."

I take one, and the four of us proceed together, up the mountain.

Awake again. The sky is now so light that I need no bird song to tell me the hour. It is full morning. The individual calls of robin, cardinal, and jay have been swallowed up in the musical cacophony of a backyard alive with winged creatures. Only the crickets are silent, or at least I do not hear them. I cannot remember whether crickets chirp by day. Isn't their fiddling a mating call, played at night upon their own backs? Surely I should know, and yet the fact escapes me. Maybe Jacob or Hannah will know. It seems the sort of fact one should learn at summer camp. I feel oddly peaceful, as if something has been settled, but I am not certain what.

I yawn and stretch, almost touching the four corners of the bed. It feels good. I take a deep breath—several deep breaths—and I realize that despite my lack of sleep, I am not tired at all. Still, I am in no hurry to rise. Outside my window, the sun is shining. A gentle breeze stirs the topmost branches of the pin oak tree. It looks strong and stately and fine.

I know what faces me at the office: all the terrified patients, bewildered and angry, unwilling to let me go, afraid to be alone. Although I ache for them, I have to help them let me go, just as I have been letting go of them, to face the inevitability of separation and of loss. Besides, despite my momentary sense of well-being, I am exhausted, nearly undone. I need my trip to Spain, my reunion with the children and Daniel.

I get out of bed. Both feet on the floor at last, I reach out and turn off the alarm. As I head for my morning shower, my mind is filled with all I have to do. Only four more days to attend to my patients, order my household, finish my packing. Oh, there is so little time! And I must make all of it count. For even if I live to be ninety, like Grampa Bronstein, I still will not have had enough of this imperfect world.

I turn on the water, pull off my nightgown, and step into the shower, thinking that on Saturday morning I will have to rise very early to leave for North Carolina. I will drive through those mountains to find my children and then, together, we will cross the ocean and find their father.